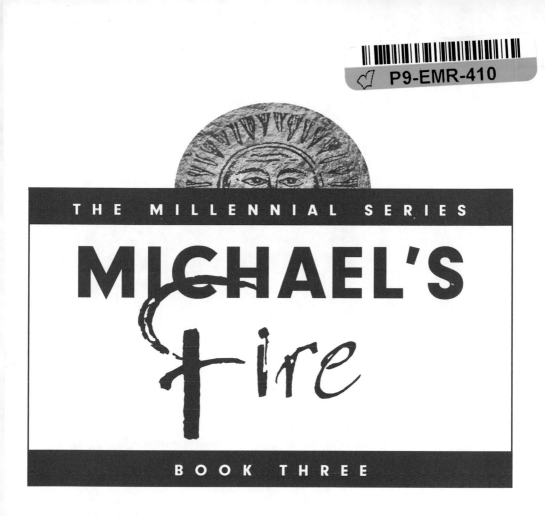

THE MILLENNIAL SERIES

MICHAEL'S Fire

BOOK THREE

PAM BLACKWELL

Published by Onyx Press in partnership with WBH Publishing, Inc.,
P.O. Box 520885, Salt Lake City, UT 84152-0885.

Printed and bound in Canada.

ISBN 0-9724547-0-5
Cover Design: Rob Davis
Cover Art: Seven Nielsen

10 9 8 7 6 5 4 3 2 1

Distributed by Brigham Distributing, (435) 723-6611

To those blessed people
who still believe
in spite of everything

Acknowledgments

Each of the books in this Millennial Series would not have been written were it not for the support of my husband, Cliff. Now when I say support, I mean everything from grocery shopping to editing. He tells me he thinks this is one of the more important things I could be doing in my life right now. And with a guy like that...

In addition, I have a longtime friend, Donna Nielsen, who knows just about everything about everything, so I can call her and ask something like, "The Hasidic Jews, do they believe in reincarnation?" And without missing a beat, she tells me they do and why and where the idea originated. With a friend like that...

I had great readers: Leila Gaskin, Chris Montour and Ramona Cutri, all friends and science fiction aficionados.

Seven Nielsen, who did the cover art, is well known. His artistic skills include designing the storyboards for the opening and closing ceremonies for the Salt Lake Olympics and brilliant set designs for stage and film. Yet, he is the most humble of men, willing to work with me as if my project were the only thing he had on his plate. So, with an artist like that...

I write for my daughter, Dana, and my stepchildren, Josh and Elizabeth. I love them, so I want to leave something of myself.

Finally, I acknowledge the presence of the Holy Spirit in assisting me in my labors. His presence comes in response to my constant *mantra*: "So, please, what happens next?"

In spite of His assistance, I add this disclaimer: I do not really know what will happen in the future. This is just a book from one author's imagination, based on the prophecies of Joseph Smith, John the Revelator, Daniel, Isaiah, Ezekiel and others.

Foreword

As I began to write *Michael's Fire*, having survived the turn of the century and entry into a new millennium, I did so with more trepidation than I did the first two books in the Millennial Series. In 1995, when I began with *Ephraim's Seed*, what I was writing seemed a faraway reality. Now I feel like I'm peering into a tomorrow that is rushing at all of us with deadly immediacy. In some ways that makes it easier to conjure images of what my characters might be experiencing. On the other hand, I have a lump in my throat as I tear out headlines to use as possible points of reference.

A number of readers have let me know that I should turn out more than one book every two years. I understand their justifiable impatience. I am touched by it. However, I can't look back for inspiration. To peer into an imaginary future is one thing. To try to match it (even remotely) with scripture is doubly difficult. This time with *Michael's Fire* I waited first until the new century began to see what, if anything, I should write about Y2K or the opening of a seventh seal. Then the bombing of the Twin Towers and the Pentagon occurred on 9/11/02 and after that I felt I had to rewrite my vision of the future. That one incident has sent me off into an alternate future reality.

Originally I thought that *Michael's Fire* would end with the world's end and Christ's return, but there was too much on the plate of this novel series. So there will be another book, yet unnamed, which will address the last 3 1/2 years of the earth's existence.

As ever, my intent is to stimulate the reader's imagination about the exhilarating times before the Lord's return.

Synopsis

of Jacob's Cauldron

ook Two of the Millennial Series, *Jacob's Cauldron*, begins with the supernatural events that surround the establishment of Zion. Ben Taylor, apostles Dawahoya and Stewart, and several other men, return from Jackson County to Puerto de Luna, New Mexico, to get the Latter-day Saints and bring them to the electromagnetically protected sanctuary that the Lord has set up under John the Beloved's direction.

Elder Dawahoya, along with Peter Butler, travels first to Hopi land, then on to Salt Lake where he oversees the exodus of the Saints to Missouri.

Sangay Tulku, a Tibetan rinpoche (holy man), returns to Tibet and his family and makes a remarkable journey across Asia to a gathering of heads of the ten tribes.

Not far away, Lu Han, soon to be China's emperor, plots with his friend and first lieutenant, Dmitri Gornstein, to take over the world…and this is not idle fantasy…these men do just that.

Ben and Peg Taylor get established in Zion, where Ben is given the job of translator of ancient plates and curator of a burgeoning collection of ancient texts.

As the many people flee to Zion, Grace Ihimaera, a Maori saint, is made General Relief Society President and helps orchestrate the influx, while Moira Dubik, her daughter, leaves her family to join the Native American consortium planning on the takeover of North America in light of the deteriorating conditions in the U.S. Laurie Winder continues to cause trouble by becoming a worshipful follower of Lu Han. She experiences his psychic abilities, after which she begins to make converts among the newly arrived refugees; but her father, Apostle Winder, makes the difficult decision to escort her out of Zion.

One of the new arrivals is Mary Margaret O'Boyle, a woman Nate Winder tracted out on his mission in Ireland thirty years earlier. Both she and Nate have had a long-distance spiritual connection, and he leaves Zion at some risk to himself and the party he travels with to bring her back, along with a shipload of passengers from Great Britain

The novel ends with the dedication of the temple at Independence and the appearance of the Savior and other angelic personages to people at the dedicatory service.

(For those who have just opened this book, I would strongly suggest you begin your reading with the first in the series, *Ephraim's Seed.*)

Characters
in the Millennial Series

Ben Taylor—Jewish convert, translator of Tibetan plates, scribe
Peg Taylor—Ben's wife, former school teacher, aspiring poet
Danny Taylor—son of Ben Taylor from former marriage
Miriam Taylor—daughter of Ben Taylor from former marriage
LaDawn Christensen—Peg Taylor's mother from Idaho

Alex Dubik—sculptor, longtime friend of Ben Taylor
Moira Dubik—Maori psychotherapist and wife of Alex
Grace Ihimaera—mother of Moira, spiritual mother to many

Nate Winder—grandson of beloved prophet
Laurie Winder—ex-wife of Nate Winder, follower of Lu Han
Ned Winder—oldest son of Nate and Laurie Winder
Mary Margaret O'Boyle—Irish mystic and Nate's love interest

Sangay Tulku—Tibetan rinpoche, meditation teacher
Pema—Sangay's wife and advanced yogini
Joseph Dawahoya—Hopi, senior member of the Quorum of Twelve
Charles Stewart—Scottish apostle, Dawahoya's traveling mate
Lawrence Ueda—Japanese prophet of the Church

Lu Han—Chinese emperor, spiritual adept
Dmitri Gornstein—head of New World Order
Hazrat Patel—general, head of armed forces for New World Order

Peter Butler—Aussie, mechanical engineer, bodyguard for apostles
Jed Rivers—outdoorsman, nurse, bodyguard for apostles
Jody Rivers—artist, married to Jed, mother of Craig and Gracie
Bobby Whitmer—returned missionary, actor, playwright
David Hunter—family physician
Robert Olsen—Ben's former bishop and mentor

Chapter One

Behold...the Lord, whom ye seek,

shall suddenly come to his temple.

Malachi 3:1

In the central temple of the New Jerusalem, Ben Taylor, a balding, bespectacled scholar, sat near the front during the dedication ceremonies. Peg, his wife, stood on the stand with the choir, while they sing a rousing rendition of the Hallelujah Chorus from Handel's *Messiah*.

It was then that Ben, the Church's scribe, felt the hair stand up on the back of his neck. When he turned to look left, a figure in a long, white robe strode across the room to the podium. With every step he took, it became more and more apparent that it was the Lord, His Savior.

Ben sucked in his breath and tried mightily not to faint. The sounds from the choir became deeper, sweeter, and more multidimensional. As he looked over his left shoulder, he was astonished to see the room filled with people in white robes, singing and floating several inches above the floor. A heavenly choir!

Turning his attention back to the podium, Ben found his wife trying to sing as she shook with sobs of joy. The Savior, His countenance powerful yet tender, stood quietly while the choirs finished their song of thanksgiving for His life and sacrifice in their behalf.

Try to remember this, Ben repeated to himself over and over. *Try to remember what He looks like.* The Master pronounced a blessing so beautiful on the assembled group that they were simply and utterly awash with the Spirit. Ben felt like the top of his head would rip off. People began to stand and prophesy about the future. Some even spoke in tongues.

Peg, the plump 41-year-old wife of Ben with a broad and open face, appeared to be conversing with an unseen person. She was, in fact, seeing for the first time in many years her daughter, Rachel, who had been killed when she was seven. Rachel was now a tall, slim young woman with arresting brown eyes and shy smile.

"Mom, I've just come to say I'm fine. It won't be long now before we'll be able to talk on a regular basis. As soon as the Millennium starts, we'll be able to visit regularly."

Peg couldn't speak at first; she tried to reach out to hold her daughter but found there was only air. "Oh, Rachel, baby, is it really you? How I've missed you! Are you really okay?"

"Couldn't be better, Mom…"

"Have you seen Grandpa?"

"Your dad?"

"Yes."

"Mom," Rachel said with a trace of impatience in her voice, "I *live* with him. We've been together with his dad and mom and a whole bunch of relatives ever since I got here."

"Oh, of course…"

Rachel's figure began to fade as two white-robed men materialized on the podium near the Savior. Peg called out softly to Rachel, "I love you, sweetheart," then was distracted by the two men who began to work their way through the choir, shaking hands and giving quick words of comfort and advice. The larger of the two with the broad face and smile lines creasing his face stopped in front of Peg and said in a baritone voice, "Margaret, how you are loved by so many saints on the other side of the veil." His handshake was firm and comforting.

"Are you...you...Peter?" Peg asked, not believing she was asking such a question of this large holy man. She dared to ask because he looked quite like the version of Peter in a temple film she had seen a number of years earlier, when the church was still operating.

"I am he, and you are much blessed for all the temple work you have done for your ancestors. I know many of them; they are among the good and noble people who have graced this earth."

Peg put her hands to her cheeks and inhaled quickly. "I had no idea I was really, *really* doing something so important."

"You have, and because you have been so faithful, the Lord will bless you with your fondest desires." He then moved on to the next woman, whom he knew by name and for whom he had a different but equally electrifying message. Next it was James, who took her hand and let her know how much she was loved by the Savior and her forebears.

After his leaving, Peg looked down to see another white-robed figure reach Ben. It was John the Beloved. Ben was flushed and shaking. This was exactly how he felt when he first encountered the translated apostle at the dedication of the temple lot in Independence. Standing in the outer witness circle, Ben remembered having trouble keeping his head down and eyes closed. *To think that John, the translated apostle, the emissary sent to the ten tribes, is here, just an arm's span away, conducting a prayer circle. And John's spiritual state? A state of divine incorruptibility! Here stands a man who lived 2,000 years ago—a divinely appointed servant of the Lord Jesus*

Christ! He also remembered the reality of the beloved apostle's handshake and the exchange about the Tibetan plates that had been given into his charge.

Now as he stood before Ben, John asked, "Well, translator of ancient plates, what do you think now?"

Ben's mind and spirit rushed to a peaceful focus on John's tender face, but he couldn't speak. He was so filled, tears flowed down his cheeks and onto his white shirt.

"Do you remember asking me if you could see the Lord?" John asked.

Ben nodded.

"He has sent me down here to tell you..." John said lovingly.

Ben looked up just in time to see the Lord leaving, walking across the stage with His arm around the prophet.

Putting his hand delicately on Ben's shoulder, John said, "Our Lord would like you to know, dear Brother Benjamin, how pleased He is with you—'for being true to yourself,' as He put it."

Ben reached for the back of the bench, overcome. The last part of that message was a direct quote from his patriarchal blessing. Before he could speak, John moved on to deliver other messages from the Lord to members of the dedication congregation.

As Ben and Peg pulled away from the parking lot and began to wend their way back to their house on Orchard Lane, Ben's arms were so leaden he could scarcely keep them on the steering wheel to drive. He now understood how Joseph Smith, as a 14-year-old boy running across a field, had collapsed before reaching home after his vision of the Lord and Heavenly Father.

Peg too was completely spent. Neither of them spoke. Both were singly focussed on making it to their house to collapse. They hoped their children—Danny, twelve, and Miriam, ten—were still with the neighbors who went to the temple dedication but sat outside on the lawn with the people who didn't have a temple recommend.

Ben's brain was so overcharged that there were no thoughts. Occasionally he would let out an "Oh," then an almost moronic, low chuckle. He drove unevenly, erratically, even weaving a bit, as they made their way down the long country road outside Independence, Missouri. When they reached their house, Peg opened the passenger side door and disappeared inside before the car had hardly come to a stop.

As she walked through the kitchen, she looked guiltily at the apples in bushel baskets on the floor that needed to be made into applesauce, but pulled herself together to get through the maze of boxes of tomatoes and zucchinis, past the freshly steamed jars on the kitchen counters waiting to be filled with the bounteous harvest, up the stairs, and down the hall to the couple's bedroom. There she fell across the unmade bed with her brown loafers still on her feet, unconscious in seconds.

Ben, on the other hand, wandered back into the ten-acre field behind his nearly one hundred-year-old, white stucco house. Like a sleepwalker, he made his way through the tomato patch that still had tomatoes hanging tenaciously onto its thick vines—colored from mint green to luscious deep, blood red—and on through the watermelons and squash which were still spreading out tendrils. He kept on, half-conscious, through the rows of desiccated cornstalks until he found a stump on which he unceremoniously landed.

There he surveyed the first autumn harvest in Zion. The electronic "net" that had been placed over Missouri had provided ideal growing conditions. The bumper crop consisted of the most delicious fruits and vegetables Ben had ever eaten.

Before owning this house in its semirural setting, Ben had not understood Peg's need for land. But as the first summer's crops began to grow in the rarefied air (the chiggers and mosquitoes had been flushed out when the electronic net was set in place), and Ben watched as small corn plants seemed to grow overnight and fruit trees went from blossom to cherry or apple, he finally understood—this was as close to witnessing God's miracles as one could get. Never before had he popped succulent peas plucked from the plant into his mouth or stained his fingers while he pulled raspberries from their prickly perch. And he had never experienced the pleasure of a sun-warmed tomato pulled from the vine and eaten on the spot.

Not that he had helped. Peg had a crew who came in the spring to plant and returned weekly to weed. Ben felt guilty, but he was kept very busy as the head of a major project for the Church. Sacred records from the ten tribes had been placed in his hands to oversee their translation. He would return home late and exhausted, not particularly interested in the daily crop report, but eager to grab handfuls of whatever luscious crop had been harvested.

Now as he breathed in the slightly dusky smell of the early autumn late afternoon, he felt filled and comforted. Instinctively, he knew this was a spot where he could find a measure of rest from the highly charged events of the last eight hours. "I have seen the Lord...I have been blessed by His presence...He is proud of me." Tears of joy streaked the face of the highly emotional Jewish convert. After a few minutes, he slid off the stump and lay down on the soft, moist, dark soil where he fell into a deep sleep.

The loud pounding on the front door finally woke Peg, who struggled to her feet and plodded heavily down the hall and stairs.

"Coming," she called out, disentangling herself from jeans and socks left in the hallway.

"Hey, Mary Marg…" Peg started to say as she pulled back the door. But it wasn't their friend with the children. Instead a broad-faced African-American woman stood in the door frame.

"Are you Margaret Taylor?" the woman asked.

"Ah, yes, I'm Peg Taylor."

"I see. Well, I'm Hilda Cotton, Amber's grandaunt," she explained, extending a hand.

Peg went numb. She stepped aside so that Hilda could enter. The large, sixtyish woman sat down heavily on the couch and gushed, "May the Lord bless you for taking care of my Amber like this."

Amber, a 5-year-old African-American girl, had appeared in a southern refugee camp with unrelated people from Alabama. It was there that Peg found her and brought her home, believing Amber was intended to be part of the Taylor family.

"I've searched and searched for my baby," Hilda continued.

Tears formed in Peg's eyes. Her secret fear had been realized. Amber wasn't an orphan. Peg struggled to be civil. "Well, I'm happy to meet you. The kids should be home any minute. Do you think Amber will remember you? She hasn't spoken of anyone from the family in the months she's been with us."

"I would hope so. I took care of her from the time she was a baby while her momma…God rest her soul…went to work." Hilda choked up a bit.

Peg fell silent. *How could the Lord bless me and then take away my baby—all in the same day?*

"Do you think I could have a glass of water?" Hilda asked.

"Oh, of course. Excuse my manners," Peg said, plodding to the kitchen, where she washed out a glass and poured water from a pitcher in the crammed-full refrigerator. On her return, she said woodenly, "I'm expecting them any minute."

Hilda drank the water eagerly. The two fell silent. Finally Peg said, "I guess I should go up upstairs and gather her things."

"Yes, that would be nice." Hilda pulled out a well-worn Bible from her large tapestry bag and settled in, reading and humming to herself.

Angry tears welled up as Peg ascended the stairs. "...not fair...I love that little girl...I was so sure she was ours."

While she picked up clothes from the hamper, pushing them into a pillowcase, the back door slammed against the kitchen wall, and Peg could hear the three kids open the refrigerator and cabinets in search of food. "I'm up here, kids," she called out.

Amber ran through the dining room, into the living room where Hilda sat expectantly. Peg hurried down the stairs and guided Amber to the couch. "Ah, honey, this is Hilda..."

"...your grandaunty!" Hilda said with great emotion, stretching out her arms.

Amber moved to Peg's side. She stuck her head through Peg's arm and gazed out at the woman.

"Honey, it's me—Gandy," Hilda coached.

"Gandy?"

"Yes. I found you!"

Amber cautiously moved from Peg's side to the waiting arms of Hilda. She slid into her spacious arms and nestled against Hilda's bosom. There was nothing else Peg could do.

"You're going for a visit," Peg lied. "You'll get to come back soon." Then the two were gone.

Peg stood with her arms to her sides and stared out at the setting sun. Finally Ben's kids' questions penetrated her depression.

"What's to eat?" Danny asked insistently.

"Find something. There's tons in the fridge."

"Where's Dad?" Miriam asked.

"I don't know. Try out back. I'm going upstairs."

Peg couldn't cry enough. She wept and wept until her stomach hurt so much she had to stop. It grew dark; Ben came up to the bedroom.

"Peg?"

"Yes."

"What shall we eat?"

"You figure it out, Ben," Peg said with a hint of anger.

He slept on the couch. He hadn't seen her quite this out of sorts. When she didn't get up to fix breakfast, Ben went to her. She lay facing away from the door.

"Peg," Ben said softly.

"Huh?"

"Honey, what's wrong? Should I get Dr. Hunter?"

"I'm not sick. I'm sick of living." Peg fell silent. Ben stood by the side of the bed, stunned. He was the one that fell into occasional depressions, but Peg was the sunny one. He felt conflicted and angry. "That was the most beautiful day of our lives, sweetheart. How could you be so depressed? Amber is back with her rightful folks. You've seen the *Lord*, for heaven's sakes."

When she failed to respond or even turn over, Ben left for work, muttering, "I'll never understand women. Why did she get so attached to that girl? She knew there was a good chance she wouldn't stay. I'll *never* understand, I swear I won't."

Peg didn't open the curtains all day, nor did she get out of bed for anything except a visit to the bathroom. It seemed impossible that she would fall into such blackness after such a miraculous event, but losing Amber was the proverbial straw that broke the camel's back.

It felt to her like an abandonment in a long string of losses. *Nothing is mine* repeated itself over and over in her mind. *Everybody dies or goes away* was the only other thought.

By the time Dr. David Hunter, a family doctor and friend from Utah, visited Peg on the third day, she had also let in the realization that the house and land she had put so much energy into was also just a temporary matter. The Lord was, after all, coming to consume the earth with fire. David reported to Ben that he thought Peg had finally let go–she had been the rock, and now she had sunk to the bottom of the lake.

"I wish I could just prescribe an antidepressant and send you to the corner drugstore," David said kindly. "We don't have access to any but the most essential life-saving drugs. I'm sure you can understand. I am so very sorry."

Ben mumbled something diplomatic to the doctor, but he went upstairs to Peg and let her know she'd better start pulling her weight around the house. "You are jeopardizing this family's chance of being ready for the Lord's return."

He regretted the outburst, but after that, Peg would get up to attend to the kids and Ben's breakfast, then go back to bed for the rest of the day. She looked awful: dark circles under her eyes, hair dishevelled, uttering occasional monosyllabic sounds as she went about her duties. People in the ward held a fast for her, but she refused to let anyone give her a blessing.

"Go away. I want to be left alone," she would intone. She wished she were dead; she would be with her Rachel and those relatives on the other side of the veil who loved her so much. Then she would-n't have to face anymore losses.

Miriam would come up to her bedroom and leave hand-picked flowers for her in a drinking glass; Danny would stand in the doorway and watch her sleep. His mother had died a few years earlier of congestive heart failure. He had just come to let himself love Peg and feared that Peg wasn't going to pull through. Ben found his son uncharacteristically surly. Peg's inactive mother was called in. This only made things worse for Peg, if that were possible. LaDawn Christensen, a critical, pudgy, narrow-lipped woman, came from pioneer stock sent to Idaho by Brigham Young in the mid-1800s. Her approach to problem-solving, one unquestioned for generations, was to get up and put your house in order. She believed there were no psychological problems; hard work would take care of any malady.

The first morning LaDawn ordered Peg out of bed after Ben left and demanded that she shape up, as she ripped off the sheets and descended the stairs to the outside washer and dryer.

"Margaret LaDawn, I'm ashamed of how you are acting!"

Peg said nothing in return, just remained seated in a chair until her sheets were returned, then went back to bed in defiance of her mother's orders.

But the rest of the family were at LaDawn's mercy. As the days dragged on, she organized them into teams to clean the house from top to bottom—throwing out food from the overflowing refrigerator, straightening every dish in the cupboards, scrubbing baseboards, filling every canning jar with produce from the garden—all this to the loud complaints from the children who were unaccustomed to being conscripted to fetch and carry.

Ben did his best to stay away; he had his archives where he could lose himself and forget what was happening back at the house. He would enter another house, the House of the Lord, to the smell of tropical flowers and sight of a profusion of gemlike flowers and exotic shrubbery that filled an interior atrium. The ruby red stained-glass design would throw crimson-colored prisms on the floor ahead of him as he walked around the outer corridor to his sanctuary. Once inside his office, he could even adjust the lighting to suit his mood, as he walked from case to case filled with ancient writings. And everything from baseboards to the tops of cabinets was cleaned by an invisible nighttime cleaning crew to whom Ben felt an overwhelming sense of gratitude. He even left them a note in thanksgiving.

After he had had a week of what he called "martial law," Ben had reached his limit with LaDawn. He paced back and forth in his office, then slumped into his chair. He reached for the phone (one of only a few in Zion at the moment) then put it down. He couldn't think of who to call to come to his rescue. Suddenly he sat straight up, slapped himself on the forehead and pulled open his phone book. "Stupid, why didn't you think of her before?" Ben asked himself as he eagerly dialled the number.

Moira Dubik was a psychotherapist and friend from Utah days when Ben and Peg were on the run from the international government. A Maori, from New Zealand, she had married one of Ben's best friends, Alex Dubik.

The tall, elegant woman with high cheekbones and long, black, braided hair strode up to the Taylors' front door. LaDawn whipped it open after just one loud rap.

"Ben said you were coming," said the sweaty woman, wiping her hands on the tea towel she had hooked over her terry cloth apron. "It won't help. Talking never does," she said with just a bit of a sneer. "Peg just needs to get some steel up her backbone."

Moira stood erect, silent against this outburst. When LaDawn finished, Moira simply asked, "Where is Peg?"

"Upstairs, but I tell ya, it won't help. I've tried, Ben has tried, the kids have tried…"

"Thank you, Sister Christensen," Moira said, dismissing her with a firm glance of the Maori warrioresses she was descended from.

She spent a half hour with Peg and, after the visit, Moira told Ben that she thought Peg was suffering from post-traumatic stress, something she was treating daily with the stream of refugees flooding Zion.

"What should we do?"

"Ride it out. She'll be okay. She's already asking for chocolate."

That was not what Ben wanted to hear. He wanted immediate results. "Isn't there anything you can do, Moira? For old times' sake?"

"Sorry, Ben. I just can't do any more. I'm swamped with people flooding refugee camps who have been through much more."

"Okay," Ben said, sagging down onto the living room couch. Then rallying his spirits, he asked, "Can I tell you a funny thought that come to me the other day? I think you'll appreciate it."

"Sure."

"There was the one about this timid girl–ah, let's make her one of our refugees from northern Europe, who goes to this therapist."

"Okay."

"He's an analyst."

"Yes…"

"And afterward, the guy writes in his notes…'She is Jung and casily Freudened.'"

Moira couldn't help herself. She rarely laughed out loud, but this time she laughed so hard, she got tears in her eyes. "That's a really good one, Benjy. I'll have to tell my colleagues about that one. We don't get many laughs these days."

"People are really that screwed up when they come in?"

"Yeah. It's pretty awful outside Zion."

Moira was now at the door, Ben behind her. As he opened the front door, painted red on the inside by Peg for *feng-shui* reasons he didn't care to understand, he asked, "What can we do here?"

"Let her be depressed for awhile. She deserves a rest. She told me she's held everything in since that bombing of the Twin Towers back in 2001. Just be nice to her. Cook for her, let her rest. She'll come around, I promise."

"Promise?" Ben asked worriedly. "I couldn't make it without her. She's been my rock."

Chapter Two

For the mystery of iniquity doth already work:

only he who now letteth will let,

until he be taken out of the way.

2 Thes. 2:7

The red silk curtain rustled as Lu Han brushed against it. His second-in-command, General Dmitri Gornstein, half-rose from the mahogany chair he'd been waiting in. The curtain of Han's inner chamber parted slightly, and Dmitri could see his mentor and "god" fold a black apron with white embroidered symbols and place it carefully into a black, lacquered box. The smell of a recently extinguished candle wafted out into the hallway of the Forbidden Palace along with that of subtle incense.

Now done, Lu Han slid open the curtain slowly along an ornate brass rod and appeared, looking withdrawn and a little distracted. His was an interesting face…not Asian, yet not Caucasian…with long, black hair tied back in a braid that hung down his back. His eyes were icy blue. And there were those lines, cruel lines that fell in creases down the sides of his mouth.

Dmitri was curious. He had learned to control his thoughts around his master, but there was too much fascination with the black apron and the quiet incantations behind the curtain to keep the impulse from coming up to his consciousness.

"The apron?" Lu questioned. "Part of my priesthood power. One day I will initiate you into one of the priesthoods."

"Priesthoods?"

Lu dismissed the question with a wave of his hand, a long-fingered, sensitive hand adorned with three costly, bejeweled rings.

The emperor had always been a great mystery, not just to Gornstein, but to others who thought they knew him. And now, well...to his worldwide following he was a living god...and so he was to Dmitri, who was no longer a fellow student at the military school they both attended as young men, but a member of a small inner of circle of Han's closest and more evolved (and politically connected) devotees.

Lu Han was born in Vladivostok, a port in the southeastern region of Siberia, where his father, Lu Jing Guo, a highly educated man, was an executive for the Trans-Siberian Railway. Jing Guo met his wife, Irina, on a trip to Moscow. She was a beauty whose parents came from Odessa on the Black Sea. When the boy was five, his mother was approached by a member of a Taoist monastic sect who told her that her son was born to be a priest, so she agreed to let him go into the countryside. Her only stipulation was that she would accompany him to the monastery. As her husband was frequently gone on long trips across the Asian steppes, ostensibly on matters for the railway, she would be alone.

Han trained in both the healing and martial arts. He grew tall and athletic. Because of his agility and flashing temper, he was dubbed "Snow Leopard" by his teachers. He was also especially sensitive to ghosts and the spirits who inhabited the area.

At age sixteen, when the priests had taught him all they could, his father stepped in and sent him to the prestigious military school he shared with Gornstein. Jing Guo was determined his son would become no introverted mystic but a man of the world. He needn't have worried. In Chinese military matters, Han also quickly excelled, so much so that he rapidly made his way up the ranks in an army that normally would have rejected him for his mother's foreign blood.

Gornstein, a small, wiry Russian Jew had sat up many nights with Lu fantasizing about how they could come to power and dominate the world. Now, remarkably, they had nearly transformed those youthful dreams into geopolitical reality—Han was the Chinese emperor and Dmitri was the titular head of the world economic organization.

As Lu adjusted his golden brocade robe and put on the black embroidered slippers next to the chamber's entrance, Dmitri couldn't help looking at the long scars that ran down both sides of Han's neck. *What a miracle,* he thought. *What a miracle that he lived after that attack.*

Gornstein thought back to the time when Han related to him how he had received those scars. The two had met in a Sufi enclave some years after their military training.

"I had wandered down to Sri Lanka on one of my spiritual pilgrimages—to the southern tip of the island where I was told Gautama Buddha made a pilgrimage over eight hundred years earlier," Han had related. "The main temple in Katrigama was the site of many reported miracles. So I went and sat inside this temple, deep inside a forest, a forest charged with spiritual vibrations. I began to meditate, and, just because of the spiritually saturated nature of the place, I found myself gaining higher and higher states of consciousness."

Dmitri looked at his emperor with eyes that betrayed his adoration. Han ignored him.

"One day, while I was deeply withdrawn into my body, a man with a machete stepped onto the temple grounds, shouting something in an Indian dialect I scarcely understood. The only thing I could make out was that he wanted to get rid of me because I was a foreigner. Before I knew it, he had run the machete straight through my neck, severing the artery. His screams brought several attendants to my side. I still was sitting upright in a lotus posture, and to this day I don't know how, but I slowly raised both hands to my neck and held them there. The bleeding instantly stopped, and all that was left was the scarring which you see. There is no medical reason why I am still alive. It was truly a miracle."

Back in the present in the Forbidden Palace, the emperor, having read his follower's thoughts, said, "It *was* a miracle, Dimi. And I was saved for this day—to bring the world together in one great whole." He slipped his arm under Gornstein's arm. The Russian, in a khaki-colored army officer's uniform complete with an array of medals, squeezed his *guru's* arm against his ribs and smiled seductively. They then walked the length of the area of the Great Hall which served as Han's private quarters.

"I've decided to make Mandarin the world's official language. What do you think of that?" the emperor asked, turning to look at Gornstein full face.

"What? But that would be a colossal, even impossible task to make the change from English!" Dmitri blurted out before thinking the answer through.

"But it would thoroughly break any hold the United States had on the world."

"But they are nothing now—and Mandarin?" Dmitri quickly calculated how long it would take for him to bring his rudimentary Cantonese into line with the demands of Mandarin and didn't like what he figured.

At that point, Han broke into a broad grin. "Just a thought. I'm not going to do it. It was nice thought, though."

Dmitri let out a quiet sigh of relief.

"But there has to be some unifying factor that helps us bring about complete world domination. Whenever one has succeeded in taking over the world, there has always been an outside threat and a ruler who has risen to the occasion..."

Gornstein interrupted, "...but surely with shrinking forests, falling water tables, rising temperatures, more destructive storms—and your power over the elements..."

Han did not wait for this litany to continue. "Perhaps I'll arrange an invasion of the Earth from another planet."

"You can do that?" Dmitri's eyes widened.

The emperor let his disciple dangle, having taken the bait, then grinned. "No, although I know someone who could."

"Who?"

"My master."

"But, Master, you are the almighty."

"On this planet and on this plane of existence. But there is one far more advanced whom I serve."

Dmitri waited for a name or just some other crumb of information, but none was forthcoming. Lu was lost in thought. "No one has to know that I don't have those powers..." He pulled his arm loose from the Russian's and began to walk more briskly. "It could crash somewhere in the remote Mongolian desert—they would contact me because I am the only one whose spiritual powers reached their own." He stopped midstep to think. "And because I've worked out a deal whereby I provide them with...ah, something in return, they've agreed not to invade."

Gornstein furrowed his brow and tried to keep up with Lu.

Lu continued, "This is only in the early conceptual stages, of course."

"It does have merit."

"Thank you, my friend," the emperor said with just a little too much sugar. "We could immediately begin denying there has been UFO contact...later, perhaps at some official function of mine, I could 'accidentally' reveal some new wisdom I'd received from our extraterrestrial hosts..."

"Or we could arrange some demonstration of their presence."

"Doesn't the Christian Bible speak of one who can pull fire down from heaven?"

"I don't know. Would you like me to research it?"

"Yes. I am sure it does. Just get me the details."

The two had reached an inner garden where a small boat awaited them. They stepped onto the deck and sat on the wooden planks while a boatman rowed them past palatial gardens filled with peacocks and a plethora of exotic flowers. Han said nothing during the fifteen-minute ride.

On the return walk, Dmitri dared open up the discussion about Han's plan. "You know this UFO theory—this could go well, since you have stopped all Internet communication. People are growing paranoid, since they've been denied the means to know what is happening worldwide."

"I want television to be pushed more. I want them to go back to watching what we present. Maybe some wholesale distribution of television sets for humanitarian purposes."

"Then we can all worship you as you should be worshipped—as a being who has ascended to higher realms and returned—to heal the sick, raise the dead…"

"Yes, yes." Han raised a dismissive hand. "And I think I'll travel. I've always said that if I did, the other half of the world would worship me, not just all of China and India. I'll go to the United States. I have many ashrams there." Han's half-smile held a malicious exclamation mark.

"Shall I make the preparations?"

"Yes!" Han dismissed his disciple with a wave and continued his walk. And, when Gornstein's hurried steps faded away, he said to himself, "And I will go to that point of mystery in…ah, Missouri, USA. I must meet for myself the only man who is a threat to my leadership, this prophet," he spit out the word, "this Asian who *claims* to speak for God." He was, of course, speaking of Lawrence Ueda, Japanese-born prophet of the Church.

He angrily wrapped his arms around his chest, made fists of his hands and pulled them into the dangling sleeves. The dark furrows that ran beside his mouth became more pronounced as he hurried back to his private sanctuary.

The world that Lu Han was planning to take over was in perilous disarray. There had been a unified but shaky world government, the UWEN, which had fallen out of world favor when it destroyed large numbers of own troops in a nuclear blast in Alaska. Since that time, Gornstein (with Lu's backing) began to set up another world government based in Constantinople—the New World Order. It took over bases and outposts left abandoned by the UWEN when its leadership was blown up by assassins in Switzerland, and it lost its dictatorial grip.

The climate was deteriorating rapidly. As Gornstein noted, there were shrinking forests, falling water tables, disappearing plant and animal species, with rising temperatures and melting glaciers that caused destructive coastal flooding. These woes were accompanied by frequent volcanic eruptions and unseasonal storms which drastically disrupted the cultivation of food.

And there had been a rash of limited nuclear bombings after years of terrorist attacks that had radically reduced the world's economic resources. These bombings worsened the atmospheric mess, resulting in a shift of the magnetic North Pole to forty-five degrees north latitude. Deserts formed in large sections of the continents worldwide; persistent weather patterns produced tornadoes, blizzards and other weather-related miseries for those people who had not fled to Zion.

Since John the Beloved had placed an "electronic" shield over the state of Missouri, it had provided an environmental sanctuary where crops could be planted and refugee camps erected—all safe from the ravages of the weather conditions and tightening dictatorial restrictions put in place by the vicious despots who ran the New World Order.

When word came that this electronic shield suddenly emerged on radar, Gornstein ordered his air force headquarters to dispatch fighter pilots to circle the perimeter. They reported back that it appeared to be a natural occurrence related to the shift of the magnetic North Pole.

As one pilot noted, "The difference between the surrounding countryside and the area under the bubble is outrageous. Outside is brown, virtually wasted. Inside is green, a lot of agricultural activity along with small isolated population centers."

Many Latter-day Saints from throughout the country had fled to Zion, along with others who believed there was a possibility of being safe with the Mormons. But compared to the overall population, the early residents of Zion were small in number—about 25,000. Everyone knew it had been prophesied by Joseph Smith that Zion would eventually house all those who would not go to war, Latter-day Saint or not. So, in spite of help from translated beings such as John the Beloved, the mortal men involved in this process couldn't help worrying about the logistics of housing, feeding, and clothing refugees projected to eventually reach into the millions.

Some Zion residents were lucky enough to move into structurally safe houses in the Kansas City area, though most of the homes had been flattened by a series of powerful earthquakes. So the majority of the population lived in tent cities in the outlying areas near entry points.

Yurts were used for temporary housing. Traditionally used by Mongolian nomads, the three-hundred-square-foot yurt could house a family of five. It was held up by wood poles rising about ten feet to a peak with a round opening. A circular lattice frame created five-foot-high vertical walls. The supporting structure then was covered with canvas and held together with a steel cable. Solar panels supplied the yurt with power.

Although the economy was based on an emergency welfare model used by the Church in earlier emergency situations, the governing Council of Fifty (apostles and other community leaders) emphasized that the actual establishment of a Zion economy would come when there was a stable enough population to elect officials and put a government in place.

These men were in accord that their mission was to create a place envisioned by Brigham Young, who said: "I have looked upon the community of Latter-day Saints in vision and beheld them organized as one great family of heaven, each person performing his several duties in his line of industry; working for the good of the whole more than for individual aggrandizement (something that twentieth century capitalistic Americans didn't learn) and in this I have beheld the most beautiful order that the mind of man can contemplate, and the grandest results for the upbuilding of the Kingdom of God and the spread of righteousness upon the earth."

A tall order, to be sure. But the Church was predominately populated by Third-World members who were far less spoiled by having too much in the way of material goods and were therefore accustomed to working together to make ends meet.

The Council was now working on repairing a highway infrastructure, creating sanitation systems, a postal and internet service, and setting up other basic necessities for a functioning society. But this one would be based on United Order principles: care for the poor through increasing employment opportunities, self-reliance, equality, consecration or reinvestment of excess funds,collective self-government, responsibility and morality.

The economy would still be market driven with currency. As the Presiding Bishop, Joseph Levine, had explained to Ben and Peg when they first arrived, "The Church will endow a bank, let's call it the Bank of Zion, with sufficient funds to start up employee-owned cooperatives, governed on a one-person, one-vote basis. Management will then be elected by a worker assembly and given a multiyear contract, subject to the support of the majority of workers.

"That bank will be the central focus of a complex of cooperatives. It will coordinate and mandate compliance with basic rules established by the majority of workers. In short, the bank will provide strong local autonomy on the operational level with strong central coordination."

A social safety net like those successful models developed by Scandinavian countries would provide the resources necessary for everyone to have the basics—food, clothing, health services—but this was not to be a communist model or even a socialist one, but one in which each member must work for what he was given or be asked to leave.

In general, the governing council looked to the scriptures and to the model that the City of Enoch provided. In *Moses* "the Lord called his people Zion, because they were of one heart and one mind, and dwelt in righteousness; and there was no poor among them." They knew their charge was to bring a people to a point where they could continue to live on this earth after the Millennium was ushered in.

And it was to this small (and seemingly insignificant) group of refugees that Lu Han, Emperor of China and head of a consortium of ten men who were undeniably the world's wealthiest and most powerful, was planning to travel. With his most extraordinary psychic abilities, Lu Han was able to telepathically track nearly anyone on earth, if he so desired. The only people not susceptible to his probing were those who were protected by the Holy Priesthood. In other words, the Holy Spirit's influence was so strong Han could not penetrate Latter-day Saint thought so long as they were living in such a way that invited in the third member of the Godhead.

Lu had been scanning the Latter-day Saint frequency for some time and was growing more and more curious about this small group of people whose movements he could not discern. Although he was a master of both Indian and Chinese astrology and could usually anticipate with great accuracy any person's decisions based on their cyclical inner conflicts, this was not true of the Mormons. It seemed to him they didn't play by the rules. Little did Han understand that his powers were limited to the telestial sphere.

The emperor was particularly interested in Lawrence Ueda—so much so, that his planned worldwide trip was largely motivated by this curiosity. He was certain that if he could just spend a few minutes with Ueda, he would find chinks in the man's armor which would allow him to intuitively dominate him.

But President Ueda wasn't to be dominated by anyone. He was God's chosen prophet. His real name was Tatsuya S. Ueda, a simple man from Sapporo, Japan. Perhaps "simple" wasn't exactly the right word for him, for although his habits and mannerisms were simple, his mind was not. He was a brilliant historian who had attended Princeton because of its Islamic department. There he was dubbed "Lawrence." His classmates used to kid him and say, "Be careful, Ueda. You'll end up going native like Lawrence of Arabia."

The prophet would just smile and say, "I thank you for your worry, but I have no intention of leading marauding bands. I have great respect for the Arab world. I only hope to add to the world's appreciation of these great people."

Ueda was converted to Christianity at Princeton, in spite of his interest in Islamic studies. When he returned to teach in Japan, Ueda accepted a *Book of Mormon* from two American missionaries at a train station in Tokyo, read it from cover to cover in two nights, then tracked them down to be baptized. He met his wife, Sachiko, a lifelong member of the Church, in a ward in Tokyo. Soon the couple moved to Provo, where Ueda was recruited by Brigham Young University to teach and research great works of Arabic literature.

Ueda was the first Asian apostle and a favorite one among Church speakers because of his rousing, passionate speeches in which he called members to live a higher law. Then the troubles came, and the Church was outlawed by the international government. He, being an apostle and the president of the Quorum of the Twelve, had to go into hiding. Shortly afterword the prophet died, and Ueda became the head of the Church in those terribly difficult times for Latter-day Saints. Under the strain, his health began to fail.

During the period of exodus to Zion, Ueda played a minor role; he delegated his duties to the chief apostle, Joseph Dawahoya, because a deteriorating kidney problem. The prophet wasn't expected to last more than a year, if he did not stress himself very much. He hated being a titular head, but acquiesced to medical authority, thus spending many hours a day in prayer and meditation.

Then, when the Lord visited the temple for its the dedication, Ueda pled with him to let him live and have a body that would take him into the Millennium. The Lord answered his prayers. "The prophet is healed!" The word spread throughout Zion like gas poured and ignited on a calm lake. And thus a vigorously renewed Lawrence Ueda led the charge to rouse people to do their best, to strive to purify themselves, in anticipation of the Lord's imminent return.

Chapter Three

I will take the children of Israel from among the heathen...
and will gather them on every side,...
And I will make them one nation in the land...
that I have given unto Jacob my servant.

Ezekiel 37:21–22, 25

President Ueda had been in temple since four in the morning. By 6:30 that evening, he was ready to go home to his beloved wife. He left his sanctuary in the temple, said good night to his loyal secretary, and began his descent down the stairs to the first floor. As he passed by the archival library, he saw the light was on and decided to check to see if Ben was still there. He was.

Ben stayed late nearly every night he thought he could get away with it. His mother-in-law (whom he had not met before her current reign as domestic despot) was so annoying to him, she had him cringing and crying for mercy to Peg. But Peg, who was still very depressed, was no help. So Ben stayed away to avoid the chores his nemesis from Idaho had in mind for him—cleaning toilets, scrubbing down baseboards, helping with bread baking, and other "unmanly" activities. It was more than a little difficult to take LaDawn Christensen straight on. Better to be unavailable.

When Ben opened the door of the library, the prophet bowed slightly to Ben. "What are you still doing here?" Ueda asked in kind, fatherly voice.

After bowing in return, Ben asked, "Shall I tell you the truth?"

"Oi?"

"Say that I was caught up with translating."

"Not so?"

"No. I've finished what I can of the Tibetan plates and just don't have the focus to begin work on the new plates—mother-in-law problems."

"And Peg. How is she doing? Is she any better?"

"Some. Don't you think it's ironic, President, that people get sick and even die here, now that they've made it to Zion?" Ben asked with a little bitterness in his voice. There was a pause while the prophet chose his words. "I believe we are tested until the very end." He spoke with detachment, yet with great kindness born of years of physical suffering. Ben, who had never become comfortable being this close to the prophet even though they had worked together for months, bowed his head. At that moment he felt like a spiritual charlatan.

"Ben, do you think I might look at the translation of those last four plates?" the prophet kindly changed the subject. "So much business has kept me away. I'd like to get a good read-through."

Ben quickly moved to the case where the Tibetan plates lay on brightly colored yellow silk in the smaller case near the windows. He lovingly pulled out the stack of plates and laid them down for the prophet's perusal. The brass-colored metal leaves were about 4"x 5", the thickness of three or four sheets of paper, and they were held together by three small metal rings spaced evenly apart on the left.

These rings had been pried apart. Additional rings had fit into the top and bottom, but they had been removed altogether. Delicately chiseled characters reflected the overhead lights.

Then Ben walked to the office area where he pulled from a file drawer a sheaf of papers and laid them out on the top of glass case next to the plates. President Ueda moved forward in quick steps. When he reached the case, he took in a sharp breath as he stared down reverently at the plates for a short moment. "What a miracle that we ended up with these!"

"Yes, sir."

The plates had been given into Ben's keeping by Sangay Tulku, Ben's meditation teacher and now head of the tribe of Naphtali in central Asia. With the help of the Holy Spirit, Ben had been able to translate them.

"The Lord surely preserved these plates until now."

"Yes, sir."

"Well, let's see what they have to say."

"Yes, sir."

"At ease, sailor. This 'Yes, sir,' is getting a little old."

"Yes…sorry, yes, President Ueda."

Lawrence picked up the thirty-page translation packet and walked to the large glass windows that faced south. The sun had already set, as it was October. But the dusk added a translucent light to the room. The prophet tried to forget Ben and disappear into the lines that had been translated from the 3,000-year-old text.

Every so often, President Ueda would make a low, throaty, "Uh huh" or a "I see." And Ben would try to make out where it was in the text that was interesting Ueda. Finally the Church president put the papers down on the case, carefully straightened them in a neat pile, and turned to the translator.

"Ben, this is very enlightening, particularly about the ten tribes. I have known most of this, but some of the details are most interesting. I know I don't have to remind you how important this information is, or how important it is that you share what you know with no one."

"I doubt they'll blow me up, President." Ben meant the remark as a joke to lighten up the moment, but Ueda remained stone faced.

"Ben, it's not those kind of people we are concerned with. You and I both know mobsters would never have made their way into Zion. It's the rumors that fly around here and sometimes are spread beyond our borders. The timing of the tribes' departure from Asia Minor, away from the despots who are desperate to stop them—this is what we must worry about. We don't want anyone to know what has been prophesied."

"Of course, sir. I'm sorry for even joking about it."

"That's okay, Ben. I know your humor." Ueda let a slight smile register on his face and then went on, "In fact, one of those, Emperor Lu Han of China has sent word he plans to visit us, if we let him."

"Lu Han?" Ben asked, surprised. "Isn't he the one that Laurie Winder was worshipping?"

"Yes."

"And she was thrown out."

"Sadly, yes."

"Are you going to let him in?"

"I don't know. I must ask the Lord. If it serves His purposes, Lu Han will come to Zion."

Ben wasn't sure why, but he shivered.

The smiling prophet paused in the doorway, turned, and said, "Ben, I know you're beginning work on the scriptures of the ten tribes, but I would like you to begin to familiarize yourself with Judah's works as well."

The translator winced. "I really know hardly anything about them…not the scriptures, of course…I mean Jews. My mother was only a cultural Jew. I heard stories from her about the Holocaust and how we lost relatives. And then there was the great-grand-mother who graduated from Juilliard and entertained on Broadway with a vaudeville act telling Jewish stories while she played the piano. I think she was from a wandering theatrical troupe in White Russia. Was that Belarus? I don't know. Southern Russia, I think."

The prophet smiled throughout the long-winded exclamation. There was something about Ben that reminded him of a Jewish stand-up comedian—the exaggeration, the pathos. When he had finished, President Ueda said matter-of-factly, "As you know, the temple in Jerusalem has been built. We have received word they are interested in talking with us about what ceremonies are conducted in our temples, we being the only other temple builders who worship Jehovah."

"Do you have me in mind as someone to meet with them?"

"Possibly."

"But, sir, with all due respect, I have an aversion to modern Israelis. Once, I was taking a Hebrew class, and the teacher was a *sabra* from Israel. After class one day, she walked out of a class behind me and said, 'So, Ben, you're a Jew I hear.' She said it with a quite a bit of warmth."

"I replied, 'Well, my mother was. I'm a convert to the Latter- day Saint faith.' To that she threw her head back with an imperious hurumph, and intoning through her upturned nostrils, she said con-temptuously, 'You're not a Jew.'"

"And that was that. One moment I was Jew, the next I wasn't. It was quite breathtaking."

Now Ueda was laughing. When he caught his breath, he said, "Well, you don't seem to have an aversion to ancient Jews."

Ben looked puzzled for a moment. "Oh, of course, what am I thinking...John." Ben blushed. "I didn't mean..."

"Of course you did. Most modern-day Jews have lost contact with their true roots. But it's time to redeem Israel, and you are to play a role."

A thrill ran down Ben's spine and the hair on his arms rose. "Of course, President, what do you want me to do?"

"Sharpen your Hebrew skills for one, and I have an article on *Rvach Hakodesh* in my office. You can come at your earliest convenience. I'll give it to Sister Haglund. Then I will let you know more as we go along. And best regards to Peg."

With that, he was out the door.

Ben called out after him, "Speak or just write?"

"Both," the prophet's voice trailed off down the hall.

Although he didn't know what *Rvach Hakodesh* was (his rudimentary Hebrew didn't cover such words), he began to weave its meaning into a wild scenario where he was called to Israel to die in the streets with the two prophets, as prophesied in *Revelations*.

What pulled Ben back to the darkened room was a sharp ache in his stomach. It was brought on by thoughts of his ambivalent relationship with his Jewish mother, Esther. He loved her whisky-throated laugh, her slightly off-color jokes, and the verbal sparring they always engaged in. But he never felt he had lived up to her expectations.

The last time he'd seen her was in a motel in St. George, Utah. It was an unpleasant scene; actually it was a titanic confrontation about his children and his religious choice. She was as usual a worthy adversary.

Although he didn't want it, the conversation came flooding back to him...

"...so, Benjamin, it's come to this, has it? Negotiating for the health of the children in a motel room in God-knows-where."

"What *do* you want, Esther?" Ben tried to sound slightly annoyed. If she thought he was at all intimidated, things would be much more difficult.

She had winced and lit up a cigarette from the second pack of the day.

"So what do you want, Esther. Let's get on with this." Ben continued with his slightly superior tone.

"I want the children returned to their home. It's not that difficult, I don't think."

"They belong here with us."

"You've taken them without permission," Esther retorted.

"I've taken them to save their lives!" Ben nearly shouted. If these two had been pit bulls, they would have been up in each other's face, growling and salivating.

"Has your wife put you up to this?"

"Her name is Peg, Esther. No, Peg has not put me up to this."

"I never liked her. Not from the beginning."

"That was obvious," Ben rejoined. "That's your problem...and your loss."

He remembered her sitting back to inhale deeply. "But this Peg person," she said coughing. "This woman has seduced you into a bizarre religion, turned you against your own mother."

"No, don't want to go there," he sadly said to himself. "Don't want to think about that. I've got to focus on Christ coming to Judah." He closed down the rolltop desk and reached for his keys in his brown winter jacket. He'd had enough for the day. But the memory of how his stomach hurt as he would daily check the refugee list for his mother's name when he and his family first arrived in Zion hadn't faded. He remembered that last day when he walked away from the long list posted outside the Church Office Building and decided she'd been killed in the great quake which ripped Chicago apart. He couldn't help the tears that ran unchecked down his cheeks.

Nate Winder stood on an open grassy plain in eastern Colorado, a brisk wind blowing in from the north. He was part of one of many companies of men sent from Zion to create a larger, solar, oval-shaped "net" over Zion. It was to extend from the Canadian border south to Panama, from the eastern plains of Wyoming, Colorado and New Mexico to the Ohio River valley as the eastern border.

He had driven out west on the plains with his friend, Peter Butler, an engineer sent out to oversee this section of the project. Farm houses stood like stark sentinels in the distance. The large herds of bison that had roamed in the large preserves were noticeably absent, driven north into the Canadian Rockies as the drought set in. The land was devoid of deer, rabbits, small game animals, and even the hordes of mice that had spread the plague throughout much of the Midwest and East. However, their remains were scattered along the pocked, unused highway.

The logistics of setting up the ionic collectors wasn't that difficult for Peter, particularly under John the Beloved's watchful counsel. They had done it once before, when they formed the electronic shield over Missouri. A couple of hours of work with the twenty-man crew and now Peter and Nate along with the others waited for the signal from Independence on their CB radio, as the placement of the last receptor was secured in the ground. Once the go-ahead crackled from the box, it was Peter's privilege to throw the switch, and the sky began to slowly fill with green spirals, alternating with shimmering white and pink lights. The aurora borealis was being "awakened" and spread throughout the enlarged corridor.

"That ought to be enough space for the ten tribes. What do you think, Natie?" Peter asked his friend, clapping him on the shoulder.

"Yeah, and I wish I knew when they were coming. It would make the second coming of the Lord a lot more real," Nate replied soulfully. "Sometimes, honestly, I think this whole thing is some kind of weird dream I'll wake up from."

The two men had travelled in one of the electric cars that Peter had converted. As Nate and he walked back to the gathering of men who were now beginning to put up a makeshift tent city, they discussed Peter's innovation—a highly efficient photo-electric battery—which made the drive possible. It was a photovoltaic battery made from several different semiconductor materials, each sensitive to a different portion of the solar radiation spectrum. This allowed a car's engine to make optimal use of all kinds of solar radiation, whether the sunlight was direct or obscured.

"We have a coating we put all over the surface of the car to collect solar energy," Peter explained. "This is directed toward the motor with a portion maintaining the battery. That way, it's even charged for night driving. We were able to use moonlight to a limited degree. And with a ninety-five percent conversion from the solar to the electrical, all we had to do is figure out how much horsepower we get on a bright day; then, as long as we remained below that power requirement, we could, in theory, drive clear across country at speeds from 90–120 mph indefinitely, depending on the terrain."

"Too bad we couldn't have made that kind of time. The roads were just so bad," Nate responded.

"No matter. They're better than the horse and buggies out there that people are using outside of Zion."

"And bicycles. I understand whole cities are reduced to using bikes with the lack of access to whatever oil reserves are left."

The two men grabbed the ends of a large tent while another pounded stakes into the hard clay. These tents would serve as home for an indeterminate time for the well-armed volunteers. This portal would serve as one of the entry or admitting stations into Zion. Even though the electronic field was in place, there was the ever-present problem of policing the portal to keep desperate people from trying anything they could to move out of the lifeless landscape in which they found themselves into green land with waiting amenities.

It would become a virtual city with all the basic services, providing the men with what they needed to survive the parched and harsh climate, until the rains came. And they would come soon now that the "shield" would stimulate the production of a moderate client, like it had in Missouri.

The tent now erected, the men sat down on canvas chairs for a last chat. "Thank heavens it's going to take less time to create a new world than it has to destroy this one," Nate mused.

"And this one hasn't taken that long. It seems like just months ago when Bin Laden and his maniacs signalled the beginning of the end."

"Modern-day Goths and Visigoths raiding Rome—I doubt they really thought they would be successful in bringing down the Roman Empire."

"And look at it now—just years after the September 11th bombing—a desolate and bankrupt nation." Peter uncrossed his legs and leaned back so that the chair rested on the back two legs.

"I wouldn't have believed it if I hadn't lived through it. I guess we were that morally corrupt. But sometimes I think the Lord brought everything down so fast because geneticists were on the edge of creating life."

"I'll tell you something else, mate. We were on the threshold of achieving immortality."

"How? Through cloning?"

"No, through gene-chip technology. Researchers were working to turn on an age-dependent gene by something called nuclear transfer. They'd already done it to cows, sheep."

"And if you were rich enough, you'd be able to do this, I suppose."

"That's why I think the Lord pulled the plug, frankly."

"Well, it makes as much sense as anything else. I just wish I knew when a new world will be in the offing. I don't feel like I can make a commitment to anyplace. Just hanging around, waiting."

"Well, we'll be seeing a million or so new souls soon. That ought to entertain you." Peter leaned forward, easing his chair back to a four-legged position. And Nate rose.

"See ya soon, good buddy," Nate said with great sincerity. He was a member of the Presiding Bishopric and now would return to Missouri because he was the head of a large, motherless family and because his calling would then take him to other areas of the United States. Peter would remain indefinitely.

"Good luck out here, Pete." Nate extended his hand.

"You take it easy with my car, mate. Watch for potholes and don't take it over a hundred, you hear?"

"You're talking to the right man. I'm a really careful driver. You wouldn't know that, because you wouldn't let me drive, jerk."

The two shook hands vigorously. They laughed and Nate climbed into the old Toyota. Peter slammed his hand down on the back of the car as his friend pulled away. He stood for a while watching the dust trail and then returned to the reality that he and his companions were like the original pioneers out on the plains by themselves. They didn't necessarily have to worry about Indians and wild animals. What they did have to worry about were hordes of desperate people who would do or say anything to get into Zion's protection. For the decisions they made, they would have to rely heavily on the Spirit because it was just too difficult to decide who would be protected and who would be left to the diminishing resources on the planet.

I could just head up north and exit up there, Nate thought as he headed out of camp. *I could use some excuse to get to Boulder. Tell the crew I had some urgent business.*

Now Nate was not an impulsive man. In fact, both Laurie Winder, his ex-wife, and his current "flame," Mary Margaret O'Boyle, complained that he was too rigid, one to march blindly following the orders he'd been given. But this was such a temptation to go northwest to Boulder that he was having trouble heading back to Missouri. In fact, he was usually successful at blocking out thoughts of his ex-wife and mother to his nine children, who had been banished from Zion six months before and whom he suspected was living in Boulder at an ashram of Lu Han's followers. He was just hours away from finding out.

Nate wasn't even sure if Laurie was alive. The last time anyone in his family has seen her alive, his son, Ned, watched as she climbed into a van accompanied by New World Order soldiers and drove out of Zion into the dark of the night.

Laurie's father, Elder Whitmer, had paid the men a handsome sum to take her where she wanted to go after a hastily called high council court had been convened when Laurie's "missionary" activities in Zion had been revealed. Everyone was shocked to learn that the apostle's daughter felt she knew more than the prophet about the

Lord's second coming and that, in fact, he'd already come in the form of the Chinese emperor.

As far as Nate knew, she could be dead—murdered by the UWEN troops and left by a deserted roadway. But he imagined now as he drove slowly down the road to the intersection that she was alive and making her way up in the ladder in Han's organization. She had always been ambitious. He was certain she wouldn't be some flunkie washing floors.

Have to be the general authority's daughter again, he thought. *And now she doesn't have me to stand in the way of her ambitions. Well, God bless and good riddance.* He looked inward but couldn't conjure up any images of the sweet but intense young woman he'd wooed with such fervor. Her constant nagging and betrayal of the family had left ashes in his mouth. So when he reached the point where he had to decide which direction to go, he thought, *Nah, I'm not that interested.*

And Laurie *was* alive. She had been taken to Boulder, Colorado, and summarily deposited outside the former Kappa Alpha Theta sorority house on Frat Row at the University of Colorado, which had been taken over by the followers of Lu Han. It was 5:00 A.M. and Laurie was cranky and disoriented, but she knew not to say anything to the two UWEN soldiers who had driven the three hundred miles in near silence. She made her way up the walkway to the three-story beige building. The familiar yin/yang symbol hung on the door, matching the one that hung around her neck. Running her hand through her stringy brown hair, she tried to pull herself together to look presentable.

An expressionless woman with a shorn head finally answered the door. When Laurie explained why she was there (to worship with the true followers of the lord), she was led to a small basement room containing a single bed, blanket, and two-drawer dresser, along with a small wooden-framed picture of Lu Han. She was asleep before her head hit the pillow but was awakened a half hour later by a gong and a rapping on her door. "Rising time for prayer and mediation." She didn't respond. She couldn't. Her legs and arms were wooden. And this was the first of many infractions of the house rules that had landed her the most "coveted" position as pot and pan washer in the kitchen—the very bottom of the work ladder…a far cry from Nate's imagined scenario of Laurie as queen of the hop.

The luster of the ashram quickly wore off—the obligatory buzz cut, the 5:30 rising time, the kitchen duty (which was to be performed cheerfully and in silence). Laurie possibly could have handled these regulations, but since she knew that she had disappointed Lu Han, she feared once this became public knowledge, the entire enclave of nearly 800 followers would turn her out, as she had been turned out in Zion.

The last time Laurie had had contact with the Chinese emperor and so-called supreme lord of the universe was the second night after she arrived in Boulder. In the past, in Zion, when he had appeared to her, he was hoping to find a spy who could supply him with information about the workings of the Latter-day Saint enclave. Laurie had been his follower for a couple of years and had experienced his presence as a small, ten-inch apparition that had materialized at the end of her bed. Now, as she lay exhausted from a day with little sleep and high physical demand, she became aware of the familiar figure first as a shimmering light, then his worshipped visage.

"What are you doing *here*!" Lu Han demanded of her after he had searched but did not find her energy in Missouri.

"I've been thrown out of Zion…by my own father," she whined. "May I now come to you, great lord?" she asked, stretching her arms beseechingly in his direction.

"Never! I have no use for people who fail me." His eyes flashed a menacing hatred in her direction. Before she could say a word more, he had disappeared.

In the months that passed, she had never seen him again, and thinner now by about twenty pounds, Laurie looked a little like a prisoner of war. She ate little and availed herself of the "synetrope," an acid/speed blend that was a popular "recreational" drug. And she was filled with self-pity. "All I did was try to tell the truth about the coming of the lord to a dumb bunch of Mormons!"

Then she was faced with a dilemma she hadn't counted on. Although voluntary, there was a great deal of pressure to become a temple consort to the sects' priests for acts "sanctioned by His Worship to further enhance the spirituality of the people" in the former Sigma Nu fraternity house.

A quiet woman who lived down the hall from Laurie knocked on her door during a lunch break when she was just dropping into a deep depression after coming down from synetrope high. "You have been selected as the lord's consort for the month of May, if you wish." Laurie agreed, but when the time came for her to leave for the ceremony, she could hear cheers and chanting from the frat house and couldn't make herself do it. She was so convincing in faking a stomach ache that she was taken to the ashram's infirmary instead.

It was there, lying in a bed after being poked by a chiropractor, that she heard the news. *He* was coming to America! Then the moans and pains began in earnest. She began to throw up and continued to do so until she was sedated and put on an IV drip.

Laurie was genuinely trapped this time. She had nowhere to go, no money, no transportation. In her groggy state, she tried to think who would come to rescue here. Near the end of her eighteen-year marriage to Nate, she had developed elaborate daydreams, a daily ritual that occupied many waking moments, an inner soap opera in which she was swept away from her present horror by a man, always blue eyed, much more powerful than Nate—a man like her father. In fact, when she was stuck in Nevada with Peter Butler, she tried the fantasy on him, but he would have none of it.

Now she couldn't even conjure up that image. She had used up her all her fantasy reserves and now lay in the smell of her vomit and her despair. *There's no guarantee Master Lu will come to Boulder. I heard them say he might stay in the East.* Tears began to form in her eyes. *If he comes, I am a dead woman.*

From that thought, she began to think about suicide. She had tried it once before in a cheap motel room in Baker, Nevada, five miles from the Utah/Nevada line. Several days after Nate and she split up in the desert, and she took half of their children and headed for Salt Lake with Peter as driver and bodyguard, she had decided to fill a tub with warm water and slit her wrists. Suddenly that scene came flooding back: As the water began to flow out of the tap, Laurie remembered searching through her black cosmetic bag for a razor blade.

It's very thin, she lamented, as she pulled one from her razor. *It might not do the trick.* She had glanced into the bathroom mirror, then stared at her sunken cheeks, eyes red-rimmed from days of crying, the straight, thin brown hair that had not had a professional cut for years.

What about the children? she asked herself again. *You know, Laurie. They're going to be happy with Nate. Everyone will be happier without you.* She ran the razor across her left index finger. It bled...

Yes, but my father rescued me that time, Laurie thought returning from her reverie to the infirmary. *And he's not coming this time, that's for sure. He's such a...* She couldn't think of word that would describe her utter contempt for her apostle father's decision to choose the Church over his only daughter.

She lay quiet for a moment, then a thought began to form into a plan. *I'll fast until I starve to death.* That will show everyone back in Zion! And my fast would bring me respect in the ashram. *Yes, I'll fast even until death.*

With that, she slowly ripped back the tape that held the IV in her very thin left arm, pulled out the tube, and struggled to sit up. She was woozy but enlivened by the idea that she would soon be dead and that her martyrdom would finally bring her the notoriety she so desperately craved.

Chapter Four

Any idiot can face a crisis,
it's this day to day living
that wears you out.

Anton Chekov

It was the smell of paint and clay, both wet and fired, that brought Peg to tears as she waited in the doorway of Alex's studio. It reminded her of the smell of the earth in the spring before planting. He was talking to one of his apprentices, a woman in jeans and a white-caked apron. She felt like such an intruder, but she was desperate. Alex was like an older brother to her, and she couldn't think of anything she wanted to do more than hang around him right now. She hadn't known what it was to be a little sister, to feel protected and inspired, without all the complications of a marriage, and she needed that now.

Soft lute music played from speakers attached to the ceiling at various places in the newly built, fifty-foot-long studio out in the newly formed Excelsior Springs where Alex; his wife, Moira; and son, Adam, had moved after Alex finished the temple art project.

Peg watched as Alex left the slender young woman and moved to another of the eight young people he was supervising. They were new members of his school for the arts and were intently working on sculpture and stained glass pieces. He turned to see her leaning awkwardly against the door frame. "Peg, Peggy…how long have you been here? Come in, come in!" he said loudly and exuberantly.

She quickly wiped her tears on her shirt sleeve and entered the workshop area. Alex was across the room in four strides. "Wow, what a nice surprise," he said with great pleasure. "I haven't seen you since the temple dedication, I think."

Peg looked down at her feet then back up again. Alex smiled in a way to indicate that he noted her nervousness. He leaned forward and looked into her eyes to see what she wasn't saying. She ventured to say, "I always feel this way when I come into your studio. It's like I've entered Hephaestus's work area—you know, the Greek god who forged thunderbolts for the gods…"

"…and don't forget he was married to Venus. Don't forget that," Alex said, laughing lightly. "Come on, Sis. Don't make this anything more than it is. What's happenin'? What brings you here?"

Tears again filled Peg's eyes. "I'm lost."

"Lost? Boy, you are, if you just happened upon us out here in the boonies." Alex indicated Peg should follow him across the studio into a far office.

"No, Alex, seriously, I've lost myself." She walked quickly to keep up with his long strides. "I even feel like I've lost my faith."

Alex pushed open the door to the book-lined office with his usual messy desk. "Sit here," he said, gesturing to a faded, kelly-green over-stuffed chair.

He didn't look quite like the Alex she first met now that he had a short haircut that exposed far more gray than the long ponytail of Pah Tempe fame. He also looked more peaceful than the tense, brooding sculptor of that time that seemed like a lifetime ago.

Peg plopped down. "I was praying this morning and you came to mind. I feel like an idiot, but I couldn't think of anyone else."

Alex, who had been leaning against a tall stool, stood up and came over to Peg. He eased down on a knee and looked her full in the face. "Peg, I've heard you weren't doing well. I'm honored you'd come to me. Now stop this apologizing."

Peg sniffed at the scent in the air.

"New incense. We've had to make some ourselves. Sage."

"Oh, nice." Peg fell silent, looked down at her hands. Finally she asked, "You remember when we talked about Jung, back at Pah Tempe? I want to do something artistic. I've got to get to the core of why I'm still so down."

"Sure. Let's set you up at this drafting table," Alex said rising and moving to take a pile of papers from the table.

"But before we do that, can I just vent for a minute? If you have the time."

Alex took a cursory look over his shoulder at his apprentices. All were contentedly working on the projects he had assigned them. "Shoot." He leaned back against the stool.

"Okay. Alex, you've known Ben a long time. I know he thinks of you as a brother. I don't know how to get him to act differently with me. I know as soon as I look and act better, he'll dump the whole load of the house and the kids on me again." This was not the pleasant and pliable Peg that Alex was accustomed to.

"What?" Peg said. "Don't look at me that way. I'm saying that I can't get Ben to see what an immature baby he is!"

"Whoa, there. Have you talked with him about how you feel?"

"Oh, yeah. But he denies he is the problem. Alex, he acts like I'm his mother. If I don't cook a meal or forget to wash his favorite shirt, he pouts, I swear."

"Well, most men I know would like to go back to the Great Mother, Sis. It's really up to the woman to tell him no."

"Well, let's take his diet. He just eats those soy hot dogs and the canned corn I put up last year. I mean at every dinner. And that's basically what he feeds the kids. And when I say something about it, he says, 'Well, then you cook, Peg." Her voice had risen nearly a decibel. "If he thought about it or cared at all, he'd figure out something decent for them to eat. But it's like he's doing it on purpose, knowing it really upsets me…"

Peg put her forearms up to her eyes and began to cry. Alex got up and closed the door, then sat back and waited. When the sobbing subsided, he said kindly, "Peg, I think you're going to have to look within yourself for the changes. Then, when you're feeling like it, you can confront Ben with what you want, and I'm sure it will work out. I know him, and I know he's crazy about you. He's just the typical unconscious male."

Peg didn't look too pleased with the direction the conversation was going, but when Alex asked about her dreams, she became animated. "Oh boy. I had a doozy last night. I woke up crying and crying."

"Tell me about it."

"Well, the first thing I remember is that there is this girl, she's about sixteen or seventeen, and she keeps riding around on a motorcycle…nude! And there is this doctor, and I think I'm in it and we are trying to help her. I don't remember what she was so upset about. I just remember that she was riding wildly around nude on this shiny red and black bike."

Alex had to work to keep a straight face.

"Well, then the dream changed," Peg said somewhat dramatically, "and I was standing over Danny's bed and in the dream I thought he had died. I began to cry and cry until I woke myself up. So I got up and rushed into his room to check on him. I stood over him and tried desperately to tell if he was still breathing."

"And was he?"

"Yes. I felt so stupid."

"What did Ben do?"

"He didn't wake up," Peg said with more than a hint of bitterness in her voice. "He's wearing homemade beeswax earplugs these days. Says he has to get his sleep. If he heard me, he didn't respond."

Probably can't handle her after all these weeks of depression, Alex thought. *Poor jerk.*

"What?" Peg asked somewhat defensively at Alex's silence.

"Well, I was just thinking that this is a good place to start with art. I'm sure that's what Jung would suggest."

Peg was miffed that Alex wouldn't join her in her invective against Ben, but she warmed to the idea of drawing her dream. After supplying the pens and paper, Alex left her to work. She was surprised to find that she didn't draw a motorcycle or a dead child, but a large tree with its roots exposed in the air.

When Alex returned, she was staring out the window into the nearly treeless forest of late autumn.

"All done?"

"Yup."

"Can I see?"

"Sure." She moved the sketch in his direction.

"No motorcycle?"

"No. But I thought about the dream as I was drawing."

"Great." Alex sat down, interested in what she had to say.

Peg began, "Well, the only thing I can think about the nude motorcyclist is that I had my kind of wild Jimmy Dean fling one time in high school. There was this guy who had a bike..."

"What was his name?" Alex asked teasingly.

"Orson Benson...middle name...ah...Peter! I haven't thought about him for ages." Peg began to smile for the first time. "He was some distant cousin of President Benson's."

"Cool."

"In the town where I grew up in Idaho, it really was like the 1950s. My dad was the town drunk; my mother tried to keep it together for my little brother and me. I was the good girl who got perfect attendance certificates all the way through the school and seminary."

"But in the summer between my sophomore and junior years, I ran into Opie at the gas station..."

"Opie?" Alex asked laughing. "Wasn't that the kid on T.V. with Andy somebody?"

"Yes. That was the joke. His initials were O.P. but he was the opposite of that kid—this was Mister Cool.

"Anyway at the gas station, I couldn't help admire his bike. He noticed my attention and invited me for ride, after I had rode in on my clunky four-speed!" Peg blushed.

"Well, I couldn't do that in front of who-knows-who. It was a very small town so I told him I'd meet him in the back of the high school...that evening."

"Ooooo, Peggy, darlin', now it's gettin' good," Alex kidded. "Remember that movie about Peggy Sue and her cool boyfriend...ah, *Peggy Sue Got Married?*"

"I was just a kid when that came out."

"Still, it sounds like life imitating art," Alex said with a laugh.

Now Peg began to be animated, gesturing and half-rising from her chair at times. "Oh, my gosh, I was so nervous. I have no idea what got into me. I had never done anything like that. I wouldn't have, except my mother was gone visiting my aunt who was dying in Utah.

"So, with no one to ask, I remember I was shaking as I pulled on jeans in case I fell off, a beige windbreaker, and tying my hair back with one of those large cloth-covered rubber bands."

Peg's energy had changed from brittle and complaining to excited warmth. "I also remember looking at myself in the mirror and saying, 'Peg, what are you doing?' And answering myself, 'I don't care. For once, I don't care.'

"I had to walk to the school. I didn't dare ask my brother…"

"I didn't know you had a brother."

"He died…Seattle…sarin gas. The terrorist attack…"

"I'm so sorry, Peg," Alex interrupted, suddenly serious.

But Peg didn't want to stop to dwell on the devastating terrorist attacks—she was on a roll. "Well, I'm trying to act normal as I walked down that long road to the school. It was dusk. I was rehearsing what I'd say if someone drove by." She leaned forward, speaking in a higher girl voice. "'Oh, I'm just going to town for milk,' or 'My dad just called and asked me to come bring him some money.'

"Anyway, I could see him, or rather the bike, flashing in the last rays of the hot July day. He was wearing—oh my heck, I haven't thought of this in so long—he had on a T-shirt with the sleeves rolled up."

Alex rolled his eyes up. "No, now you're making this up."

"I am not. Swear to goodness. It was white. I remember worrying that he'd fall off and skin his elbows. I was mothering even then." Peg paused, lost in uncovering the memory.

"So go on. What happened?" Alex came on like an eager daytime soap opera fan.

"Well, we rode up into the hills, my arms wrapped around his waist, wind in my face, the whine of the engine. I was scared, but he was careful to take the corners slowly."

"And did you stop and lie down in the tall grass and…?"

"NO, nothing like that, for heaven's sake! No, we just rode around until it started getting dark. He left me a few blocks from my house as I requested and I walked home."

"No kiss?"

"No kiss. Sorry to disappoint you. But I'll tell you what. I lay on my bed for hours with my sweaty clothes on, smelling my blouse, my windbreaker. I wanted to hold in my memory the proximity of a man—someone strong I could trust. Oh, my. Was I transported! There was a song in my step that summer, believe you me." Peg gave out a big sigh. "And that's what I miss so much with Ben. He's always so distant. He'd never get on a bike, much less ride it."

"Hey, let's don't go to Ben. What happened to Orson Bean?"

"Benson," she corrected him, then looked to see if he was teasing her, but he kept a straight face. "I heard he graduated from high school in Malad and joined the navy. That's all I know."

"But did you go riding again, before he left?" Alex asked, this time with a different tone in his voice. He'd come to even more appreciate this dear woman.

"I did, twice, but then it got too dangerous. I'd go down to the gas station hoping to run into him, but sure as shootin' somebody I knew would drive in for gas. I couldn't risk having people see us together, so I stopped going."

"How do you feel about that?"

"Now? Sad. Then? Relieved. I wasn't really the type to do much sneaking around."

Alex got up to change the CD player. Miles Davis's silky tones from *Sketches of Spain* began spilling out into the studio.

"How about the Danny part of the dream?" he asked as he resettled onto the stool.

"Okay, ah… Danny was dying in the dream…you know he's been so sweet to me during this time. I mean he brings me flowers—always trying to cheer me up. I guess it's an uncomplicated love." Peg now blushed. "And he's not like Ben. He's a good athlete."

Alex looked away, carefully considering his next words. "Mothers, if they are not careful, use their sons to fill in the holes in their relationship with their husbands."

Peg looked startled. "I don't think I'm doing that."

Now it was Alex's turn to look down at his hands. He straightened up and took a deep breath before continuing. "It seems to me the question here is not how to get Ben out on a motorcycle, but how to get *Peg* on one. Then, I think, you can let the Danny relationship change to a mother/son one. Does that make sense?"

Peg stared straight ahead, obviously struggling with Alex's answer. The studio grew quiet momentarily, then Davis's horn began sounding low with longing.

When she did speak, Peg said in a hushed voice, "I just want a mother—not my mother—she's too toxic for me, but a mother who cooks and cleans and cans and gardens. Then I could go riding."

"Don't we all?" came a quick retort from Alex. "I think the real question here, Peggy, should be, 'How can I mother less and take more exciting chances?'"

"I don't know." Peg leaned back.

"Look. I'm going to use a Moira voice here. Let's review the dream. You and a doctor are trying to help our naked motorcycle girl…" he smiled at Peg, "…trying to find a way to help yourself bring up the energy you experienced with Opie. And the nudity usually represents the natural self."

"And the tears over the thought of Danny dying?" Peg asked.

"Lost love. Lost opportunity. Lost youth. Many of us come to dead ends, to depression as you have. I almost destroyed myself in Japan after Vietnam."

Peg began to cry. She reached for a tissue on the desk and wept. Alex sat straight backed, intensely present. Several minutes passed; then Peg took another tissue, wiped her red-rimmed eyes.

"Can I stay here, Alex…all day, if necessary? I won't be in the way."

Alex stood and took her arm. She moved woodenly into the adjoining room. "You can stay as long as you like. Instead of drawing, let's get you into some clay. It's as close to getting on a motorcycle as I can pull off right now."

"Further humiliation," she muttered under her breath as she watched Alex pull out a block of clay and wet it down. "First I couldn't draw, and now I'm going to demonstrate my complete idiocy as a sculptor."

But after Alex left her with the clay and she began to roll out pieces into long strands, something shifted, and she let her shoulders relax and sway a bit to the jazz beats. The tan color and the smell of the clay took Peg back to her kindergarten class and the pleasure she had taken with her clay creations that her teacher, Mrs. MacIntosh, took home and fired in her kiln. With this memory filling her, Peg found herself humming.

She began work on a tree, one like she had drawn. As it began to take shape, it was obvious this wasn't an ordinary tree; although it had a very broad trunk, its roots rose high in the air, twisting and gesticulating in the process.

After a half hour, Alex interrupted her reverie with, "The Tree of Life! What a great symbol."

"It's just a tree that's been overthrown," she replied somewhat sourly.

"Well, it may be that, but in the Zohar of Hebrew tradition, the Tree of Life spreads downwards from above and is entirely bathed in the light of the sun."

"No! You're making that up to make me feel better."

"I'm not," Alex retorted as he walked to the bookcase and pulled out a dictionary of symbols.

As he pulled out of the temple parking lot, Ben drove slowly. He dreaded going home. He assumed this night would be like the others in the month since Amber had been taken away by her grandaunt—a month in which Peg spent a great deal of time either in bed or be emotionally unavailable. He had his routine. He would get the kids to finish their chores, eat, do homework, bathe and be in bed by 9:00. Then he'd settle down to read, and it was then, really, that he missed Peg. Occasionally she would read along with him. Yet even though she might be in the same room with him, it just wasn't Peg.

He assumed he knew what he'd find when he pulled in the driveway: dishes in the sink, kids at someone's house, Peg upstairs in her robe. *I have to admit she is getting a bit better, but, tarnation, I'm the depressive here. It's Peg's job to keep me going, not the other way around.*

"Danny? Miriam?" Ben hollered as he came through the back door. Dishes were not in the sink, but cleaned and stacked in the drainer. "Dan the man? Miriam, honey?" No answer. Ben sighed, put down his briefcase, and went to the phone. He looked through the ward list taped to the wall and began phoning.

Peg's mom came thundering down the stairs and into the kitchen, bucket and rag in hand. "I thought I heard you come in. That upstairs bathroom was a pig sty."

Ben felt his stomach tighten up involuntarily. Before he knew what he was saying, he blurted out, "LaDawn, it isn't that we aren't grateful for your help, we are. But I want you to leave now and not come back for awhile. We're going to be all right."

She opened her mouth to protest, but Ben dropped the phone and lunged into the living room for her coat on the coat rack. He returned, holding the powder blue, knee-length coat out in front of him. He indicated he wanted her to put her arms into it, which she did obediently but reluctantly. The truth was she was a little afraid of Ben at this moment. He didn't look like the snivelling private in the Taylor army she had generalled. In fact, he didn't look like he wanted to be trifled with at all.

"Well, bye. Tell Peg and the kids I said bye," LaDawn said mournfully as she made her way down the front steps half-turning at every step, hoping he would mellow.

Ben shut the door the minute she turned her back to walk down the sidewalk. "And good riddance," he said as he leaned against it.

He waited a minute to see if Peg would come downstairs, but she didn't, so he walked up the stairs, dreading the scene in the bedroom—curtains closed, Peg lying on the bed in her red bathrobe.

But she wasn't there! He went back downstairs and looked in every room. No Peg. He called the Winders and found his kids, but no wife.

As he waited in the living room for the kids to come home, he tried to throttle the panic. *Okay, Father. I'm really sorry. I really hadn't realized all the things Peg did in the course of a day to keep this place running. I promise no more, 'Peg, I'm out of underwear,' and expect them to magically appear several hours later. I've got to be more tuned in on the physical plane. I've got to do my share.* Ben's eyes filled up with tears. He began to feel the full force of the guilt that began to consume him. *I just pray she hasn't done something terrible to herself.*

"Hey, Dad, what's to eat?" Danny called out playfully as he thundered through the back door out of breath.

"'What's to eat' isn't the question. It's 'What chores would you like me to do before dinner, Dad?'"

"Yeah, but there's this great game of basketball going on down the street. Can't I play until supper?"

"Nope. Sorry. Hey, do you know where your mom is?" Ben asked a little too lightly.

"Dunno, sorry." Danny's shoulders sagged as he dragged himself into the living room and pounded mournfully on the piano.

"Go upstairs and clean your room, son."

Miriam arrived on the heels of Danny and asked with a definite hint of sarcasm, "What *is* for dinner, Daddyo? The same hot dogs and beans?"

"No, I thought I'd surprise you and we'd have beans, hot dogs and *corn*!" Ben said in falsetto. "Now go do your chores." Ben lowered his voice.

Minutes later, Miriam was at the top of the stairs, hollering. "Where's mom?" Pause. "And where's Grandma?"

"I don't know and gone," Ben replied curtly. "Now go on. Get your chores done."

Ben focussed on writing out a shopping list for the bishop's storehouse. *Not much variety, but at least they eat on time and they're learning discipline.* He was still flushed from the encounter with LaDawn. *She's probably the only one who knows where Peg is. She did say to say good-bye to her,* he reasoned. *But I can't call LaDawn. I won't stoop that low.*

He picked up the phone and called the Dubiks. "Moira?" Ben asked after he heard her voice. For just a moment he thought it might be Grace, her mother, who had passed away months earlier.

"Yes, Ben. What can I do for you?"

"I'm looking for Peg. She doesn't happen to be there, by any chance?" Ben asked, controlling his panic.

"Alex is driving her home right now. They should be there in about twenty minutes. Okay?"

"Yeah, thanks." Ben hung up the phone and sighed with relief. His stomach rumbled, so he put on the beans and hot dogs. *No, not okay.* He was irritated with her. No note, no nothing.

He sat in the kitchen and looked out the side window for car lights. He didn't get up when she opened the front door and thanked Alex profusely for the ride and time he'd spent with her.

Ben felt jealousy rise up in his belly. He stayed at his battle station. Peg called out to him and the children. The kids came bounding down the stairs with complaints they were hungry. All three entered the kitchen simultaneously. Peg said pleasantly, "There you are, sweetheart. What's for dinner?"

Ben turned to see a different wife than the one left in the morning—she was flushed with a definite curve to her smile. And he registered jealousy once more. *She must have had a great time,* he said to himself darkly.

Chapter Five

It is much safer to be feared than loved.
Because in general men are ungrateful,
fickle, false, cowardly, covetous…

Nicolo Machiavelli

It didn't take long for the word to spread that Master Lu had arrived. It was just after dawn when his plane landed in Bangkok. Tawny skinned men in white shirts and pants bustled through the nearly empty airport (made that way by extremely tight security) to greet the large entourage. The emperor was dressed in an ornate gold kaftan over black silk "pajamas."

He was annoyed at the cloying and grabbing of the people as he emerged into the street. The crowd of several hundred people pressed forward—some with hands outstretched. When a woman with a face hideously marked by smallpox thrust her emaciated baby in his direction, he ducked into the waiting black, '60s model taxi. He sat for a moment. *I hate crowds. Remind me again, why am I subjecting myself to this?* The Thai woman, like half of the population of the Asian continent who were exposed to the bioterrorist release of smallpox, was one of the lucky ones who survived.

"I don't want to have to touch this scum," he barked at his aide up in the driver's seat. The man winced at the ferocity of the delivery of words. "You go. You touch them with this." He pulled out a red silk handkerchief from within his long sleeve and brought it to his nose and mouth.

The emperor emerged from the car with a broad smile and gestured to the crowd that the lanky aide would be moving through the crowd with the handkerchief. Lu nodded his head to the cameraman who was following behind and said in a low voice, "There's going to be some fireworks. Get everything on tape."

The burly man hustled off after the red silk being waved above the heads of the masses of Thai people, who now pushed and shoved frantically to get to the scarlet object.

The cameraman got plenty of good footage. Lu's handkerchief was used to heal at least thirteen people in the crowd—some as dramatic as bringing sight back to a blind woman, repairing a cleft palate, and the most remarkable, the growth of a hand from a man who had lost it years before. All this before a crowd which had swelled to about 5,000. And all this would be played and replayed on ITN, the international television network owned by a consortium of ten men, all in positions of power throughout the world and all Lu's initiates. They used the network for Lu's privately declared purpose of bringing the world into his hands.

The next stop was Bombay where he was already worshipped by many Indians as Krishna reincarnate. The trip was planned to coincide with the festival honoring Druga, the Fire Goddess.

As his caravan of taxis serpentined their way out of the airport and down the wide boulevard that led into the city, the early evening shadows cast an ominous black on the labyrinth of hovels nearly a half mile deep that lined each side of the road. The black was relieved by pyres, some two stories high, that flamed high into the red-orange dusk. Fire and sparks shot fifty to sixty feet into the air. Han's nostrils flared and his pupils widened as he approached the celebrations. Men in loincloths threw wood on the pyres. The atmosphere was so primitive it brought the emperor forward in his seat.

"Look at those peasants, Xao," he exclaimed to his driver. "This could be twenty centuries earlier." At the next pyre on the right, he saw dancers whirling and dancing near the flaming altar. "Stop!" he ordered.

Lu nearly leaped out of the car. His breathing was heavy from the excitement of the scene. The sun dropped below the horizon, and the shadows began to deepen. The dancers outside the light of the fire became mere black silhouettes.

"Xao," he barked. "Go get that cameraman." He walked with firm determination to the edge of the light, paused, and waited for the television crew to catch up.

"I want to demonstrate to this people that I am superior to this fire goddess. Keep your cameras rolling and skyward when I point!"

The emperor stared into the huge bonfire momentarily; the yellow of his silk jacket seemed to exaggerate the color and illuminate him. Raising his arm heavenward, he called out in a loud voice in Hindi, "Come, ye fiends of fire." He pointed into the spark-filled sky. The camera followed his trajectory.

A half mile above the horizon, a fiery orb, like a comet, began shooting across the sky in the Fire Goddess's direction. In its tail, flame. The crowd gasped and pointed.

Then Lu Han pointed in the opposite direction. The camera followed his every move. From seemingly nowhere, another brilliant round fiery object with a tail of flame and sparks began converging on the spot where Lu Han stood.

He continued to hold both arms in the air; a slight breeze ruffled his long jacket. The crowd, now silent, began to fall to their knees.

Like an airplane mechanic guiding a 747 into the docking area, the emperor brought these two brilliant objects together overhead. With a boom and explosion rivaling a building blown up with dynamite, the fire and ashes rained down on the now-prostrate, terrified people of Bombay. Some were singed with embers; others ran crazily through the crowd—clothes on fire, but in ecstasy. The camera crew got plenty of close-ups.

The last leg of the journey ended in Indonesia, the third most populated country and Muslim to boot. By this time, his plane had only to touch down on the tarmac before thousands of people risked injury to swarm his plane before it came to a stop at the gate in Djakarta. Word of his spectacular abilities had arrived ahead of him, even without the planned television shows. This time there was a slightly different spin—he was arriving days before Ramadan, and the word on the street was that he was, in reality, Mahdi, the messianic figure scheduled to return at the end of time.

Han managed beneficent smiles as he alternately healed people with the ashes (*vibuti*) that he miraculously produced from the palms of his hands or gifted the crowd with precious jewels that also materialized from the middle of his long-fingered, carefully manicured hands. The cameraman was exultant with the footage of a beaming Lu Han blessing and healing, someone the masses longed for in a world gone wrong. The tour was a rousing success.

On the flight back to Beijing, the emperor lay back in the large, sumptuously decorated chair he had built especially for his travels and reflected on the journey that had brought him to such a pinnacle of political and religious power. He had been a longtime fan of Machiavelli, the Renaissance Italian who wrote the textbook on the craft of ruling, *The Prince*. This book came into Lu's hands when he was student in military school. His prowess in English paid for itself many times over that night, that sleepless night when he devoured the book in one sitting. Here was a pragmatist! Here was a how-to manual putting forth the secular truths necessary to form a powerful state. Han, then twenty-two, grinned widely as he read the unsentimental lines in the seventeenth chapter, "But when it is necessary for him (the Prince) to proceed against the life of someone...he must keep his hands off the property of others, because men more quickly forget the death of their father than the loss of their patrimony." He remembered he had to look up *patrimony* just to make sure it meant what he thought it did...and it did. That slim volume of political science formed the basis of a plan to satiate Lu's thirsty desire for ultimate power.

He devoted himself to the military after returning from India and the incident where an Indian attempted to kill him while he was meditating. Han decided that he'd had enough of the passive life, and he swore he'd never find himself in that position again, where a man might come up upon him to take his life.

The emperor, now paranoid, literally watched his back as he made his way up the military ranks. He became known for his genius, but also for his barbarous cruelty in wars with North Koreans, Tibetans, Russians and skirmishes with Asiatic nomads. He was feared, and therefore respected, just as Machiavelli had predicted. Having arrived at the rank of general in the Chinese army at the same time as a rival named Zhu Hao, he cleverly decided that he would be beloved as well as feared. This was what he felt was lacking in the Italian's text in order to survive as the ultimate leader.

Lu knew Zhu Hao's weaknesses and knew that, although he could best him in battle, the square-faced, squat man had the love of the men in the army he commanded, whereas Lu didn't. He offered a compromise to Zhu. "I'll leave you to the field if you acknowledge my spiritual leadership in the resurrection of the emperor/king. You will rule in day-to-day matters; I have other goals." Although suspicious, Zhu had little recourse. Even in those days, Lu was known as a wizard. The general didn't want to die a slow death from some exotic poison, like several of Lu's rivals had in the past.

"I must contact Dimi," he said quietly to himself as the plane soared across the night sky. "He'll be pleased." Lu snapped his fingers and ordered a warm nectar drink. The crew hurried to do his bidding, for he was a cruel master. After slowly sipping the drink, he leaned back and laced his fingers behind his head. *Fortune is a woman…it is necessary to beat and ill-use her…She is a lover of young men, because they are less cautious, more violent, and with more audacity command her…*words he had carefully put to memory many years before. They pleased him now. He wished Machiavelli were alive to see the perfect princedom he was creating—a princedom on a grand, planetary scale.

Halfway across the world, Nate travelled the arduous road back east toward the center of Zion, struggling with stretches of tortured road—potholes, twists and turns, ravines and washed-out highway. Each portion seemed to symbolize some aspect of his relationship with the women in his life—Laurie and the irrational fascination he had for Mary Margaret O'Boyle, an Irishwoman, whom he had first met when he was a missionary in Ireland and she a young, tormented teenager.

Nothing about his present attraction to her made sense to Mr. Rationality—she wasn't a member of the LDS church, she was probably crazy, and he didn't need any further trouble in his life: he was trying to raise the younger seven of his children by himself as it was. But there she was, bigger than life, dancing before his eyes as he drove along. His heart beat faster as he envisioned her quick smile, her large blue eyes set against alabaster skin and that ebony hair. *Oh, Miss O'Boyle, if you only knew what you do to me!*

He had revealed to her a few times what he thought about her, and once he quickly sat down beside her on the couch at her house and said with great intensity, "You know I love you, don't you?" But he didn't look at her—he just stared straight ahead. She put her blue-veined hand on his and said in her brogue and tender voice, "I feel the same way about you, you know." The two then sat in silence for a time until they were interrupted by her oldest daughter, Eilean, who had just returned from a date. They quickly moved apart on the couch and changed the tone of their voices.

Nate played through that scene several times as he made his way across the flat lands of Nebraska—each time feeling the thrill that began in the pit of his stomach and ended in his throat. The memory of that almost ecstatic, electric moment caused him to catch his breath. He felt so weak in his arms, he let the left one drop into his lap. Then he was jolted out of his reverie when he hit a particularly difficult patch of washboard-like road. To his surprise a light rain began to fall.

"Boy, that was fast. It hasn't been twenty-four hours since the net went up." He turned on the wipers and found himself right back with Mary Margaret. "It's really a pity what life has dealt her. What would she be like if she'd had a normal LDS life?" he asked rhetorically. "She wouldn't be bleeding from her hands and wrists on Friday nights." *Why are the women I'm involved with so crazy? I've ended up with the nut cases! What does this say about me?*

The rain now came down harder, and Nathan Winder, grandson of a well-known general authority, adjusted the wipers to a higher speed. "Maybe they are attracted to me because I'm so dull. Or rigid. But this pretending to talk for dead people…that's where I draw the line."

In his mind, Nate was back at a dinner party the Dubiks' had invited him to—a house-warming party for their new house and studio. There were a lot of people mingling around—Ben and Peg, Jed and Jody Rivers, the Martinezes, some of Alex's apprentices. Nate had brought Mary Margaret, who was dressed in a brown and blue print dress of some kind of clinging material and smelled of violets—all of which caused him to ache to his very bones to kiss her and hold her close enough to his body until she felt faint with desire. But he was a disciplined man, so he drove back the very thought. Looking at him, one wouldn't guess that he cared for her any more than he did for his other friends who came to talk and shake hands before moving on through the crowd who were admiring Alex's and other artists' work hanging on the gallery walls that connected the large dining room with the workshop.

Then dinner came and Moira put out cards in front of plates, deliberately breaking up couples to further "warm up" the party. Mary Margaret was seated across the table and down two from her date. They were eating the dessert course. Alex had whipped up some great-tasting delicacy from Jell-O, canned peaches and ice. (He had taken up the challenge of creating gourmet meals from the food distributed from the Central Food Warehouse. Women were always asking for his recipes.)

Suddenly and loudly, Mary Margaret began to speak. "Moira, you're very lucky to have such a good man and chef, or so says your mother."

The buzz of conversation diminished. People looked from Mary Margaret to Moira. Several leaned to their dinner partners to ascertain what the handsome Irishwoman had said.

Moira flushed. "Well, thank you. I think he's quite extraordinary." She was going to let the rest go, but that was not to be.

"And your mother is reminding you that you should be doin' more of the domestic chores...(pause)...ah, and she's sayin' to remind you that a way to a man's heart is through his stom..."

Mary Margaret hadn't finished the proverb when Moira rose from her chair and rushed from the room. Alex excused himself and went after her.

"Maggie, what are you saying?" Nate blurted out, greatly embarrassed. He was a very decorous man, after all. And Grace Ihimaera had been dead for less than six months.

"I'm sorry, Nate. I certainly didn't plan to say anything about Grace being at the party. It just slipped out. I think Grace was worried that we'd finish eating and go home without havin' her say."

Back in the master bedroom, Moira had begun to cry. "It's not that I don't know she's like some nutty medieval saint. And I'm not embarrassed about what she said...it's just," she blew her nose into her handkerchief, "that I haven't heard from Mother. And this is not the way I expected to hear from her—in the middle of a dinner party, for heaven's sake, by some nearly psychotic woman who should be my patient."

Alex paced back and forth in large room dominated by the large bed he had constructed along with a carved bedstead, matching the one he had done in Pah Tempe. On it was a large eagle with talons raised skyward, clutching a vigorous snake. "Well, I'm not comfortable with this," he said intently. "I never was completely at home with all of Grace's purported telepathic abilities."

"You believed in them. Come on."

"Okay, I had to. She was too good. But I don't want to have to deal with some medium who falls into a trance at dinner and brings back my mother-in-law, of all people." Alex was usually more diplomatic, but he had planned this party down to last homemade candlewick. And this was definitely unwanted entertainment. "Okay, so what do we do? We've got to go back out there."

"Why don't you go and see if she's still doing it?"

"Okay." Alex opened the bedroom door and purposefully strode back to the long dinner table. He clapped his hands and said, "Okay, then. Who's going to help clear off this mess?"

"Grace wants you to know that you're going to get the greatest desire of your heart," Mary Margaret blurted out, then turned red. "I'm so sorry. I cannot help it. She is very insistent that I pass this information on. I'll leave if you want me to."

Everyone looked to Alex. He struggled. He didn't believe it was Grace. And he thought Mary Margaret needed badly to see his wife.

"Grace says to remind you when you were standing on the balcony of your house in Utah and you thought about throwing yourself over because you thought you were going to lose your baby. Do you remember?"

"No one knows about that! I never told anyone...not even Grace!"

Then Mary Margaret's voice changed, and she said in a decidedly New Zealand accent, "But God knew, Alex, and he told me," in a voice so much like Grace's that a few of women in the room shrieked and put their hand to their mouth.

"Okay, guys. That's it," Alex barked. "Party's over. It's been fun. Never mind about the dishes." He began herding people to the coat rack in the large stone entry. Moira came out of the bedroom and also helped people with their coats.

Nate had driven Mary Margaret to the Dubiks' and didn't see how he could get out of taking her home—a good thirty-minute drive. The air was thick with tension as they drove for nearly ten minutes in silence. Finally Nate spoke. "Maybe this is the way you do things in Ireland or with your Catholic friends, but in this world, that was in very bad taste."

Mary Margaret sat with her arms folded around her waist tightly.

"We've been told from early on to stay away from soothsayers and astrologers," he continued in his church voice.

"And yet your ancestors consulted the *Farmer's Almanac* which is based on astrology, I've been told," she shot back. "And I have it on good authority the early pioneers had phrenology readings on their heads when they came to the Great Salt Lake." Big tears began to form, and her mascara began to drip past the lower rim of her eyes. "It's a gift," she said quietly. "I'm not some passin' gypsy, you know. I'm a real person who just happens to have this gift." Her voice trailed off, as Nate tightened his jaw and adjusted his arms so that they were wrapped higher around the steering column and away from her knee.

They rode on in silence for a time; then Nate spoke. "I want you to take the missionary lessons. If you want to continue with this relationship, I want that commitment from you—right here and now."

"I am talkin' to the missionaries. I didn't want you to know so I wouldn't be feelin' any pressure to join your church because of how I feel about you."

Nate felt like someone had grasped his heart and manually squeezed it. He didn't know what to say.

"I know I'm a burden to you," she said sweetly. "You bein' in the presiding authority and all. And I know you say I'm a wild Irish mystic like that was something indelibly romantic, but it isn't like that.

It's more like what happened at dinner. Sometimes someone who is dead is so insistent, I can't help myself."

Nate found a smile spreading across his face against his will. He reached down and patted her knee. "I guess that's your appeal, Maggie. I come from sturdy, logical stock. I wouldn't know an angel if one lit down right in front of me."

"Would you like me to use the Sight to help you in some way…to make amends?"

"How's my daughter? How's Cristina coping with the orphans in the camp down south? This is the first time she's been away from us."

Mary Margaret straightened her spine and leaned back against the seat. It looked to Nate as he glanced over at her that she had some-how shrunk. She'd withdrawn into herself that far. After a quiet minute, she said, "Well, she's fine, just fine. Would you like me to tell you what she's doing right now?"

"Sleeping?"

"Very funny. Now do you want to know?"

"Isn't that like spying? If she knew, she'd say, 'Oh, great. I can't even leave home without Dad snooping on me.'"

"Well?"

"Okay. Okay. What she's doing?"

"Putting babies to bed."

"Good guess."

"Want specifics? I can see her in a tent, humming to herself. She's just put pajamas on little boy with dark curly hair…"

"Maybe he's Irish," Nate said as he eased the car to the side of the dark lane outside of Independence.

"Now what are you doing?"

"I'm going to look you in the face this time." He pulled up the brake abruptly. He turned and leaned against the door. She did the same. "God help me, Mary Margaret O'Boyle, but I do love you."

He had to find his handkerchief. She couldn't contain her tears.

Nate hadn't counted on being divorced—under any circumstances. He was the first to have a marriage fail in a line of men that stretched back to Hyrum and Joseph. And it was Laurie, not he, who had left the marriage. But it still was more than he could cope with. And he couldn't imagine the problems of remarrying—especially to Mary Margaret. Besides her delicate state of mind, she had three girls to add to his nine children.

Yet this woman had such a hold on him; it was like he was fourteen again when he first held Christy Rogers in his arms at the school dance. He couldn't break away, no matter what the chaperones said.

Nate was brought back to the present as the Honda suddenly flew over a bump in the road, lifting Nate up off the seat and then slamming him back down with an audible thud. Nate smelled a familiar scent. *What is that? Lilacs? No, violets!* He couldn't quite believe what he was experiencing. *It must be the driving and the rain. I'm hypnotized.* The odor grew stronger. And with it, the sense that he was not alone in the car. Although he couldn't quite see her, he "knew" his Irish goddess was sitting right beside him…had just arrived, in fact. At that, he let tears trickle down his cheek for the first time in nearly fifteen years. "My love and my heart," he said and reached for the formless form. "I'm coming home."

Chapter Six

Sangay Tulku, Tibetan rinpoche and translated being, stood in the celestial room of the central temple of Zion. He looked up at the golden reflector and the dome beyond. The lighting from within the room made the dome seem to float. It was late evening after the staff had gone home. He was one of ten men, all dressed in white, who were waiting for two honored guests, one of whom Sangay had not met. Then came the sound of slippers sliding across the white carpet and the entrance of three men: President Ueda, John the Beloved, and a large, muscular, dark-haired man with intense brown eyes. This was the man Sangay had longed to meet.

The Tibetan smiled with pleasure, showing the gap between his teeth. He looked a lot more like an imp than the head of the tribe of Naphtali. He obviously liked to laugh, as the smile lines around his face attested, especially the ones near his gentle brown eyes. He was obviously pleased when signalled by the President to sit down on the assembled couches. They made an unusual quorum—the prophet and heads of the tribes of Dan, Reuben, Simeon, Levi, Naphtali, Zebulon, Issachar, Gad, Asher, and Benjamin, along with John the Apostle and the head of an earlier dispensation, Moses the prophet.

"Let me introduce everyone. This is Rudolf Grudzinski of the tribe of Dan, Michel Dyachenko of Issachar, and Alec Hovanec of Reuben," the prophet began. Sangay laughed to himself, remembering back when he thought that these men would somehow not look human when he met them, but they were just ordinary men from Eastern Europe and Eurasia. *These are my comrades-in-the-Lord, my brothers!* He longed to touch foreheads in the Tibetan manner of greeting.

"And I think you all know our brother John. But not our brother Moses." Sangay looked eagerly into the face of this man of mystery. Like the others, his body had a definite glow. He appeared to be twenty-five or thirty years of age, in perfect health. Moses' presence in the temple marked a new chapter in the rapid conclusion of the earth's telestial existence.

Sangay couldn't remember being this excited since the remarkable priesthood event that changed the bodies of the ten heads of Israel's tribes, himself included. It had been in Siberia, near a lake, when John the Beloved had informed them, "This change in your body will allow you to travel at a thought and without any great expenditure of energy."

After they had become acclimated to the novel feeling of having tremendous energy, the Lord's beloved apostle asked them to gather up their belongings and stand in a circle around a large stone up on the bank. "Can you imagine yourselves in the center of the United

States? You'll find the place by the electronic force field placed over it." Then he gave exact coordinates for Adam-ondi-Ahman. In less than a second the men had been transported to Spring Hill, where President Ueda greeted them with his enthusiastic handshake.

Now with the scent of tropical flowers wafting in the open doorways from the atrium in the middle of the temple, President Ueda began. "There is just one item on the agenda tonight. First, let me give the floor to our newest guest in this temple, Brother Moses." (It was Moses, of course, who appeared to Joseph and Oliver in the Kirtland Temple, giving them the keys to commence the process of preparing the tribes to return.)

"Brethren," Moses began. "The Lord has indicated that the time has come for your tribes to begin your journey to Zion."

There was an outburst of joy. Moses quietly waited for them to absorb the news. "It is a time of rejoicing, but unfortunately we must act quickly. We have only a small window of opportunity to move the nearly 500,000 people who are determined to come to Zion. We must execute this transition in a few months' time. After that Gornstein's government will have in place the most sophisticated satellite surveillance system the world has ever seen. Then no large population movements of any kind will be possible."

"I assume, sir," said Alec Hovanec of the tribe of Reuben, "the Lord intends some miraculous means for this to occur?"

John let a little smile fill the corners of his mouth and replied with, "Well, let's say that most of what's to be done will be telestial—just a little help from the miracle department."

The men leaned forward in anticipation. Moses nodded to the prophet to begin.

Lawrence Ueda spoke in the most humble of tones. "Most of you know of Central Asia's dust-storm zone."

There was subdued laughter. Ueda continued, "As you know, in the past years the spring dust storms have increased in severity. People in northwestern China, in particular, desperate for work, have plucked huge tracts of land clean in search of "facai," a dried, black, fibrous mass. Elder Chou, can you give us your first-hand account of what you've observed?"

"Yes, sir. I have been moving my tribe, most of whom come from nomadic backgrounds, across the steppes in anticipation of this return to Zion. I have seen tens of thousands of Islamic Chinese scraping the landscape—millions and millions of acres are left with no ground cover to speak of. All so they can sell this moss to support the whims of buyers in southern China and Hong Kong who believe that ingesting it will bring them good luck and good fortune."

"Thank you, Elder," Moses said. "And Elder Wenyuan, you come from the Tongxin area; can you tell us about the history of this?"

The head of the tribe of Gad blushed slightly as he began. "There have been severe sandstorms going back as far as we have recorded such events, at least the sixteenth century. But since the end of the last century, when this commerce started, the destruction of the vegetation cover on the glasslands has been disastrous. The UWEN tried to stop it, but the word *facai*, also means "get rich," and the people who have any money to spare want to put it in their soup or their rice to get more money. Superstition overcomes government every time."

Chuckles emanated from the translated beings. The prophet briefly rested his head back against the brocade beige couch and looked up at the golden reflector and the dome beyond. *I really don't believe I'm sitting here with these men*, Ueda thought. *It's almost too much to take in.* Then he was brought back to the moment by John, in his melodious voice, who picked up the story. "And as we know, most of China and Mongolia are now blanketed with a thick, yellowish mixture of sand and dust each spring, so thick, people can't breathe the air if they go outside. And each year, as President Ueda has indicated, has become progressively worse. I think we could count on a couple of months' worth of dust storms that would not be produced supernaturally—storms in which we could hide our tribes and travel to the Bering Strait."

The group talked to each other quietly, wondering just how they could take their people through such a catastrophic event.

"As I took my people through the Red Sea, so shall your people be led," Moses spoke up.

"Are we as translated beings to be visible to them?"

"Yes, when necessary," he responded with a kindly tone but still sounding like a general in the war room, bringing the men in his command up to speed. "Let each of the leaders of your tribe take on most of the responsibility. It will be his duty to have the faith in the Lord to go through this. And why? It is always the case that the Lord leads his people out into the wilderness and through testing times so that they may come to lean on him, and his leaders, in preparation for living a higher law."

"And what about Lu Han?" asked Rudolf Grudzinski of the tribe of Dan. "His powers are such that he will know telepathically when this migration takes place."

"The Lord has assured me He will distract him. I'm told the emperor has begun to travel, to convert the masses," Moses said somberly. "He's preoccupied with conquering the world."

President Ueda said, "I'm told he's headed first for Thailand, India, then on to Indonesia, targeting half the world's population."

"Africa is an empty continent not worth visiting," Michel Dyanko added.

"True, and Western Europe is now predominantly Islamic, if any-one there believes in anything these days," Sangay said with some sadness.

"How marvelous to know what he's doing, and he doesn't know what we're up to!" Elder Grudzinski exulted.

Moses quickly retorted with, "It won't be that easy, believe me."

A deferential silence filled the room as each person pondered on the great struggles Moses had endured with the children of Israel.

Sangay's mind wandered to the scripture about the highway of ice melting before them. Moses read his thoughts. "Yes, dear brother, the scripture that reads, 'and they shall smite the rocks, and the ice shall flow down at their presence, and an highway shall be cast up in the middle of the great deep' shall also be fulfilled. But right now we're dealing with dust."

That brought a hearty laugh from everyone. After an hour or more of discussion about this massive undertaking, the prophet found himself sitting alone in the celestial room, in quiet meditation. He had become accustomed to the comings and goings of translated beings…barely.

While the others returned to their tribes and duties, Sangay lin-gered in Jackson County. He had two of his meditation students to visit before returning to northeastern Asia.

Ben got a phone call early, around six in the morning. Staggering down the stairs, he muttered under his breath, *This had better be good…better be the prophet.* Ben, a confirmed night owl, had only been in bed three hours. He had been reading Kierkegaard, a 19th-century Christian philosopher, and couldn't put the book down.

"Ben?" Alex asked, not sure if it was Danny whose voice was changing.

"None other. Is that you, Alex?"

"You gotta get over here, man."

Now Ben was awake. "What's happened? Can I help?"

"What's happened isn't an accident. It's good. Come right away."

Alex hung up before Ben could badger him into telling him that Sangay had materialized in his living room a few minutes earlier. While the two waited for Ben, they sat for awhile in the spacious living room with floor-to-ceiling windows and watched the rain fall outside. Both sat erect, silent. Alex's face was serene, but there was a definite hint of delight. He hadn't counted on seeing his meditation teacher.

After a meditation in which Alex found himself being quieted and filled with a sweet nectar of bliss—from the base of his spine through his heart, throat and filling the interior of his cranium—Sangay moved to undo his legs which had been folded one on the other in a full-lotus fashion. "You haven't been meditating enough, friend," he said.

"No, I haven't. It's been crazy here with the construction, new school, family…"

"You haven't been meditating enough."

"No, I haven't."

"Back when you thought I was a heathen." Sangay leaned over and squeezed Alex's knee in jest, "I carefully followed the words of your prophets when they spoke every six months. I had a number of Mormon men in the monastery, as you may recall."

"Of course."

"I remember the delight I felt when the prophet Hinckley spoke about meditating. I memorized it, so that I could quote it in my instruction," Sangay recalled with fondness in his voice the memory of the monastery days on Mt. Nebo. "It went, 'You need time to meditate and ponder, to think, to wonder at the great plan of happiness that the Lord has outlined for His children...' I heard President David O. McKay say to the members of the Twelve on one occasion, 'Brethren we do not spend enough time meditating.' I believe that with all my heart. Our lives have become extremely busy. We run from one thing to another. We wear ourselves out in thoughtless pursuit of goals which are highly ephemeral. We are entitled to spend some time with ourselves in introspection, in development."

"That's a great quote," Alex said enthusiastically. "I was a heathen then, too, as you may remember."

The two chuckled and then fell into a long moment of silence, remembering the times before becoming members of the Church.

"Good," Sangay said abruptly and clapped his hands. "Now that that is out of the way, I'm here. It's your prayers and concerns that have brought me here. What's up?"

"Let me say first how great it is to see you. I forget how fabulous it is to be with you. When are you coming to stay?"

"Not for your ears."

"Ooo...kay. Next question. How good are you with marital impasses?"

"Yours?"

"Ben and Peg's."

"Better than I was when you knew me in Nepal."

"Why's that?"

"I'm married now."

Alex's jaw dropped so quickly that Sangay reached over and pushed it back in place with a light laugh. Then he quickly covered his own mouth to suppress his glee, not wanting to wake Moira and Adam.

"I'm sorry, *rinpoche*, but last I heard monks were renunciates. I'm flabbergasted."

"Well, I know that you are aware that one cannot attain the highest levels within Christ's kingdom without being married. So I am. I couldn't be translated. Translation is a temple ordinance that must be preceded by temple marriage."

"Oh, of course. I hadn't given that any thought. But it's just…"

"Just can't see me as an old married man."

Both men laughed.

"Who is she?

"Her name is Pema."

"A former nun?"

"Yes, and a truly remarkable woman."

"I wouldn't expect anything less," Alex teased. "Tell me about her."

"She was given over by her family to be raised in a nunnery when she was three. She exhibited remarkable spiritual abilities from birth."

"How so?"

"I'm told that when she emerged from the womb and was laid in her mother's arms, she struggled to sit up and did so in a full lotus position for nearly five minutes."

"No saggy head?"

"No."

"No wobbly spine?"

"No."

"Witnesses?"

"Several reputable ones."

"Wow." Alex leaned back against the couch to take that picture in. "I wish you had it on videotape. We could get rich—sell it to the *National Enquirer*."

"What *Enquirer?*"

"Oh, yeah. I forgot where I was. That was so amazing. And I thought my son Adam was precocious."

"You know when the Chinese came into Tibet and imprisoned and tortured the mendicants, along with destroying over 6,000 monasteries with their contents—libraries of sacred scripture, statues, paintings...well, Pema, now an adult, was among those imprisoned. The Red Guard were exceptionally brutal to the nuns—raping and torturing them. Many of the women who had been dragged repeatedly through these awful scenes simply and quietly retired to a corner of their cell, and taking up the meditation position, left their bodies."

"Died?"

"Yes, in a way. They were practicing *powa*, a 'transference of consciousness' technique used by adepts to exit their bodies and propel their spirits into a different realm of existence."

"Pema did the same thing, but when she left her body, she reports that she was met by a woman of exquisite beauty who told her she must return to the earth, that she had a mission to perform. She also told her she was pregnant with a guard's child."

"Really?!"

"Yes, and in that society, that was another kind of death—social ostracism. Yet she returned to her body. And miraculously she was left alone...they must have sensed that she was pregnant...and after six months, she was released."

"And obviously pregnant, I assume."

"That's what she told me."

"So what did she do?"

"She and her blessed mother walked to Nepal..."

"In her condition?" Alex, now agitated, stood to pace. Then the sound of a car on the gravel driveway outside took them away from the story and to Ben's rumpled arrival.

Ben stomped into the stone entryway, ridding his shoes of the rainwater in such a way that told Alex that this wake-up call had better be good. It was not until he had rounded the corner into the living room that he caught sight of his teacher in simple traditional gold and deep red robes.

"Whoa, I don't believe my eyes. Sangay! What brings you in this direction? I thought you were tramping across the steppes."

Ben took several large steps to reach Sangay and took the rinpoche's hand to shake it vigorously. Ben had gone from dark circles under half-opened eyes behind his wire-rimmed glasses to bright-eyed wonder at being in the presence of a translated being.

"You are the reason I've come," Sangay said, gesturing to Ben and Alex to be seated on the long, beige couch. He sat down in a chair with large, wooden arms. As he settled, Ben noticed that even in repose, the corners of Sangay's mouth turned up.

Ben first felt guilty, but then he couldn't help but feel the tension in his body melt away. *Why do I always forget that there is nothing in this world to worry about?* he asked himself with irritation. *You'd think I couldn't forget that rather important point, having known this incredible human being.* Sangay broke his reverie. "Alex tells me you've come to a sort of marital impasse."

Ben swung around to face Alex. He was both embarrassed and a little bit angry that Alex had given away secrets that Peg probably told him.

"You gave up being alone with your secrets when you agreed to let me be your teacher, Ben. Don't blame Alex. It was only that his prayers to our Lord were so direct. You haven't seemed to ask for the Lord's help with much fervor."

Ben hung his head. He felt like a little boy who was headed upstairs to his room for a time-out.

"Herbal tea, Ben?" Alex asked and rose to go to the kitchen. "I'm sure I can convince Sangay to join us." Alex suddenly stopped and turned. "I haven't had you for tea, *rinpoche*, since your ah...transformation. Do you still imbibe every once in a while?"

"I can and I will," Sangay said with a gentle lilt in his voice. He retucked his feet under him and sat in the chair with his legs crossed in lotus posture.

"Ben, I was just hearing from Sangay about his wife..."

"Wife?" Ben interrupted. "Now I have heard it all. I thought you were the number one confirmed bachelor of all Eurasia."

Sangay chuckled. "That was then. This is now. Her name is Pema."

"I'll catch you up later," Alex said. "We're just to the part of the story when Pema and her mother walk to Nepal."

"Uh, okay. I'm sure this will begin to make sense. Please go ahead," Ben said, bowing slightly to the impish Tibetan holy man.

"Pema had been raped by a Red Guard and decided to keep the baby..."

"How awful!" Ben exclaimed.

"That's what I said," Alex said. "She had a vision that told her to keep the baby."

"She had an out-of-body experience, to be exact," Sangay gently corrected Alex.

"And?" Ben asked, his interest piqued. "What happened?"

"They made it without incident. Pema had her baby. A boy," Sangay related. "This is about the time when two Tibetan lamas came to Nepal to set up their spiritual practice near the great *stupa* of Boudnath, considered to be the most powerful Buddhist shrine outside Tibet."

"And that's when I come into the story," Alex said, returning with a wooden tray, three mugs of steaming water, silver tea balls, and a honey jar. "Just like old times," he said warmly, nodding to each of these men who meant so much to him.

The three sat in silence for a few moments while they dunked the tea balls, added the honey, and stared out at the rain until the tea water had cooled sufficiently to sip.

"I have never heard this part of the story—how you two met," Ben broke the silence.

"The two lamas, along with a Western woman named Zina, established a center on a hill called Kopan overlooking the *stupa*…"

Ben interrupted, "Sorry. *Stupa*? I forget what that is."

"It's an elongated pyramid-shaped building. The dimensions represent the holy mind, body, and speech of a Buddha," Sangay replied.

"Oh, thanks."

"Anyway, I think I told you that I was pretty suicidal after 'Nam and while I was travelling in Japan. But having decided against that drastic action, I decided to go further into Asia. Not sure what I was looking for. Just knowing I was incredibly unhappy."

"The place overlooked Kathmandu valley with the towering Himalayas in the background," Sangay volunteered. "Pema raised her son until he was three, and then she gave him to the monks to raise, just as her parents had done."

"Wow, that must have been hard. No matter what the circumstances of his birth," Ben said.

"She's a stoic. She told me he exhibited an uncanny spiritual sensibility from the time he was born. She knew he wasn't hers to be attached to. So, after her son was accepted to go to Sera, which was the largest Tibetan monastery in southern India, she asked her master what she should do. He told her she was to go to a cave high in the Himalayas for at least two years."

"That is amazing," Alex said, awestruck.

"While she was there, she had a vision of what her next mission in life was to be." Sangay took a sip of his tea. He looked out on the autumn foliage and seemed to slip away for a moment. Neither of the other men moved. Finally, he spoke. "She was shown that her path would take her away from the *yogini* life she had so planned on—that she would one day marry and become a Christian."

"Boy, I bet that was hard to take," Ben said sympathetically.

"I've kidded her that she had to stay in that cave for two years just to get her mind wrapped around that idea."

The men chuckled.

Alex picked up the narrative. "I came to Nepal several weeks after Sangay had arrived from Sera. I heard there was an amazingly spiritual American, a former movie starlet from L.A. who had become a Buddhist nun. I wanted to meet her. When I went to a class she was teaching, Sangay was sitting in the back of the room. I couldn't pay attention to the woman—I just wanted the meeting to be over so I could talk to Sangay. That was the most amazing electric attraction I've ever experienced, except maybe when I met Moira. And I asked him right there if he would be my guru."

"And I said no."

"So I found out where he was living, and I kept bugging him."

"Until he wore me down," Sangay said with a light laugh. "No, not really. It was until I could see that he knew what he was asking for and that he was committed to learning what I had to teach him."

"Good for you, Al," Ben said. "And thanks for all the early spade work. I certainly didn't have to go through that kind of initiation."

"Oh, yes, you did," Sangay interrupted. "It was just in a different setting under different circumstances. I assure you I have quite high standards for my students. You didn't get in on Alex's coattails."

Ben sat for a moment taking that information in. He always believed he conned people to get what he wanted. But that was not what Sangay was relating.

Sangay went on with tale. "When Pema came down from the mountain, there was quite a buzz in the Tibetan community, so I went to see her, just out of curiosity. I was headed for the center, when she boldly walked up to me on the path. She said in a matter-of-face voice, 'We have a destiny together…later. Right now I want you to know my name.' Then she told me a new name she'd been given while in the cave by a man who materialized before her, calling himself by a Western name, John."

Ben began to laugh softly. The light was dawning in his head. So that was how Sangay knew John the Beloved and Alex, and even perhaps why John singled him out at that dedication to talk to him. *He* was part of this larger cosmic pattern. His heart beat faster just thinking of all the "coincidences" that had taken place to bring him to this living room, this early morning.

"So when the Dalai Lama asked Sangay to open the meditation center in Utah, on Mt. Nebo," Alex offered, "Moira and I were looking for a place to settle, and the rest is history."

"But when did you get married?" Ben asked Sangay.

"Before I was translated, but after I'd met you."

"So where do you live?" Ben asked, trying hard to grasp this whole new picture.

"We're nomadic right now. We have our yurts, sheep and extended family. And we're headed toward the Bering Strait to meet with the other tribes and come swooping down from Canada when the time is right. And, frankly, I can't wait."

"And you've come to see me?" Ben was overwhelmed with that realization.

"Yes, Ben. You are an important student of mine. It's time for you to get on with higher spiritual practices."

For the next hour, until a sleepy faced Adam wandered in, the three meditated silently. Ben was psychically lifted up by the two men so that he began to feel tingling sensations throughout his body and a pulling sensation between his eyebrows. He wondered if Sangay would thump him on the chest as he had done in St. George, but nothing like that happened. What did happen was… He became happy! A state he rarely let himself feel.

"You are to meditate each day until you feel the high energy vibrations you have felt here. I will help you. So will Alex."

At their parting, Ben agreed on a time to meditate in the middle of the night when he was up and the family was asleep. The other two agreed to stop and send him energy at that time.

"I don't know what feeling this good will do," Ben kidded. "I'm sure I'm flawed on the depression gene—got it from my mother's side."

"Yeah, but who knows. Maybe you'll be the first Jew who ever becomes a blissful saint," Alex said with a straight face. "You'll become such a celebrity, they'll ask you to play the Palace in Vegas."

Chapter Seven

When the earth begins to tremble,
Bid our fearful thought be still;
When the judgments spread destruction,
Keep us safe on Zion's hill.

LDS Hymn #83

If a high-flying plane were to head down the middle of the United States, from Canada to Mexico just weeks after the electronic "net" had been raised, the occupants would certainly be astonished to see that the newly expanded land of Zion was already a mint green from the growth of grasses on plains that had previously been just burnt, arid wastelands. And from that perspective, they might be able to see the crowds of people pressing at the gates to get in—thousands and thousands at each of the twenty-two entrances.

The central storehouses were abuzz with activity as yurts and supplies were loaded onto trucks and sent out in all directions to camps newly established. The immigrants had fun giving these settlements Book of Mormon city names like Bountiful and Liahona, biblical names that mirrored towns in Israel like Bethsaida and Bethlehem;

and some humorous ones like Yurt City and Dodge City. Within days of settling in, boys formed ragtag athletic teams and were competing in soccer and a new favorite—Aussie rules football. Because electricity was very scarce, children had to return to entertaining themselves with simple games of their own making.

And while this joyous immigration was being orchestrated throughout North America, an earthquake in Tangshan, China, with a magnitude of 9.0 shook the region with such force that the ring of volcanos that made up Ryukyu Islands in the South China Sea erupted. Four major volcanos spewed ash into the air, along with the contents of a huge complex of warehouses in which Lu Han's network had stored a virtual stew of biochemicals designed to aid his worldwide terrorist organization. It included anthrax, botulinus, alfatoxin (theoretically enough of just these three to kill everyone on Earth). They had "weaponized" them by loading them into bombs and missile warheads. They had also mass-produced mustard gas and nerve gases, including VX, a terrifyingly deadly agent.

The prophet was informed as soon as the earthquake occurred. He was seated at his desk, reading in the Koran, Surah 99: *When the earth shudders and shakes, And the world throws up its internal burden, And man cries, what is this? On that day, there shall be tidings; On that day men will proceed in masses, sorted out.* President Ueda was at first quite startled at the synchronicity of the moment, even though he knew what had been discussed in the meeting with the heads of the ten tribes.

His mind raced to remember what had been written on the Tibetan plates. *And surely God will provide for our people in our flight when the earth is burned, not with fire, but with air.* That scripture seemed to fit, especially since it was prophesied to occur immediately before the tribes' migration was to begin.

Pretty good description. I don't dare to think about what this will do to people, animals, even the vegetation. He had to turn from these thoughts and go out into the hall to talk with his secretary about other matters—he had such a tender heart, he couldn't help being touched by each person's sorrow and misery, let alone huge sectors of the population. *Just when we enlarged Zion, this!*

It wasn't the first dose of the deadly "brew" over the populated land masses of the northern hemisphere that did them in. It was like a first spray of DDT from a crop duster. The plants and animals still looked fresh for a time. It was the second and then the third pass that did it. Because there was no long-range weather surveillance, no one knew except high officials in the worldwide government headed by Dmitri Gornstein. And, of course, those who needed to know in Zion.

The very air, as predicted in the Tibetan plates, sickened cattle, sheep, poisoned crops, and made people violently ill. It was like a silent ghost, passing overhead, dripping deadly poison. The plume, an elongated carrot shape, headed out across the Pacific on November 8th and reached the west coast of California by November 13th on its first pass around the world. At that rate, it would circumnavigate the world in a couple of weeks.

After hastily consulting with individuals within the New World Order organization in Constantinople where he just happened to be visiting when the earthquake occurred, Lu Han calculated that he would have less than a week to get to safety. He decided he'd travel into the Southern Hemisphere. None of this North American tour to visit the head of Zion. That would have to wait. Although he wouldn't admit it to anyone, he was feeling fright-ened. *This* was not part of his plans. Too agitated to sit down, the emperor paced Gornstein's private quarters in the Hagia Sophia, a sixth-century basilica and masterpiece of Byzantine architecture. It was world famous for its lavishly decorated interior, and high placement of windows around the top of the dome engendered in the viewer upon entering the ethereal sensation of being lifted into light, even into heaven. Now it served as the administrative and electronic center of the New World Order's worldwide net.

"How did this happen?" Han asked no one. "Fortuna. It's Fortuna."

"What's Fortuna?" Dmitri asked as he knocked then entered.

"Fortuna…ah, it's like Fate. Machiavelli talked about the fact that you can plan and plan, but you can only control part of your destiny. The rest is left to Fortuna. How long do you calculate before we can go back to normal?"

"Can't say. Maybe months, a year, two."

"And the Southern Hemisphere?"

"From what we know at this point, that will be pretty much spared, as will the very northern climes. At least from the wind patterns that are usually occurring at this time of year." Han raised his hand to indicate Dmitri was finished speaking. "Leave." He commanded his protege to leave his own quarters.

Where should I go? How to turn this to my advantage? Those were the burning questions in Lu Han's meditation even into the early morning hours. He refused food. He needed complete concentration to receive the messages from his otherworldly master.

Twelve hours later, Lu threw open the doors to the outer area and said with exaggerated bravado, "I'm going to Argentina—you can announce that…ah…it's a continuation of my worldwide tour. Say that there are so many faithful followers there that I've felt the need to visit them."

"Great," Gornstein replied, signally to the male secretary sitting at the desk in the foray to pass the word on.

"Like the Pope of the Catholic Church used to do when there was a Catholic Church. Go out to the masses in different countries. Remember?"

"You're kidding, right? Have you forgotten what pains we used to go through to try to assassinate him?" Dmitri asked with some incredulity in his voice.

"No, my dear Dimi. I haven't. I thought maybe you had. Now, what about you and the others of our brotherhood? Will you accompany me or head to the polar regions?"

"I've spoken to all but two. They said they prefer to follow you. We'll create a cover with the announcement that there will be a conference to work on world health or something…"

"I want to leave tonight. Not tomorrow. I want out of this city tonight. Is that clear?" Lu Han carefully modulated his voice so that he did not betray any of the curious sense of urgency that he felt— not since the specter of the machete attack that he suffered in India.

At least eight of the members of the Order of the Dragon, a secret society of men who were utterly devoted to his Lordship of 10,000 Years, would be leaving from different parts of the world to follow him. Each man held tremendous economic or political power. All presented themselves as altruists working to save mankind, yet they were some of the most evil individuals alive, denying all allegiance but to the emperor and all for a slice of the world domination pie. They would go to Rosario, a large city northwest of Buenos Aires. Drug business acquaintances and former terrorist contacts would provide a very comfortable setting for a temporary headquarters of the New World Order.

Laurie stopped fasting when she heard the emperor wasn't coming. She tried eating, but she was only able to take in soup and tea because she had gone without food for nearly two weeks. The apostle's daughter was bitterly disappointed. And, when news circulated around the ashram that portals to the newly-expanded Zion had been erected as close as Limon, Colorado, she was brought to a sobering standstill.

"New plan," she said to herself as she tried for the second day to get out of bed and walk to the bathroom down the hall. She held onto the beige wall with chipped plaster and made it more than halfway, before she collapsed. She lay helpless for nearly five minutes before someone noticed her and helped her to the toilet with the permanent brown ring around the stool.

She looked like a skeleton. Her joints ached with each step that she took. Light-headed, it took all of her considerable will power to return to bed on her own.

Lying in the cot in the sickroom of the ashram, cold and without an attendant, she found tears flowing down her sallow face and onto her light orange robe. *My mother would take better care of me, no matter what I've done*, she said to herself with considerable force.

Each day she ate a little more and walked to the end of the hall and back. She was determined to get out of the ashram and back to Zion if that were possible. However, with the first passage of the great cloud of Death, she had a setback. She contracted a severe rash and a raspy cough. For a day, she was delirious. There was no one around to help her. She lay in the middle of an infirmary filled with a hacking, vomiting population.

Those devotees who were less affected just put food and water next to her bed and checked on her a couple of times a day. In her delirium, she thought her mother had come for her. Another time, she was sure that she was being rocked by her mother.

A week later, she perked up when someone a couple of beds down made mention of Salt Lake City, where it was reported that nearly 100,000 people had died. It seems the volcanic cloud had dipped down and slammed into the Wasatch Front range, dropping its bio-chemical load before moving on over the Rockies.

John Taylor in a dream or vision related, "I found myself wandering about the streets of Salt Lake City and noticed on the doors of every house…badges of mourning. No one seemed to be passing along the streets and everything was as still as death, except the prayers of the people that could be heard in the houses." This might be the tragedy he was envisioning.

Rumors around the ashram were that there had been a biochemical attack by some anonymous terrorist group on the West Coast, and it was spreading east. Laurie, now able to eat solid foods, was strong enough to walk about. One evening she heard someone upstairs shout that Lu Han was on newly expanded coverage supplied by ITN, the New World Order's network.

She struggled upstairs and into the sitting room where most of the followers of the emperor had gathered. She pushed her way to the front and sat down, cross-legged, near the screen. There was the man she had adored and risked her life for, the man who appeared in her bedroom as a miniature apparition, a man with blue eyes that she had longed for in the waning years of her marriage to Nate. But images of him moving through crowds of desperate people, smiling, sending out handkerchiefs for healing, no longer moved her.

The crowd in Boulder alternately cheered and were stunned into awed silence as the camera got close-ups of *vibuti* streaming out of the palms of his hands and being applied to the eyes of an obviously blind woman—a woman whose eyes were changed right before the world-wide audience to clear, bright, and tearful in gratitude for her sight.

Something's missing, Laurie thought, as she leaned back against the couch. *It feels flat. Maybe it's just because I've been so sick.*

But, as the telecast continued, she became more and more despondent. Feigning the need to throw up, she struggled through the crowd of orange-clad worshippers and headed back down to her small room in the basement. She was a little worried that Lu Han might be reading her thoughts and be displeased.

"Oh, god incarnate, if you want me to continue to worship you, please give me a sign," Laurie said fervently as she dropped to her knees beside her bed. "Please…just something."

Laurie's prayers didn't reach Lu Han in Argentina. He was preoccupied with the masses who were discovering his magic. The emperor had long forgotten the woman he branded as a traitor because she left Zion and thus removed his only inside source of information about the mystery city.

And what an answer to his prayers from Master Mahan! This was the perfect location to begin winning over the people of South America. Rosario, and all of South America for that matter, was in the heart of a spiritual revival—a group of healers and purported visionaries had grasped hold of the collective consciousness. Centered in Rosario, they travelled from town to town putting on the kind of revival that Billy Graham and Benny Hinn were famous for, only this was not to convert the people to Christ but to an amalgam of spiritual traditions, Christianity being only one. And they had pyrotechnics, healings and blood sacrifices right on stage. So when Lu Han arrived, emperor of China! Oh, my, how they were interested!

In the Spanish-style villa that Han and his entourage took over, Dmitri met daily with his master.

"How are you this fine morning?" the Russian asked solicitously.

"I am so pleased with how this world tour is going. I think the New World Order needs to put into place some kind of economic guarantees if people pledge their loyalty to me," Han said as he leaned back in the cane-back chair and laced his fingers behind his head. "Make it pay to belong."

"A cash incentive?"

"No. Nothing that costly. Something like a card or stamp that they could carry, guaranteeing a certain price for goods and services...that kind of thing."

Gornstein's eyes lighted up. "Remember when we worked so hard to get the Smartcard technology? What if we revived that?"

"That really didn't get too far, did it?" Han asked rhetorically.

"A few countries got into it—people were beginning to use the E-purse, I think that's what it was called. I know it was a rechargeable and disposable card that used electronic cash instead of coins to pay for groceries, parking, libraries...that sort of thing."

"If I remember they had got as far as using it with fingerprints." The emperor rose suddenly to his feet, pushing away the glass coffee table. "Even better! I remember when the *al Qaeda* broke into some Russian plant. The plant was manufacturing ID chips that were implanted directly into the bodies of their operatives."

"That's exactly what we should do," the Russian said, breaking into a grin. "And not get stupid like the Taliban did. Left behind maps, computer manuals in Kabul..."

"...detailed designs for nuclear weapons. I told Bin Laden never to grant interviews or give any hint of the extent of his organization. But, no, he wouldn't listen. What a stupid egomaniac!"

Han's deep blue silk pants rustled as he moved across the room—a well-built, moderately handsome man were it not for deep frown lines above his eyebrows and on either side of his mouth. Gornstein looked at him with longing. Lu picked up on his thoughts and turned, "Dimi, I cannot sully this with human desires. This is the ultimate *jihad*."

Dmitri quickly dropped his eyes and mumbled, "Sorry."

"Report on the satellite system," Han barked, sounding nastier than he intended.

"Well. We're set to launch eight satellites from the South Pacific. They will have unblinking surveillance capability over the far corners of the globe. They are to go into deep orbits where they are hard to detect—if there is any one left out beside us who can do such a thing. The only problem it looks like we'll have to deal with is maneuvering around all the space debris that's out there."

"So...we can tighten the noose, so to speak. Watch what people do and control what they buy and sell. Sounds like a Utopian solution to me. But when?" the emperor asked with great impatience.

"We've got some really sick engineers. People dropping out there like flies. We've got to find alternate personnel. That will take some time. I'm so sorry." Gornstein looked like a young dog about to be whipped for making a mess.

Han dug his fingernails into his palms kept his cool.

"This will be like the quantum computer I had you build."

The Russian hurried to change the subject. "Oh, yes what a stroke of genius!" he exclaimed in worshipful tones. "A single atom that switched between different quantum states...speeding up computations so that we could break electronic bank codes."

"I must admit that was sweet," Han said, letting a smile with wicked satisfaction spread across his face. "Certainly helped finance that short-lived war with Israel." He dropped his smile. "Got to get that system in place. Then we can get back there and finish off those infernal Jews!"

After lunch and a stroll through the luxuriant garden that adjoined the house, the two resumed working.

"How is the castor bean project?" Han wanted to know.

"That is moving along nicely. Production is up."

"The plant isn't anywhere near a volcano, is it?" Han asked maliciously.

"Not if I have anything to say about it." The two laughed a hollow laugh.

"One of three most toxic plants…"

"…With no antidote. I know. I just haven't decided how I want to use it."

"I thought we were…"

The Chinese emperor raised his bejeweled index finger to indicate he wanted Gornstein to stop speaking. "Dimi, I'm feeling really creative. I want to keep all my options open. I'm still thinking about how we can use it to our best advantage."

"Of course. I'm sorry."

"No apologies necessary. Let's finish with the electronic implant. How soon can we start? Shall we include newborns?"

"I'll get back to you about that, sir. We are, after all, in South America. My contacts take a little longer to reach me here. We'll know in a day or so. While we're fantasizing, what about your UFO idea?"

"Haven't thought another thing about it. What do you think?" It was unusual for the emperor to ask advice of his longtime friend, but he was suddenly in a good mood.

"I have given it some thought. I know you have power over fire and air. You demonstrated that in India. So it would not be much of a stretch for people to imagine that you had contact with UFOs. With this, you could captivate those who until now have been unwilling to worship you. You could lead them to believe you had the ultimate weapon…something they haven't imagined, from creatures far more advanced than humans."

Lu Han paused for a moment, his consternation breaking into a wide grin. "Let me see if I understand you correctly. I would announce that I had made contact. This is fabulous, Dimi. A simply fabulous idea! I knew this would be an auspicious time. I checked the astrological charts before we came down here. Now what kind of weapon?" The animated emperor laced his fingers together, then bent them back with a crack. "What kind of demonstration? Maybe we could kill two birds with one stone and blow up the Red Sea, so the Jews would think I'm Moses returned. I can imagine that they will resist any UFO ideas. Along with those bloody Mormons!" He always got worked up when he thought about the prophet and the people who had escaped his grasp.

I wonder if I should tell him about the expanded dome over the United States, Dmitri couldn't help but think even though he knew the emperor could read his thoughts at will.

"I don't want to hear about any expansion of their power! I'm in a good mood. Let's talk more about UFOs."

"Well, I'm certain you know the persistent rumor that a UFO crashed into the Siberian forest in 1908."

"No, frankly. I haven't followed UFOlogy. Enlighten me." Han settled into a small couch, tucking his feet under him like the snow leopard he had been nicknamed after as a boy.

"I think it was June of 1908 when a thermonuclear explosion—the equivalent of a ten-megaton hydrogen bomb—destroyed a vast section of the Tungus forest in Siberia. The blast could be heard in Kansk, five hundred miles away."

"Kansk, eh?"

"Yes, and in that city windows were shattered and roofs were blown off houses. For three nights afterward, an eerie glow lit up the night sky all across Europe. In Moscow, for instance, you could take pictures at midnight."

"I wonder if my great-grandparents witnessed it. They would have been old enough, I think."

Gornstein was stopped by the reference to Lu's Russian parentage. He knew it, but his guru and master acted so thoroughly Chinese, the fact of their shared ancestry usually escaped him. "Now here is the interesting part. You would think meteor, right?"

"Right."

"No. Local villagers reported seeing an enormous ball of fire—as dazzling as the sun—traveling slowly through the sky, when it slowed down and changed direction! Destroyed tens of millions of trees, incinerated vast herds of reindeer, and left twelve million square miles of soil *lifeless*."

The emperor's pupils dilated with interest. He shifted his weight so that he lay the other way and waved his hand to indicate he wanted more.

"At first Russian scientists claimed it was a meteorite, but expeditions to the site failed to uncover any fragments of space debris. And, if it were a comet, it surely would have been sighted by astronomers or casual observers long before it plowed into the frozen forests of Siberia."

"And, of course, a meteorite wouldn't slow down and change course within the earth's atmosphere."

"Exactly. Well, whatever it was, was highly radioactive. Soviet scientists conducting flora studies of the area back in the 1960s discovered that new-growth trees germinated in the wake of the explosion were four times as tall as would be expected."

"Definite sign of radioactivity."

"What will interest you the most is this: Soviet scientists, in examining more than a hundred sections of trees from the disaster area found...not just radioactivity, but evidence of *artificial radioactive isotopes.*"

Han leaped up and nearly slipped on the Oriental rug under his feet. "Man-made components of nuclear weapons!"

"In 1908. Thus the UFO theory."

"So other than the obvious, where are you going with this?" the emperor asked, reseating himself. "What good does this do us?"

"I'll have to tell you another short piece of history in order to demonstrate what I'm thinking."

"Go on," Lu said impatiently. "I have nothing but time, particularly for something of this magnitude."

"Does the name Nikola Tesla ring a bell?"

"Just that he was some crackpot American inventor."

"Maybe not."

Lu moved his shoulders back and forth against the couch to settle in. He was luxuriously immersed in this telling.

"Sometime in the middle of the 1930s, Tesla had an interview with a *New York Times* reporter in which he made the claim that he had invented a weapon capable of generating and transmitting highly concentrated particles of energy..."

"Particle beams?"

"Yesssss," Gornstein exaggerated his pronunciation for dramatic effect. "According to Tesla, his weapon would bring down a fleet of 10,000 enemy airplanes and cause an army of millions to drop dead in their tracks."

"So?"

"So, in another interview a few years later, Tesla talked about being capable of destroying aircraft at 250 miles. And also indicated that he had tried out two of his inventions."

"On the Tungus forests."

"That's what some believe. Evidently Tesla, after being rebuffed by American financier J. P. Morgan, decided to direct his energy device at Admiral Peary and his expedition who were exploring the North Pole for the United States Probably wanted to put on some dramatic energy show for the public…"

"So did he have the particle beam technology?"

"No one knows. The day after Tesla died, FBI agents broke into his home and confiscated all his scientific papers. And, of course, the files 'disappeared' immediately after that."

"Can we get our hands on the technology?" Lu asked greedily.

"We can. Since the fall of the U. S. government, many of their files have fallen into terrorists' hands. I have only to ask for them, if it pleases your majesty."

"It does. We could recreate the Siberian disaster and say that aliens have come again to demonstrate their superiority, but this time they are staying. And that I am their designated 'Ambassador to the World,'" Han concluded with a mock flourish.

Chapter Eight

No other success can compensate
for failure in the home.

David O. McKay

ost people in Zion were ignorant of the catastrophe that was floating high above their heads and outside the dome. Only those who managed to get to the "portals" after the earthquake related stories of the horrible things that the sick and dying were going through. But the immigrants to Zion had no idea why. There were many theories, but none of them were right. Who could imagine such a lethal brew of biochemicals.

Because of the healing techniques taught to the "portal" medical staffs by John the Beloved, no one came into Zion with a communicable disease. The procedure was quite simple. Someone like Jed Rivers and a companion who were stationed in Colorado would examine the individual and, if it was determined that their health would pose a threat to the community, the two men would use a sweeping, healing motion with their hands for about a minute. It was that simple.

After being screened for health problems, each adult was interviewed and asked if they would be willing to abide by the law of Zion or the Ten Commandments. If they were, they were next asked if they would live the Word of Wisdom as laid out in Doctrine and Covenants.

If they agreed, the applicants were then processed by another set of Melchizedek priesthood holders who, by laying their hands on the top of the potential immigrants' heads, could discern by the Spirit whether to accept them. Some, but not many, were turned away. For by now, people who managed to make their way to Zion's entrance had some understanding of what this "world in a bubble" required.

Once inside, the new citizens found that they joined most of the others in Zion in collectively looking forward to each new day, which brought with it the promise of the return of the Lord. The common assumption was that it would yet be anywhere from three to seven years before the resurrection or translation of Zion's populace and translation of the earth.

They talked among themselves about the rumors that the ten tribes were on the move. The scuttlebutt was that a half million or so people were coming to Zion. That being the case there would be little opportunity for anyone but them to do temple work in the various temples that were now being reopened. As a result, Latter-day Saints who lived near a temple were encouraged to go weekly at a minimum. The Church had compiled so much data that every Latter-day Saint could connect with a family line and find many of their ancestors who needed their temple work done. Many worked hard to get these records taken care of, for there was the promise that all would be revealed once the Lord came and then there would be far more temple work to be done.

And that was what Ben and Peg were scheduled to do the afternoon after he met with Sangay. On Tuesdays and Fridays, they had a standing date: she would meet him at his office in the temple, and they would do work that Peg had compiled. She hadn't seen him since his encounter with the Tibetan leader. She felt an indescribable shock when she walked in on him, leaning over one of the glass cases.

"Hi, honey," she said in a somewhat timid voice, not wanting to break his concentration. Instead of a "Just a minute. I'll be right with you," she was met with an exuberant husband with tremendous grin who gathered her up in his arms and kissed her soundly on the mouth.

"Have you been ingesting some museum glue?" Peg asked half-seriously.

"I am ingesting you," Ben said moving her away from his hug to look lovingly into her face. "Margaret Taylor, you are so beautiful, you know. I really can't take it all in."

"Ben Taylor. What has gotten into you?"

"Energy! Life! Love!" he said, raising his arms up high in the air and turning around several times. His face was flushed with pleasure; he looked different. In fact, he slightly resembled the blissful Yiddish saint Alex had kidded him he might become.

Peg couldn't make out what had happened. "We are going to do the temple work, aren't we?"

"We are going to do baptisms and initiatory work and endowments and sealings!"

"But you don't like to do baptisms and initiatory work."

"I do now."

Peg slightly staggered over to his desk and sat down, dropping her purse with a loud thump to floor. "Come sit down here and tell me what in the world has happened to you, Ben. I'm not going to play this game. Tell me!"

Ben laughed lightly and came to sit on the corner of the desk, where he had more maneuverability if he wanted to walk around as he described the effect that the meditation had on him. "Sangay and Alex are truly astonishing men," Ben related in a kind of dreamy, singsong voice. "It really felt like someone had put a purely delicious electrical shock up my body—from the bottom of my spine into my head."

He got up and began to wiggle his hips. "I'm happy. I see life *in potentia*. I'm in love with you and the Lord. Shout hallelujah!"

"Shhh," Peg cautioned, clearly embarrassed by his outburst. "Someone will hear you."

"I want people to hear me." Ben pulled his wife to her feet and into his arms where he began to dance the two-step. "I want people to know how much I love you." When he dipped her, she squealed with surprise.

They took two names of Peg's ancestors through an endowment session. Peg looked over at Ben several times. He seemed to glow. Usually he would be nodding off by the time it came to stand up. Yet he was focussed, sitting upright. What in the heck had happened to him? In all the years that she had known him, Peg had only seen him act this way once before. And that was when he returned home from the St. George Temple having met Sangay for the first time.

All the way home, Ben's mood continued to be exultant. Peg wondered how long it would last. He did, after all, suffer from hypoglycemia. She kept waiting for the inevitable "crash" after a few hours without food. But this time it didn't come.

She remembered Ben telling her, when he returned from his experience in St. George, that the *rinpoche* suddenly reached over and thumped on Ben's chest right above his heart. Startled, he opened his eyes, but instead of seeing Sangay, he found he could see through the thick walls of the temple. He also insisted he had 360° vision for several minutes.

Ben said his body felt like it had been pulled down and rooted by the end of his spine to the earth. He also claimed that he had stopped breathing. Then, Ben's most amazing assertion: He said that light seemed to be pouring in and out of his every pore, and indescribable joy flowed up the center of his spine—up into his head. As it reached his crown, waves of liquid, blissful light played in patterns in front of his open eyes: He watched fire burst into "gaseous galaxies," she specifically remembered the phrase. Peg had dismissed much of this as typical Ben hyberbole.

"Why are you so quiet, love?" Ben asked tenderly.

"I know you said that Sangay and Alex helped you get up into a high state, and now you know how to get there and stay there, but I guess I really don't understand what you're talking about. I was just remembering the time back in Utah..."

"...and you think I'll return to my grumpy, jealous, mean self like before."

"Now that you've said it...yes."

Ben made the turn down Orchard Lane. They both looked out the right side of the car to see what was going on at the Winders, their next-door neighbors. Nate's car was in the driveway. That was a novelty these days, because the Church sent him on the road all over the newly expanded Zion in his calling in the Presiding Bishopric.

Before Ben could assure her further, they were pulling into their own driveway. Danny was out shooting baskets, which was absolutely no surprise to either of them. What was surprising was that Ben got out and headed for his son. "Hey, Danny. How's it going?"

"Fine," Danny replied in monotone and tossed the basketball in the direction of the basket.

"How about we play a little one-on-one?"

"Nah, that's okay." Danny ran over to the grass and picked up the ball. As he headed back, he expected Ben to leave. But there was his dad, smiling, waiting.

"Toss it to me."

"Nah, that's okay." Danny threw the ball toward the fruit basket. Ben jumped up and grabbed it midair. "Hey, what are doin', Dad? I'm trying to practice. I've got a game tomorrow."

"Daniel Abraham, you deaf? How long is a little one-on-one going to take? You need to work out against a stronger opponent anyway."

At that Danny began to smile and look at his dad curiously. "Yeah, right!" Danny said with mildly sardonic good humor.

But Ben just kept smiling, so Danny moved to a defensive position and signalled him to start a run at the basket. Ben was out of breath after a few minutes of the high-energy exchange, but Danny now had a grin on his face, along with the goofy one that was widely spread across the usually tired, scholarly face of his dad.

Peg hadn't left the car. As she watched the two, she felt a stab of guilt. *My gosh, how long have we been millstones around the necks of these children? Weeks? Months?*

The male duo sauntered to the house, calling each other names, and Danny swatted his dad on the back.

"Okay, dude. Let's get this dinner going," Ben said. "How about you and me cooking the ladies some dinner?"

Peg went upstairs looking for Miriam. She had her door closed. After knocking lightly several times and getting no response, Peg pushed open the door slightly.

"Don't come in," Miriam said with force.

"Why not?"

"Because I want to be alone. That's why?"

"Honey, we're home now, and we'd like you to come down."

"I don't have to."

"No, but we miss you and it's dinnertime."

"I can stay in here as long as I want to. You do."

Peg winced. She didn't know what to say to the twelve-year-old who'd stayed on a fairly even keel while her mother was depressed, but now that Peg was up and feeling better, it seemed it was Miriam's turn.

Saying a silent, quick prayer, Peg was then impressed to respond, "Okay, sweetheart. Have a good time. We'll save you some food." She left reluctantly and went down stairs.

"Where is she?" Ben asked. "I've made her favorite, hot dogs. But tonight with Danny's help, we've changed the menu to include canned applesauce and chicken soup."

"She says she's not coming down."

"Why?"

"I don't know. Maybe it's just that she become a teenager."

"But she's only twelve."

"Girls mature earlier than boys."

"May I say something?" Danny interrupted.

"Of course."

"She told me it was boy trouble."

Ben immediately began to fall back to his old hysterical ways, imagining his sweet girl pregnant. He headed for the stairs. "I'll take care of this," he said menacingly.

"No, please, Ben," Peg begged. "Leave her. She'll come out when she feels like it. Take a deep breath."

Instead of his usual response, which was to override her advice, Ben did take a deep breath, then let out a laugh.

"Whoops. Almost got me." He jumped down the two stairs and headed back to the kitchen. "You're right. I'm sure it's nothing."

Peg and Danny looked at each other in disbelief.

"What?" Ben said with a malicious gleam in his eye. "It's nothing."

"No, it isn't nothing. You are wonderful. Come here and tell us what has happened to the old Ben," Peg said, pulling him down into a kitchen chair.

Rain fell steadily, creating a rhythmic tapping on the roof of the Taylors' old home. Ben built a fire in the dining room fireplace, and Peg dug out a game of Pictionary which the kids used to love to play. It was a bit battered and smashed, but Peg refused to throw it out on the move east to Missouri.

Miriam, coaxed out of her room, ate and then joined the other three around the dining room table for the first time in months. Ben and Peg jumped into the game enthusiastically, trying to beat each other, while the kids began to play halfheartedly. But it wasn't long before they were making fun of Peg's lack of artistic ability and hooting at Ben's inability to guess answers. A real game was afoot!

Peg and Miriam won, and the "girls" decided to cook up a batch of cookies to help the losers get over the shock. While they were in the kitchen, Danny started to ask Ben a question, then withdrew. Ben pretended to be putting the game away, so his son could work up the courage to ask whatever it was that was on his mind.

"Ah, Dad?"

"Yup." Ben was now rustling around in the closet, finding room for the game.

"Can I ask you something?"

"Sure." Ben turned and sat back down.

Danny twirled a pen on the tip of his finger. Ben waited. "It's about Mom."

"Okay. Shoot."

"Why did she die so young?"

Ben was startled. It had been a year at least since Danny had spoken about his mother, Linda. After a moment to gain his composure, Ben replied, "I don't know for sure. I know that she always fought her way through life. I think she may have just run out of gas."

"Will I die that young?"

"No."

"How can you be so sure?"

"Because, my son, unless you have some kind of accident in the next couple of years, your body is going to be changed and you will become immortal, not going to die, not going to kick the bucket, not going to…"

"Okay, okay. I get it…then I have another question. Why did God let Mom die so early, when she could have had an immortal body in a few years?"

Normally Ben would get irritated and defensive at this point in a discussion about Linda, his first wife who died at age thirty-five of heart failure after their divorce. But tonight he hung in there. "I really don't know. Been thinkin' of your mom a lot recently?"

"Not a lot."

"Some?"

"Yeah."

"Miss her?"

"Sometimes." Danny twirled the pen faster.

"Especially when Peg hasn't been there for you?"

Danny blushed. Ben took that as a yes.

"You know, I haven't been around much either. We've been crummy parents. I'm sorry."

Danny didn't say anything. He took the black pen and began doodling on his jeans. Time passed. The sounds of clanking bowls and high-pitched half-sentences wafted in from the kitchen.

Finally Danny spoke. "You know, I didn't like being left with Grandpa because he was so mean. Mom had to work, and I had to take care of Miriam. Protect her. Cheer her up. I was okay, somehow, because I believed that someday you'd come for us."

"And I did."

"Well, sort of. Your friends kidnapped us."

"Exaggerator."

"Not."

"Yessss. And…?" By now Ben was usually ready to slug his son. This kind of conversation brought up so much guilt, he felt he had to strike out or run.

"Well, I don't know exactly what I'm saying. I guess I want to hear from you…

"…your rescuer," Ben said kiddingly, trying to deflect what he assumed would be an emotional blow—the kind his mother would deliver after getting in close.

"Don't do that, Dad. This is serious."

"Sorry."

"I want to hear it from you, that you really believe that we are going to be rescued by Jesus Christ from this awful world. Do you really and truly believe that He'll be here by the time I'm eighteen?"

That was not what Ben thought he was going to hear, and he teared up with great tenderness. "Oh, my dear, dear son," Ben said, reaching with two hands across the table toward his son. "How much I want to assure you that He will come for all of us. No pain, no death. Just the holy presence of our Master."

Danny smiled, looked down, and resumed the pants writing routine—even more energetically than before.

"Life that bad?" Ben asked.

"It has its moments."

"I see. Hey, Mom, ah, Peg is going to get after you," Ben said pointing to the right thigh of the jeans that was becoming completely filled with doodles."

"Nah, I'll do the other one and tell her it's a new fad. She always believes me about that kind of thing."

"Kinda gullible?"

"I wouldn't say that," Danny said, rising to Peg's defense. "She's okay. She's on top of things…usually."

"Except for this bad patch."

"Yeah."

Then voices from the kitchen grew louder, and Peg and Miriam appeared with flour all over their hair, faces, clothes, even their shoes.

Ben and Danny burst out laughing. So did the other two. "Are these our cookies?" Danny wanted to know, pointing at the two figures.

"They are certainly sweet and tasty," Ben said and choked with laughter.

"Dad!" Miriam complained, half-jokingly.

"You are! You're beautiful and yummy and sweet. And it's your bedtime. Do we get cookies as well as this floor show?" Ben asked Peg.

"Yes. You'll have to take them out in five minutes. We're headed for the shower. Oh, and watch the floor. We had a flour fight. I'll clean it up later." Peg said.

Both were laughing out loud as they ascended the stairs to the upstairs bathroom. The Spirit had so permeated the walls and filled the crevasses of the Taylor home, if someone stuck out his tongue, he might be able to taste it.

At two o'clock A.M. on the dot, Ben left his bed and walked purposively downstairs to the living room. He wrapped himself in a large pink and maroon shawl Peg had crocheted and crossed his legs. "Father, I come before you to be edified."

Then the Jewish convert grew quiet and sat, spine straight, for nearly an hour. On his face, a light and a blissful smile.

When he slipped back in bed, Peg was awake. "Now can you tell me what's happening with you? I know something's up when you play board games with kids. You hate playing games like that."

"Hated. Use the past tense." Ben didn't want to talk. He was sleepy and filled with profound images that hadn't been processed into words. He pulled Peg into his arms. "Honey, I want to go to sleep. When I awake, and if I haven't changed back into Rasputin, I will tell you. I will even go in late to work. Okay?"

This time Peg didn't feel the panicky tug in her stomach that she usually did when he said no to her. He felt so soft and available, she snuggled up against his back and slipped one arm around his stomach.

Chapter Nine

People are going back and forth
across the doorsill
where the two worlds touch.
The door is round and open.
Don't go back to sleep.

Rumi

The dream Ben had that night had to be classified as one of the most profound he'd ever had. "Jung would have been proud of me," he related to Peg over breakfast.

The usually driven scholar kept his word—he didn't go into work—and Peg felt like a new bride, waiting for the kids to leave so they could be alone.

"Well, I'm proud of you," she assured him as she ladelled out steaming oatmeal into his bowl.

He didn't respond. He was still back there. "...so it starts that I'm in an open car thing, and I say as we enter this huge amusement park, 'I've been here before.' As a large number of people and I ride around, somehow the choices we make lead us to either higher or lower realms of the park. I'm headed straight for the lowest realm, which means I end up in a ghetto. Looks like a rundown street in northern England or Europe. I think, *That's the way it always goes.* I see a beautiful young girl, who's sort of tragic, pulling away in one of the cars. I'm very sad as I watch her pass out of sight."

Peg's face reflected her absorption and concern for Ben.

"I wander around, have some things happen which I can't quite remember, but then...this is the amazing symbol...I hear music, I think it's Mahler. But in the dream the composer is Puccini, and I find myself on a train slowly moving out of the park. I stare out of the window at this enormous operatic set, like a German opera. It is black, but beautiful and ornate. And I realize, as we pass by, that I've been an actor there, but now I'm leaving. And I feel very sad. Even though it's dark and imposing, it's been all that I've known..."

"A Jewish dream," Peg said quietly.

"What?" Ben asked.

"Sounds like a Jewish dream. Being forced to the bottom of society, in a ghetto. The German opera."

"Wow! Darling, I think you're on to something. I was going a whole other way with it."

He pushed back his chair and rose to pace around the kitchen.

"Yes, that's it! And I'm the clown, Pagliacci. Learned that from my mother. Keep 'em laughing. Then they won't kill you. I do come from a long line of Jewish comedians after all."

"But please don't give up being funny in this transformation you're going through. I count on your humor."

"Not very likely, sweetheart." Ben touched her face affectionately, then continued. "You know, I used to listen to Mahler, before my conversion to the Church, in Eugene. Sat in the library on campus, watched the sun set and thought about suicide." Ben sat back down and shook his head. "Stupid."

"It wasn't. It was understandable. And besides, in your dream, you're on a train out of there."

"To the gas chambers," Ben said woefully.

"To a new life!" Peg said with irritation. She lightly banged her spoon down on his hand. "I'm sick of you always seeing the dark side of things!"

"That's what Sangay dinged me for, too." Ben said, rubbing his hand and looking like a boy who's been caught dipping the family cat's tail in the toilet.

"Which brings me to ask you...notice how patient I've been? What *did* happen with Sangay and Alex?"

A loud rapping on their front door startled the two. Ben walked briskly to answer it, while Peg dropped her head and shook it. *Totally typical*, she moaned to herself. *We never have time alone.*

"Nate?!" Ben said, surprised because his neighbor and friend was hardly home, much less came to visit. "Come in."

"No, thanks, Ben. I saw your car and wondered if I could call upon you to use your priesthood."

Ben glanced back at Peg who now stood in the living room. She shrugged and gestured to him to go. *Probably one of the kids is sick,* she thought as she returned to the kitchen and the half-warm oatmeal. *Won't take long. Then I will force it out of his hide. No interruptions.* Lost in thought, she slowly pulled the oatmeal-filled spoon out of her mouth. *Why has my husband taken a turn for the better?*

"Thanks," Nate said again, affectionately tapping Ben on the back as the two walked along the road.

"One of the kids sick?"

"Not really."

"Oh?"

117

"It's…ah…Mary Margaret. The kids are in school."

"Is she not feeling well?"

"Not exactly. Look, let's just wait until we get there, okay?"

As the men entered, Ben noticed that the curtains hadn't been drawn that morning in the Winder household, which was a lot more chaotic than his own house in terms of toys, clothes and other items strewn about the living room, dining room and up the stairs. *Seven kids and little support. His mother comes a couple of times a week, I've heard,* Ben thought with a sudden pang of guilt that he never offered to help. *I'm going to come over here and do something at least once a week. I have time to help out my friend.*

The two men made their way through to the kitchen, where Mary Margaret sat, a cup in her hand, sipping herbal tea.

"Well, that didn't take long, did it?" she asked. "Nate wasn't sure where he'd find someone at this hour of the morning."

"How are you, Mary Margaret?" Ben asked with a new kind of attentive affection in his voice.

"I've been better."

Ben pulled out his key chain and began to unscrew the top to see if it still held enough consecrated oil for a blessing for the sick.

Nate said, "We won't be needing that. Thanks."

"Oh?"

"Mary Margaret has asked for the blessing to help with her faith."

Ben looked quickly in Mary Margaret's direction and saw big tears forming in her large blue eyes.

"I just can't go on pretending. I just don't believe that God cares for me when he let me suffer for all my life."

Ben looked to Nate with raised eyebrows. Nate shrugged.

"Heaven knows, I prayed to Him, to the Holy Mother, to know that they cared for me when my da was murdered."

"But you knew ahead of time, Em. You were forewarned," Nate argued. "Who told you if not God?"

"Little good that did me."

The trio fell silent. Ben said a quick, silent prayer for heavenly help, while Nate looked like a prize fighter who had taken a staggering blow to the gullet in the fourteenth round.

"I know He's real," Mary Margaret continued. "I've been bleeding for him every Friday for years. You'd think he'd appreciate it. But I didn't even get to see him when he supposedly appeared to you two in the Mormon temple."

Ben, still on his Sangay-induced high, moved over to the bereft woman and kneeled down next to her chair. "Dear, dear soul, I think I can help."

She didn't pull away, but looked up at Nate, who looked relieved that someone else was trying to get through.

"I have seen the Lord, briefly. I bear you my witness that He lives. He is very much alive and aware of each of us. As his servant, I feel I must tell you that He *does* love you and wants you to have all the blessings of His gospel."

She looked straight ahead, chin jutted out, teeth clenched. Then she suddenly looked at Ben in the face and said, "You're a convert, aren't you?"

"Yes, ma'am."

"How can you tell? When can you let go and believe these people?"

"How about right now, in the company of two of his humble servants?"

She ignored him and began to rock and sing,

> *I am but a little child,*
> *Yet my mantle shall be laid*
> *On the Lord of the World.*

The King of the Elements Himself
Shall rest upon my heart,
And I will give Him peace…

Ben stood and rubbed his knees. "Here's a way to look at it," interrupting the singing. "The Lord said that you can tell a tree by the fruit it bares. You've known us now for a good period of time. Right?"

"Yes."

"Have we been good to you?"

"Oh, yes," Mary Margaret said, tears returning in great drops.

Ben reached out his hands. "Come on. Take that first step. Come into the company of His humble servants. You certainly qualify; you are a wonderful woman."

With a wild sob, she stood and fell into Ben's arms. Nate quickly joined them. Rather than hugging Nate, she clung to Ben, letting herself feel the body of a man who didn't desire her, taking in the high intuitive "vibes" Ben was emitting. They stood there for over a minute. The only sound was the bonging of the father clock marking the hour in the hallway.

Abruptly, the Irish mystic pulled away, turned to face Nate and said forcefully, "I'm not promisin' to marry you. Just because I get baptized."

"I don't want you to even think that is part of the decision," Nate said with great earnestness.

She pierced him with the look that seemed to penetrate his very soul. "I don't believe you. I don't think you would still be my friend, if I wasn't involved with you romantically."

"But I am willing to back off completely. Just be your friend," Nate replied.

She stared at his face again. This time she liked what she saw. "Okay. I want that. I want you as a friend. No strings attached. That makes it easier to decide."

Nate stuck out his hand, she did the same. He covered hers with both of his large, square ones. "Holy friends, it is."

"Good, now I have another condition," she said, pulling her hand away and walking to the back of the kitchen, badly in need of cleaning.

"What is it?" Ben asked solicitously.

"I'm not givin' up my gifts."

The two men looked at each other. Nate couldn't help but think of the disruption she caused at the Dubiks' dinner party.

"Well?" she asked impatiently.

Ben looked to Nate then back at her. "You have remarkable intuitive and healing gifts, I understand. I wouldn't want you to stop using them. I would just ask that you get help in refining them."

Mary Margaret began to cry. She threw the apron up to her face and wept and wept. The two men stood like midwives; the Spirit restrained them from comforting her, letting her do the "pushing."

When the sobs subsided, she lowered the apron and said quietly, "I'd like that blessing now."

The dust storms over the northeasterly corridor of the Asian continent grew fierce in their intensity and size. While Lu Han and his crew worked away in Argentina with their nefarious plans, the ten translated heads of the "lost tribes" moved their charges swiftly into place. Amazingly, the occasion of moving thousands upon thousands of people from place to place was of no note to the Chinese emperor. There was such chaos throughout the northern hemisphere when people learned about the contents of the deadly cloud, they were streaming out of cities to get to sparsely populated higher latitudes.

Sangay's tribe of Naphtali had left India, China and other parts of Asia and were now gathering at the far end of the Gobi Desert. These were not city dwellers, but people accustomed to long-distance travelling on foot. They also knew to avoid these storms at all costs. But they believed in the Lord and in his servants, so, against all their natural instincts, they plunged their way into the stinging, howling dust storm. They knew the prophecies—this was part of what had been foretold for centuries: a man would rise up from among their ranks whose body would be changed. He would lead them like Moses of old to the promised land. They knew it meant they needed to muster a courageous faith.

Sangay's family, who were *Dropkas* (wanderers), had spent their life wandering throughout a vast western valley in search of good pasturage. The land and their animals had given them everything that they needed. Yaks and sheep provided cheese, milk, yogurt, along with sheepskin clothes, yak leather boots and tents. Now that had been stripped away, and they were eager to go to the promised land where it was prophesied milk and honey would pour forth without effort.

Two yaks pulled their nearly black yak-hair tent with its wooden stake poles tied with thick twine dragging behind. The red and white prayer flag which usually flapped in the breeze when the tent was up had been folded carefully and placed in one of the bundles the women carried.

"Greetings, Father," Sangay said as he raised his hands, palms together in a traditional greeting of respect as his father approached, moving in line to enter the heart of the storm. He looked up at the eight-feet-high beige and orange wall of dust just ahead. Above it there was blue sky. *What faith they have to have!* he thought.

Sangay didn't need any protective covering on his face. The dust didn't bother him—in fact, the dust danced around him, but didn't cover him at all, a fact that was not missed by the travellers as they passed by him.

His father, Yeshi, raised his hands in response and pulled down the scarf that was wrapped around his face. He was dressed in a fur cap, gray clothes covered with a dark-brown fur coat and trousers, red and gray boots, and walked with a staff in his hand. A gray goatee danced on his face as he grinned broadly. The two touched foreheads in the traditional Tibetan greeting of affection. His father then quickly pulled the protective scarf back over his face.

The elderly man was assisting a younger cousin of Sangay's with a herd of milking goats which were looped together by a long rope. They were long-haired, white, black, gray, and brown and had foot-long curving horns and "smiling faces." Right before they disappeared into the maelstrom, the two men gave Sangay a thumbs-up sign. He returned it along with a broad grin. Two women followed behind—the older was assisted by a younger one in a traditional pink, blue and green striped dress with her hair bound in a braid woven with cloth of bright colors and tied around her head. The younger wore no covering to shield her from the dust storm. This was Sangay's wife, Pema, walking next to Sangay's mother. She who could move from one location to the next with just a thought chose to make the journey on foot with his family. She carried a niece's baby in a sheepskin pouch on her back. The four-month-old struggled to peer out at Sangay as the translated being weaved through the line of people to greet each member affectionately. Sangay knew he didn't need to worry about his translated wife, but, although he knew he shouldn't worry about his extended family of fourteen who were originally from Khamin in the southwest part of Tibet where the men were noted for their size, strength and rugged features and the women for their sturdiness, he wanted to touch them and reassure them that the Lord was watching over them.

"We move one step closer to the promised land. The Great Lord calls to us," Sangay said repeatedly to each of his family members.

With this encouragement, they covered their faces with their long scarfs and pressed forward. They could see nothing more than three feet in front of them as the caravan disappeared ahead of them. They struggled for a quarter of a mile in the stinging, howling monster when the dust began to lighten up and soon they could see clearly ahead. To their astonishment, they found themselves walking in a 300-yard-wide corridor—blue sky overhead, dust all around—but they could breathe and move without the horrible impediment that they feared and detested. One-thousand-foot-tall dunes stood as sentinels as they moved toward a salty, spring-fed lake, which looked an azure jewel against the coarse sand. Camels, yaks and goats hurried their owners to the water's edge. It was the surefooted Bactrian camels, able to carry 500-pound loads and go for days without water, that had aided these travellers so ably.

Back at the fringes of the storm, Sangay and a number of Church authorities yelled encouragement to families who hesitated to move forward. "Trust in the arm of the Lord. He will protect you," shouted a Tibetan district president from Dharmsala, India.

"'Come. Follow His humble servants," Sangay shouted above the storm.

Thus the tribe of Naphtali, consisting of about 50,000 men, women and children, worked their way to the Bering Strait in the same miraculous way that Moses led his people through the Red Sea. The elements served as both protection and deterrent to any who would foolishly follow.

The same sort of circumstances surrounded the movement of the other nine tribes. In all, nearly a half million of the Lord's children were moving to fulfill the many prophecies regarding the ten tribes—not only contained in the Bible and Book of Mormon—but in their own scriptures which were more detailed about this time which had been foretold when Christ visited them, after he had left the saints in Central America.

Lu Han, in the meantime, was busy with the large terrorist nest in South America—a tri-border area where Brazil, Argentina and Paraguay meet. Using the huge maté factories in the Barrio Martin area of Rosario, the Chinese emperor converted these into bio-chemical factories which produced the same ingredients for mass destruction as did his island "kingdom" in the south China Sea which had blown sky high.

These deadly products were shipped to Ciudad del Este, a border town in Paraguay, where Colombian drug traffickers and European and Asian mafia lieutenants would purchase these highly prized goods—now more lucrative than the drug trafficking that had previously characterized the region's economic exchanges. Not that drugs weren't still in demand. They were, in fact, more in demand than ever with a world population so discouraged by worldwide war and terrible economic conditions. Similar conditions resulted in Russia after the fall of communism, when a man's life span dropped to about fifty principally because of his deteriorating health habits and increasing consumption of alcohol. Now those numbers spread to the rest of Europe, the former United States and other First and Second-World countries. The popular drug of choice was synetrope-a deadly combination of LSD and speed. People could stay high for days, not eat, not feel their exposure to the elements, and very quickly lower their life expectancy while remaining in a nearly ecstatic state.

Gornstein also set up rallies with the large Middle Eastern expatriate population who had been already been converted to Hezballah, Hamas, or al-Queda propaganda back at the turn of the twenty-first century. "It's like the Wild West there," a senior Pentagon official had complained. "Crime, religious extremism, and politics are all linked…" It was a perfect combination of factors for Han's plans to commandeer the world's economy.

Lu Han's only complaint was the size of the mosquitoes in the section of Rosario where he was staying—they were the size of small bats and were horribly efficient at sucking blood. These insects proliferated because of the surrounding Parana River and the humidity. And, if one were new to the area, he would not have built up the immunity to the bites that the natives did.

The emperor became obsessed with avoiding mosquitoes after his first bite when his forearm swelled with a lump the size of a baseball. Two of his security guards were conscripted for the job of stopping the bugs. They knew their lives would be taken if they failed, so one stayed awake all night hovering near the mosquito-tented bed of the emperor. The other man took his place during the day. They soon learned something they dared not reveal: Han was delirious with the bite. With a raging fever, he cried out for his mother, screamed for water to quench his thirst and spoke of promises and covenants to his master. Although Han made no sense, the guards intuited that what they heard could be repeated only on pain of death.

Chapter Ten

Thou art thy mother's glass, and she in thee
Calls back the lovely April of her prime:
So thou through windows of thine age shall see
Despite of wrinkles this thy golden time.

Shakespeare's 3rd Sonnet

Peg watched as the figures of Ben and Nate disappeared across the large field that separated their homes. She sighed as her eye fell on that field behind her house; she had given nine of the ten acres back to the Church. *But there are roses, a couple of fruit trees and, of course, a garden*, she consoled herself. After meeting with Moira and facing the reality that she was, after all, acting a great deal like her mother, she reluctantly had let the acreage go.

"Funny thing about trying not to be like a parent," Moira had said. "The more we try, the more we end up being like them."

"And I complain about my mother in all of her manic projects and cleaning, and here I am overwhelmed with a million of them. Wow, I really hadn't seen that before," Peg had said. "I'm going to have to redefine myself."

And she had been true to her word. She finished all the canning and streamlined the housework by delegating chores and insisting that both she and Ben reinforce the schedule the two had set up for the children. Danny and Miriam grumbled at first, but then fell into line.

Now she looked at the small garden she had planted and teared up. "I'll be fine," she said aloud as she caught a glimpse out of the corner of her eye of a man walking up the driveway. She quickly turned around to see the stranger in suit and tie approaching. He had a kind smile on his face, but she was a little panicked, seeing that no one else was at home.

"Sister Taylor?" the tall, well-built man asked as he approached.

"Ah, yes," she replied, searching his face for recognition, but finding none. "My husband's just next door..."

"It's you I've come to see. My name is Andrew..."

"Are you new to the area?" Peg cut in nervously.

"Not exactly," he replied. "I've come on an errand from the Lord..."

"Oh, my goodness," Peg exclaimed and indicated to Andrew that he walk with her to the back porch where they could sit and talk. "I'm so embarrassed. It's just that I didn't know you." Her voice trailed off as they reached the porch. She quickly wiped the small glass table with her sleeve before sitting down. "Could I get you something to drink?"

"No, I'm fine, really," he said in a quiet, reassuring voice. "I've come to talk with you about a possible calling for you and your husband."

"Yes?"

"I believe your husband has been approached by Elder Sangay."

"Yes?" *If he was, he hasn't said anything to me,* thought Peg.

"I know that he hasn't said anything to you. He was asked not to until I could come."

Did he just read my mind?

"Yes, I did. It's a function of being in the state of consciousness I'm in. I guess you haven't made the connection to my name. I'm sorry—I'm Elder Andrew, Peter's brother...Peter, the head of the Lord's church in the meridian of days."

Peg threw her hands to her cheeks which had just brightened to red. "Oh, my heck," she blurted out, then spent several minutes apologizing profusely for the what she thought was a profanity.

Andrew tried to assure her that she had not offended him. But he just had to wait until she calmed down before he could say, "The Lord would like to ask you if you would consider being called along with your husband as mission president and wife to the people of the tribe of Judah."

Peg couldn't speak. Finally, she asked in a little voice, "Where? Israel?"

"No, it would begin in the Los Angeles area. We aren't sure if you would serve the entire duration of your mission there..."

"Yes, of course," Peg again interrupted. The fact that she was sitting across from a messenger from the Lord was beginning to sink in. In all the times that Ben had seen Sangay and the children reported talking to an angel, she had only seen Sangay briefly one night in their bedroom. She had admitted to being a little jealous of the attention that Ben received. Now it was her turn.

"The reason I've come is that I work closely with the Lord regarding the tribe of Judah, and I would be supervising your work."

This isn't the way people used to be called to be mission presidents, Peg thought.

"No, these are exceptional times. And you and Ben are exceptional people."

"Well, I'm not sure about that. I've really been messed up recently."

"You have suffered, but your suffering has meaning, we know."

"Oh, my gosh. You've known about my depression?"

"Yes."

"And do you know my thoughts?"

"We choose not to know—to respect your privacy."

"Good," Peg said and let out a sigh. Then her face darkened. "I don't know if we'll be good for you. We certainly don't fit the formula for mission presidents. I mean, I had an alcoholic father..."

"...whom you cared for until you left home."

"And then I got married to a guy who ended up a drunk..."

"...as often happens when a parent is an alcoholic and you are only nineteen."

"And then my daughter was killed, and I'm not sure but what I could have done something more to prevent that," Peg said in a husky voice.

"It was Rachel's time to leave the telestial sphere. She has served admirably as a guardian spirit for you. Do you know that she was the one who influenced Ben to sit behind you that fateful Sunday?"

Peg's mind was spinning. *How does this man know so much about me? I have known thee of old,* was his telepathic reply.

Now tears came—spilling down her cheeks and wetting the white blouse she was wearing.

"But I've kicked my own mother out of the house."

"Ben did that, and it was both a necessary and healthy thing to do."

"Well, that's true, but..."

"Sister Peg, I know how it feels to be plucked up and asked to do the Lord's work, believe me. And I know that everything we have ever done in our shortcomings comes spilling out, but, unless you have strong objections to this calling..."

"I'm sorry to keep interrupting, but why would Jewish women want to hear from me? I can see Ben, but me?"

"I assure you that you have a great deal to teach."

She looked across the field to the Winders, wishing Ben would come home. *So that's why he's been so different...*

He's been challenged to work toward certain goals as a priesthood holder.

Oh, I see, she responded without realizing that they were not speaking aloud. "Oh, my, that's spooky," she said aloud, realizing she had just been communicating telepathically. She rustled around in the metal chair.

"Your say will have a greater weight with the general authorities in this matter," Andrew said gravely. "You must consider the children—the effect that this will have on your family."

"I see. Well, I'll have to talk to everybody. I don't want to make this decision without knowing how everyone feels."

"Exactly as it should be. I will await your decision," the tall, well-built man pushed back the chair and stood up and bowed slightly in her direction.

Peg, thrilled at his gesture of respect, asked, "Okay, then, so how do I contact you?"

"A thought will do."

"Wow. No kidding," Peg said, her eyes growing wider. "All right then."

Andrew bowed again and turned to walk back down the driveway. She glanced back at the Winder house, wondering if Ben was walking back down the road. When she looked back, Andrew was nowhere in sight.

When nothing came from Lu Han despite a week of her prayers and protestations, Laurie made up her mind: She was returning to Zion, if that was possible. She forced herself to eat more and more. Her eyes, which hurt when she tried reading anything but large print, began to be able focus for longer periods of time. Even her hearing, which had also been affected, began to respond to her new diet and exercise regimen which consisted of longer and longer walks around the grounds of the ashrams.

After two months of determined effort, Laurie was in much better shape. The word was that Lu Han was in South America working to alleviate the poverty and promote well-being of its people. But she didn't hear from him. And her desire for him finally began to fade. *I want to be healthy,* she repeated to herself. *Healthy in every way.*

When the driver of the delivery van who brought the produce to the house flirted with her, she knew she was back and looking good enough for men to notice. *I wonder what Nate would think of me now,* she pondered. Against ashram orders, she was letting her hair grow out, but to her surprise it was coming in mostly white. She took to wearing a headband around her head, looking like a cancer patient undergoing treatment. And thoughts of leaving, escaping, percolated to the surface of her mind unbidden.

"Hi, Larry," she called out to the delivery driver one autumn afternoon six months into her recovery.

"Hi, Laurie," he called back.

She shuddered with surprise at the use of her real name. "Hey, how do you know that?"

"I've asked around."

Laurie walked down the driveway so that they could speak without others hearing. "Oh, and what is your real name?"

"Larry Reislander."

"And Reislander spelled backwards means...?" Laurie was now definitely flirting with the tall, lanky man with acne pockmarks. His long, stringy hair hung down the back of light blue shirt.

"Never thought about it," he said, smiling at her as she walked around the truck and pulled herself into the passenger side of the old bakery truck.

"Where you headed?"

"Downtown."

"Can I come with you?" Laurie asked seductively.

"Not supposed to have riders."

"And?"

"And I'm not going to break the rules and get fired. But I could come around after work. Maybe we could figure something out." Larry began to cough, a raspy cough that seemed to follow nearly everyone who survived the months of biochemical fallout. And, if he were shirtless, it would obvious he was still suffering from the rash that accompanied the cough.

"Of course, Larry. I was just testing you," Laurie said a little petulantly as she slid down out of the seat and shut the door. "I'll see you later. Whenever you can get off."

It wasn't more than 5:15 P.M. when Larry pulled up out front of the former sorority house in a old Ford Fairlane that clearly had been lovingly worked on. Laurie was out in the car by 5:17.

"Where to?" Larry asked innocently.

"I'd like to drive out in the plains for a ways. Will your car go that far?"

"A lot farther than that," Larry bragged.

Laurie kept up the sexually charged chatter as they drove farther and farther away from Boulder, east out into the empty plains and nearer to the portal into Zion at Limon. She had done her research and guided them unerringly to the portal that Nate and Peter had established.

"Hey, what's that?" Larry called out when the tent city came into view.

"Looks like one of those places where people are supposed to be able to be safe from all this fallout," Laurie replied, trying to sound innocent.

"Well, I don't want anything to do with it," was Larry's response as he began a slow U-turn in the bumpy road.

"I do!" Laurie popped up the lock and pulled down hard on the handle. "I'm really sorry for tricking you," she said with great sincerity. She landed on her feet, but the side door was left banging in the wind as Larry slammed his foot on the gas pedal and sped off in a cloud of dust.

The guards, a hundred yards away, watched with interest at this little drama as it unfolded in the darkening night. There had not been as many people coming to this portal as there had been in the days and weeks after the release of the gas cloud. The joke among them was that the latecomers were cockroaches, capable of surviving any kind of thermonuclear radiation. Now this. It looked to them like this skinny, white-haired woman had been dumped out on the plains...and she was now making her way to them with a sad, but determined look on her face. They hoped they wouldn't have to turn her away. It was a long walk back to some kind of civilization.

Peg was sitting on the couch, hands folded, in a kind of delirium of delight when she heard Ben and Nate's voices as they approached the front door.

"...really couldn't have done it without you..." Nate was saying.

To which Ben replied, "It was the Spirit. Really, I don't think there is any other explanation."

Peg wasn't even the slightest bit interested in whatever the topic of conversation was. She was in her own blissful world. The door opened. Ben stuck his head inside. He was half-afraid to come back to her, having left so abruptly and returning in such a great state of mind.

"Hi, sweetie," Peg called out.

"Oh, hi," Ben said to her, then pulled his head back out so that he could shake Nate's hand. "What a great day. She'll be a marvelous saint," said the Jewish convert who knew what it was to make the momentous decision of becoming a Latter-day Saint.

"She already is. I can't wait to see what the Holy Spirit does for Maggie." Nate looked a little starstruck as he turned to walk down the uneven sidewalk.

Ben tried to wipe off the grin that had nearly encompassed his face as he stepped inside and shut the door. *Mary Margaret in the Church! What a thrill to play even a small part in her decision. But now, back to Peg.* He sat down on the couch before he really looked at Peg's beatific smile. *Whoa, what happened here? Did Mary Margaret call after Nate and I left?* he wondered.

"Ben, I know," Peg said earnestly.

"Oh, she called?"

"Who?"

"Mary Margaret."

"No. I think we're talking about two different things."

"Just what are you talking about, sweetheart?" Ben replied. Peg noted that Ben asked this in a steady voice. He had not lost his cool.

"About our calling. What are you talking about?" Peg asked.

135

"Oh, how did that happen?"

"First you tell me what you were talking about."

Usually by now, Ben would be boiling inside, so frustrated with her lack of direct answers. But he checked himself, took a breath and her hand. "Okay, sweetheart. Let's take it from the top."

"No, I insist. Benjamin, you go first. What happened when you went to the Winders?"

"Mary Margaret has decided to get baptized. Just in the last half hour. But she laid down some pretty stiff rules for Nate...no romance...just friends..."

"I am so glad. Well, the rules will hold up, at least for now."

"You know how women's minds work. You think she'll change it after she's settled into being a Latter-day Saint?"

"Indubitably."

Ben let out a sigh. "Good, because I think Nate really loves her."

"And he can prove it by being a holy friend."

"Her words exactly!" He paused to look a long time into her brown eyes. "What a wise woman you are."

"That's what *you* say," she demurred.

And finally, after the two patiently struggled with each other's very different discourse patterns, Ben learned that Peg was committed to the idea of their going on a mission, if it could be worked out that the children would be blessed in the process. The two momentarily basked in the spiritual light that had been conferred on them by the Lord's servants. It sweetened and lighted their way as they discussed the details of leaving and waited for Danny and Miriam to come home.

Chapter Eleven

It's not that I'm afraid to die.
I just don't want to be there
when it happens.

Woody Allen

A fondness for a certain treat, baklava, that his mother used to make, nearly became an obsession with Lu Han. And time. He was obsessed with that, too.

"I'm wasting precious time. What am I doing in the outskirts of hell?" he nearly shouted in Gornstein's direction.

"Saving yourself, so the world can have the messiah they so long for."

"How long am I trapped here?"

"We've monitored the air and ground quality daily, as you know. Nearly two billion have perished..."

"...yes, yes. I've heard it all." Han began to pace. "And in Beijing? Will we be able to put together an army?"

"Right now winds are whipping sandstorms across the city, your Highness. There's a ghostly haze to add to the people's misery. From reports I've received, the streets are deserted. And the cough that they normally get under these conditions is severely aggravated. It's so much worse than last year."

"An army. What about an army?" Lu Han's voice rose menacingly.

"Once these winds die down we can round up enough to suit our needs."

The emperor's robes swished as he turned at the end of the well-appointed room and walked back to the seated man and confidant who headed the World Council. "The rest of the Mormons are on the move! They're halfway across Siberia. They are going to escape to the biodome in America." Han shouted and banged his fist down hard on a side table. "Master Mahan has repeatedly sent me messages that I must do something about their escape. And I can't do anything about it!"

Gornstein looked to the ceiling. They had been through this discussion so many times, he was worn down. "But Master, we have intelligence, and they say they have no indication of any mass movement."

"I don't care. I know what I know. And if we don't act soon, they will be out of my reach."

Dmitri let Han go through this daily tantrum and then tried to divert the conversation to a subject that delighted the Emperor. "All the technology is ready to go at your return. And think, with one-third of world's population decimated, it will make our job a lot easier."

That mollified Han momentarily. "Yes, beginning with newborns...computer implant...necessary to feed the hungry...clothe the poor. I will be their savior. They will, of course, assent to such a population accounting in order to receive these boons!"

"You will make the announcement upon your triumphant return. Worldwide audiences will thrill to your very words." Gornstein's emphasis on the last two words let bleed into the dialogue the fascination, attraction, even worship that he accorded Han.

Lu smiled a little seductively in Dmitri's direction.

"I want to get packed. I want to go now. We'll fly into Moscow. Just behind the storms. You can visit relatives, Dimi."

Sangay's ability to bilocate served him well in this crisis situation. While he sat in his tent on a round pillow, legs crossed, in a deep state of relaxation, he could materialize his body anywhere else in the world that he was needed. And he *was* needed—in the front of the caravan, to each side, in the rear—he appeared simultaneously, as did the other heads of tribes, to the leaders of each band of a hundred sojourners.

Pema, his short, black-haired wife, knew a yogi who had mastered this ability in his telestial body, but it still was a bit of a shock when she came into the enclosed part of the tent where her husband was meditating to see him look so still. It was as if she was looking at an upright corpse. But she quickly calmed her fears by recalling once when she herself had been blessed with such an experience.

On that occasion, her guru sent her a telepathic message that she should walk to a courtyard behind the *stupa*, which she did with a little trepidation. But to her utter amazement, no sooner had she arrived than the sunlight turned into intense brilliancy and against this dazzling background, Lama Dawa-Lharje appeared.

Bewildered, she knelt before him and touched his shoes. They were real to the touch, scuffed. She could even feel the outline of his toes. She stood up with her mouth open, speechless.

"Good. I'm pleased that you trusted your intuition," he had said with much kindness. "I am about one day away by foot, and I need you to instruct several of my *chelas* about arrangements that need to be made for my stay."

After giving her precise directions about this upcoming encounter, the lama said, "This is not a ghost as you may imagine. This is my flesh and blood. I have been allowed to show you this manifestation of bilocation, rare to experience on this earth."

Then he placed his hands on her head and gave her a blessing. The pressure of his small hands on her head was real. Then she heard a kind of rumbling sound, which she was told later was typical of the sound that bodily atoms make when they begin to dematerialize. His body began to melt before her very eyes. First his feet and legs melded into the intense light, then his mid-section and head. It reminded her of a scroll being rolled up.

To the very last second, she could still feel his fingers resting lightly on her hair. Then there was nothing but a sweet aroma like honeysuckle in the air. She sat down with a thump on the stone sidewalk and waited for some sense of sanity to return. She was sure she had fallen victim to some hallucination or other.

Finally she went and told her friends what the lama wanted prepared, and he appeared, just as he had said, on the following day.

So it was very easy for Pema to believe that Moroni appeared the boy Joseph in the bedroom. In fact nothing about the miraculous events surrounding the establishment of the Church seemed at all ridiculous or unbelievable. And now that she and her husband were translated, such "miraculous" experiences were so commonplace for both of them. Nevertheless, just because her body had been supercharged with energy that allowed her to remain in a sleepless state of joy did not mean that she was completely accustomed to a translated life, one of the perks of which was the ability to travel at will, not only on this planet, but to other telestial spheres as well. She and her husband were too busy helping this mass movement to go off on such a jaunt.

Sangay, this afternoon, had projected himself into two locations: one in the middle of the migratory pack which was moving through a narrow valley surrounded by low hills made of curvaceous, shifting sand. This might have been a moonscape save for the presence of the brilliant azure elliptical water that bordered the trail for a half mile. Amid the noise of the animals and the singing of members of the tribe of Naphtali, Sangay walked with the travellers and encouraged them and told stories of what was happening in the front, where the tribe of Dan had nearly reached the Chukchi Sea.

At his next manifestation, he was touched by the sight of Tibetan prayer flags, flapping in the breeze, tied to backpacks and animals' halters.

Sangay searched until he found his extended family. He hurried to catch them. "Hello," he called out as he neared the cluster of twenty or so pilgrims.

"Sangay," his mother called out with much affection. She was much happier to have her son appear and disappear than when he "disappeared" as a young boy to become a monk. The sacrifice had clearly paid off.

After the traditional head-touching greeting, Sangay walked in the middle of them. "You are about one week from the gathering place at the sea." This announcement was greeted with enthusiastic laughter. Although these nomads were accustomed to walking over vast pieces of land, they had never travelled this distance.

"What will we find there?" his cousin asked anxiously. "I know we've been told the Lord will provide. But that is a wide ocean between one land mass and another."

"I assure you, Lhamo, there is nothing to fear. After all, you are walking in the middle of one of the worst and prolonged sand storms ever experienced in Asia. Look up at the sky." His younger cousin looked up and smiled.

"And you, of all people, a *repa*," Sangay scolded. *Repas* or "cotton-clad ones" were those who had passed a rigorous yogic test whereby the neophyte sits on the ground, cross-legged and nude in sub-zero temperatures. Sheets are dipped in icy water. He must wrap himself in one of them, and the sheet must dry on his body. The rule requires that the yogi must have dried at least three of the wet sheets in one sitting in order to be pass the initiation.

Sangay's family all gazed into the bright blue sky. "It's easy to forget God's miracles, isn't it?" he asked and flashed a broad smile. His cousin agreed, but his mother replied fiercely, "No, it is not. Every minute of every hour I say my prayers of thanksgiving for such a thing."

Sangay lost his grin and quickly apologized. "I am sorry, Mother. I must never forget where my spiritual zeal originated." He bowed to her. "I must be going, but I'll return soon." And with that, he dematerialized and instantly began to stir in his body in his tent on the western outskirts of the migration.

The back door of the Taylors' house flew open and slammed against the wall. "We know!" rang out throughout the house. Ben and Peg rose from the couches and took ten steps toward the kitchen, but Danny and Miriam beat them to the doorway of the living room. They were flushed and out of breath. "We know!" the duo repeated.

"We were just walking along as usual, talking about people at school, when suddenly this dude was walking along with us," Danny exulted.

"And we both were freaked out!" Miriam added breathlessly.

"I mean, jees, one minute you're just a normal person, and the next, you're somebody who's talking to angels."

The four had reached the couches and sank into them like they were small life rafts, bobbing on an ocean of uncertainty and adventure. "Who was it?" Peg rushed to get a word in edgewise.

"Timothy," the two said in unison.

Danny put out his hand in Miriam's direction to indicate he wanted to tell the story. She fell back in agreement, but with her arms folded, ready to add any little detail that he missed.

"You two have seen him a couple of times, haven't you?" Ben asked, knowing the answer.

"Yeah, once that time in New Mexico when Miriam thought he was talking about rock and roll..."

"...well, I was little then," she said with exaggerated defensiveness.

The family laughed again. "And you saw him at the temple dedication, right?" Peg wanted to continue, anxious to hear what Timothy had to say, and more importantly the kids' real reaction to the announcement that they would leaving their home, their friends and the safety of Zion.

The two quickly agreed that they had seen the Central American apostle at the dedication, but what they said next came as a surprise to both Peg and Ben. "What you don't know, Mom, is that he told us that we would be called to a great work..."

"...even in our youth," Miriam added.

"At the dedication?" Peg asked dumbfounded.

"Yes, and he told us that because we were one quarter Jewish, that the Lord would want us to serve the tribe of Judah," Danny said, somewhat proudly. "And that I held the Aaronic priesthood. So I could speak with angels and baptize people."

"And that I could teach people the gospel and help prepare them," Miriam chimed. "He said that was as important as Danny's job."

"And why have you guys kept this secret?"

The two looked at each other. Miriam shrugged her shoulders, then Danny looked down at his tennis shoes.

"Come on. You can tell us," Ben insisted.

"Well," Danny began. "You two haven't been in the best of moods lately and besides, we thought none of this it would happen for lots of years to come."

Peg gave Ben a quick look. He took it to mean he should share their recent experiences. When he was done, the two young people sat quietly, almost reverently. "Wow," Danny said and exhaled. "You two are amazing. I never knew..."

"Yeah, we thought we just had ordinary, neurotic parents," Miriam cracked.

That brought down the house—and led to an hour-long discussion of what each knew about their calling.

After the kids had gone to bed, Peg sat on the couch with her bare feet tucked under Ben's legs. "Can I admit I'm a little bit scared?"

"Sure. So am I."

"Just now, out of nowhere, I remembered that face of a devil that appeared in the smoke and fire of the Twin Towers' explosion," she said, voice quivering.

"The one that was passed around on the Internet?"

"Uh, huh. I remember I downloaded it and carried a copy around for awhile. That event, probably more than anything else that's happened since..."

"...and that was nothing compared to what happened afterward with the terrorist attacks," Ben interrupted.

"I know, but that first attack felt like I'd been raped. Can I say that? I guess so. Completely surprised, my faith in America's invincibility gone, ripped from me—I was never completely relaxed ever after that, until we got here to Zion."

Ben pulled her feet from under his legs and placed them on his lap. He began to rub them and she began to relax. "But then I came along," he teased.

"...and now I'm facing going out into a world where, I hear, nearly two billion people have died—a world where radiation sickness is still the number one killer."

"And where people are probably desperate to hear about the Lord and Zion."

"Maybe," Peg demurred. "But if they haven't come to Zion by now, why would they listen to us?"

"We're not going to be teaching that much. We're to be Mom and Pop to a missionary force, remember?"

"Oh, I know. I guess I'm trying to be realistic, that's all."

The two dropped into silence as Ben massaged Peg's feet. Then he broke the silence with, "Know what I've been thinking about? Returning to Lakewood when we get to southern California. What a trip. I haven't even thought of that place for years. And then I started thinking about my brother. Probably too much to think that he survived the fallout. Still..."

"Have you checked recently to see if he's here?"

"A couple of months ago. Not here."

After consulting with his irritated and invisible master, Lu Han flew from Argentina to Russia. But instead of settling in Moscow for a season, he went south to the Black Sea to Odessa, the hometown of his mother. His arrival was unceremonial and not publicized. He and Gornstein descended the steps of the large cargo plane dressed in yellow protective rubber clothing from booties to gloves to bonnets. A plastic windowed mask prevented the emperor from breathing any contaminants. He was whisked away to a containing area where he was washed down, and a technician waved a radiation counter up and down his lithe, athletic body. Then he entered a home whose construction had been altered to filter out the radionuclides that may try to invade his shelter. A more sophisticated radiation detector was located and installed for a daily pass over his body.

When Gornstein was scanned, it was revealed that his body held an unusually high amount of radioactive cesium. The lab official attributed it to reindeer meat Gornstein had eaten many months before in a part of Russia still contaminated by the Chernobyl disaster in 1986.

"What have I told you about eating meat?" Han kidded Dmitri.

"But the women were so gorgeous, I couldn't just refuse them."

Once Lu was settled in, Gornstein left for Constantinople and a similar bioengineered situation. His first act was to get ITV online. His second was to issue an edict that all members of the world's population would now be economically cared for by the world government. All newborns were to be implanted with a computer chip in the forehead. All others on their left hands. The government would begin distributing irradiated food and goods. Within a month's time, most countries were in compliance with this decree. China and India would take longer given the size of their populations.

The government workers who oversaw this economic cattle call also were privy to seeing some of the newborn children who were grossly malformed in the wake of the disaster. Most, thankfully, did not live, but the ones who did looked like aliens with two heads or only partial appendages growing out of their chests or necks.

And Han considered his alien invasion ruse very carefully.

Chapter Twelve

Seven years before the Judgment
The sea shall sweep over Erin at one tide.

Ancient Irish prophecy

ary Margaret looked particularly anxious when Nate picked up her and her three girls to go the bishop's house for a baptismal interview.

"What's wrong, Maggie?" Nate had finally settled on a nickname for her—one that she would agree to be called. She had been named for her two grandmothers and did not want to slight either. "Are you worried about the interview?" Nate had also picked up a slight Irish accent which only evidenced itself when he was around her.

"No. There is nothing he can ask that I don't believe. It's not that." She lowered her voice. "It's that something is coming to the world that's worse than even happened recently."

"What?"

"If I'm hearin' correctly, a comet is going to hit the earth very soon," she whispered.

Nate, who had become accustomed to many of her prophetic

utterances, was unprepared for this one. He involuntarily tightened his stomach and let out a loud breath. "Wow. I'm glad we're here."

"And pity's to those who aren't. You remember, I'm sure, when we'd just arrived in Zion and I told you that the prophecy about Ireland had come true. And you didn't believe me?"

Nate blushed and nodded.

"And then we received word that a tidal wave had swept over the isle as a result of an underwater volcanic eruption, killin' half the population?"

"You don't have to rub it in."

"Well, I'm tellin' ya the earth is moanin'. It knows it'll be hit. It's got so many other injuries and sicknesses, I know it will be so happy to be changed and healed. I know I will."

Always a little uncomfortable with Mary Margaret's paganism, Nate was happy to be taking her to the baptismal interview. *Maybe the Holy Ghost will calm her down,* he thought. As if to confirm his thought, she continued in her low, conspiratorial voice. "I haven't bled from my hands or sides since you and Ben convinced me to become a saint."

"Oh? What about your forehead?"

"No, not that either. I guess I feel I don't have to anymore."

'Why is that?"

"I realize that He's got others who love Him and care for Him."

Nate shook his head slightly. *I don't know if I'll ever understand where this woman is coming from,* he thought as he maneuvered the car into the driveway of Bishop Olsen. Once a bishop in Salt Lake City, Olsen had been called again to serve in that capacity. And as he had helped Ben and Peg in their distressful flight to Zion, he was once again called upon to minister in his particular fatherly fashion in this situation.

"And who are these beautiful young ladies?" he asked as he led the group into the living room.

"This here is Eilean. And Mary. And Sarah," Mary Margaret said proudly. Each curtsied slightly.

"Honey, the O'Boyles are here," the bishop called out in the direction of the kitchen. His wife, Elizabeth, emerged with a platter of homemade cookies and a teapot. Radiant and healthy, she had been healed during the great outpouring of spirituality at the temple dedication.

"You can't have people over without a 'cuppa'," Elizabeth said, falling into a bad imitation of an Irish brogue. "This, of course, isn't your strong black tea, but I thought that mint tea with honey might please the girls."

The girls fell to eating and drinking, but Nate was too nervous. *What will she say or do?* he fretted as he watched Olsen and Mary Margaret walk silently down the light turquoise carpeted hall to a back bedroom where the bishop kept his office. It was there because there was no room in the high school where his ward met on Sundays.

The bishop signalled for the Irish mystic to sit down in the straight-backed chair next to a large, dark oak desk, which he sat down behind. Tears began to form in Mary Margaret's eyes. She couldn't think why.

Although he was out of pain, Robert Olsen still had gnarled fingers from the years of arthritis that had afflicted him. These he laced together and looked at the still-beautiful, middle-aged woman in the print dress seated before him. As he searched her face, he could see the tragedies she had endured. He thought it was a haunted face, and yet there was both a peace and a determination that shone through.

149

Finally he spoke. His words were very tender. "My dear daughter, I can see that you've suffered a great deal…"

"I have, Father, and I have sinned. May I tell ya about the sins first?"

"Well, yes, of course." Olsen was taken aback by her straightforward eagerness to confess.

"I gave away a newborn baby boy. Didn't look back. Just gave him to the arms of a stranger woman and took my girls and boarded a ship," Mary Margaret's voice quivered as she told this. "I've lain with a man not my husband to save the life of my children. I blame myself for the deaths of my parents…both killed…," and she continued in this vein for several minutes.

Finally Bishop Olsen stopped her. "Sister O'Boyle. I'm certain that you are used to confession in the Catholic faith. But let me reassure you that you have told me nothing that cannot be forgiven and washed away clean in the baptismal font." She paused to look at him for just a moment, then she continued. His tender heart nearly broke for all she had suffered.

When she finished with her confession, the Spirit moved into the room and filled every corner with an almost palpable fire. Both figures seemed to be enflamed with an intense light. Mary Margaret knew about this state of consciousness, but she'd never had anyone stay with her in this type of energy rush she now felt. She did not count on Robert Olsen accompanying her, he whose spiritual experiences were more profound than hers.

"What are you doin' way up here?" Mary Margaret managed to joke.

"I am often privileged to have the presence of the Holy Spirit in my life."

"Is that what this is?"

"It is."

"It has a subtler, finer feel than what I've experienced before."

"And you can have this with you all the time. Perhaps not in this great a dosage."

"I dearly want that, I do."

Basking in this light, he asked her the standard baptismal questions; to each she emphatically answered in the correct manner. Olsen stopped to consider her expressive face once more. It appeared she had something to ask.

"Do you know that the earth will be hit with a comet shortly?"

He looked startled for just a moment; she was pleased to see that he was somewhat human under that bishop's mantle. "I'm not sure what to say about that. How is it that you have this information?"

"I have a voice, or rather there are several voices."

"I see."

"You haven't answered my question."

"I'm deliberately being evasive." Now it was the bishop's turn to make a joke. "If I say I do know, will that satisfy you?"

"Yes. I believe you."

"And if I told you that the prophet is apprised of what is happening and going to happen, would you believe me?"

She thought for a moment. "Yes, I believe you."

"Sister O'Boyle, it is clear to me that you are a remarkably spiritual woman. You have worked and worked, I imagine, to reach the state of spirituality that you clearly demonstrate. Now let me tell you one more thing. You don't have to work so hard anymore. There are people who know more than you do, and they are in charge. You can relax a bit and be an ordinary human being." He said this with great tenderness.

Of all the things Bishop Olsen could have said to her, that was the most important and most piercing commentary he could have made.

He watched as she visibly changed. She sat up straighter, the worry lines receded a bit, and a slight smile emerged from her down-turned lips.

When the pair returned to the living room, Nate nervously scanned both faces. *Nothing there to worry about, old man,* he told himself and audibly exhaled.

"Brother Winder, although it took more than twenty years, you've converted a remarkable young woman," the bishop said as he crossed the room to shake Nate's hand. "You never know what your tracting may unearth. I am satisfied."

"So am I," Mary Margaret said softly to herself.

Because they were due to have a home leave anyway, both Ned and Cristina, Nate's older children, returned from the outer regions of Zion for the baptism. Their arrival caused a stir in the Winder household. The two had served as surrogate parents to the rest of the seven children, and in their absence, no one had stepped forward. The children were ecstatic; the level of spirituality rose exponentially. These two were returning heroes. Both Ned and Cristina had stories about incoming refugees—people who had sacrificed so much just to reach Zion. The children, ages twelve through eighteen, were sobered by the realities of what they were being spared living in the center stake.

"People came to the portal. They were so sick from the nuclear fallout, they looked like skeletons. One lady I saw recently had had her hair turn white," Ned recounted, not knowing that he had stood within twenty feet of his mother and did not recognize her. "We have this great system that John, the apostle, inspired—and Peter Butler built—that scans for the amount of radioactivity and then adjusts the body's levels to within a normal range. It's really cool."

The baptism took place at the baptismal font on the temple grounds. Nate decided he would not be the one who baptized Mary Margaret. He wasn't sure he could be entirely focussed on the spiritual elements of the service when she would be so close and wet, lying in his arms. He had never had this kind of longing for a woman; it was not his experience with Laurie, even in the beginning of their marriage. His ex-wife simply did not have the emotional depths that his Irish beauty had. Nate battled with telling Mary Margaret of his problem, then decided to ask Ben to do the duties. He, the general authority's grandson, would confirm her. She was none the wiser.

It was no idle phrase that angels attended this ceremony. In fact, standing behind the telestial audience, in spirit, were two of Mary Margaret's favorite Catholic saints—Teresa of Avila and Hildegaard von Bingen dressed in white. Mystics themselves, they had taken special care of this Irish sister from the other side.

Mary Margaret looked almost translucent, she was in such a spiritual state. When she walked down in the water, for a moment it appeared she would just walk across the font on the water. Ben was nervous. He had not had the opportunity to baptize any living people in recent times. Plenty of work for the dead, but this was something different—a live ordinance. He worried he would not get every part of her under the water; he worried that he would drop her; but, for the first time in his life, he did not worry whether he was worthy. Being called to be a mission president had somehow wiped that all away.

As soon as she came back up out of the water, Nate felt an energy rush through his system as he had ever experienced before. He was nearly giddy; the old depressive was now officially banished. As she glided up the stairs out of the baptismal font, she appeared to him like a female Merlin. He leaned back against the marble wall and closed his eyes.

Mary Margaret was not aware of Nate. Her foot on the top stair, she stopped and stared for a long moment. Then she gasped and began to cry. Peg quickly threw a towel over her shoulders and led her back to the women's changing area.

As soon as the two women reached the stall-lined room with the dripping shower, Mary Margaret blurted out in a strong Irish brogue, "I've seen Him, Peg. Now I've really seen Him!"

"Him who?" Peg asked, distracted by finding dry towels and getting Mary Margaret to keep walking to the shower.

"The Lord. He's come to me and approved of what I've done. I cannot believe it."

Peg handed her three towels. She could not think of anything to say. She knew about the Friday bleeding and Mary Margaret's state of mind when she first came to Zion. She feared the Irish woman might be having a setback.

"As I came up the stairs. There he was. Big as life. Really, Peg," she said with great emotion.

"Oh, I believe you. Really I do. I guess I'm a bit jealous. I wanted to see Him again. I just saw Him that one time at the temple dedication."

"And I did not." Mary Margaret hugged the towels close to her chest. "But now I am a real Latter-day Saint."

Peg gave her a hug. "Boy, I can't wait 'til you get the Holy Spirit permanently. You are going to rip, girl."

The laughter coming from the dressing area spilled out into the waiting area where Nate sat with his nine children and at least two dozen others who had come for this occasion. Bishop Olsen was there with his wife. All were beaming.

Mary Margaret stepped through the doorway from the locker area in a simple, white gown provided to her by the baptistry staff. Her long, dark hair was slightly damp. Her smile was radiant; her step was light. And Nate knew that no matter how long it took, he could never love another woman. *She's already a goddess*, he thought as he tried to breathe but was unsuccessful.

His heart pounded loudly in his chest as he laid his hands lightly on her head and pronounced the simple words that accorded the greatest gift he could give her. The shift in "atmospheric pressure" was so palpable that he expected the wall to open up in front of them and saints pour in from the other side.

It was Bishop Olsen who commented on the presence of others unseen. "My, my. It's been quite a time since I sensed such a party of heavenly revelers as we have today."

Nate squeezed Mary Margaret's shoulder for just a second, but other than that, he acted like they were just acquaintances. And she was very grateful for his keeping his word.

Then it was her turn to speak to the gathered crowd. Her three girls sat close together up front. Although what she had to say was brief, most remembered the moment for the rest of their lives. Mary Margaret, newly gifted, spoke to them in the tongue of the first people on earth—Adamic, and Bishop Olsen translated for her.

Because of the turmoil in the world, the satellite system which had been first the pride and joy of the United States, then the UWEN, had fallen into disrepair. So there were no midnight prowling astronomers on the Big Island of Hawaii or at the Jet Propulsion Laboratory in Pasadena searching the night sky for more solar systems like ours. (Twelve of the orbiting comparable suns had been located by the time the U.S. finally fell to its knees first from terrorists attacks, then the Chinese invasion.)

Late in the twentieth century, scientists sounded the alarm that the collision of the earth and a comet the size of a football field would be responsible for global catastrophe. They warned the crash would kick up a lot of dust, debris and soot from fires started at the impact site. These would form a dense cloud, which could surround the earth and plunge it into darkness for months. As a result, most plants would die and so would most living beings up the food chain. Many scientists believed that this is what happened to the dinosaur population.

What heightened the general population's anxiety was the tabloid coverage of a collision of a string of comets that hit Jupiter. The gigantic, fiery red plumes from the explosion were shown on television and in numerous newspapers and magazines.

A congressional panel called for a ten-year program to identify and catalogue all space rocks over one kilometer in size floating within hailing distance of the earth. They also decided that, with enough notice, a spacecraft could be sent to nudge any of these objects off course. As a last-ditch survival technique, intercontinental ballistic missiles could theoretically be sent up to blast them out of the sky, high enough to cause no damage to the earth.

But they did not succeed in this cataloguing, and the time for such expenditures had long since passed. In fact, there were no orbiting telescopes in operation. Only intuitives like Mary Margaret and Lu Han, and of course the prophet, knew what was coming.

Lu Han's comet was not so large as a soccer field. It was about fifty yards long and ten yards wide. Not enough to bring the whole world to a halt, but enough to do real damage to a significant portion of any continent. The emperor, hearing from his master that this event was fast becoming a reality, paced back and forth in his hermetically sealed house. Gornstein was in Constantinople. This was first time in quite a while that the Russian, the titular head of the world government had left him for a period of time. The anti-Christ had not realized how frequently he had used Dmitri as a sounding board.

"Okay, either I use the information ahead of time to warn the world, so that they will worship me..." He paced back across the large, dark red oriental rug. His black slippers made a small swishing sound as he walked. "Or...I can have it do its deed and then offer to hold off more by my connection with the aliens."

He was nearly fifty now. He had not counted on being lonely or ill. Yet here were pangs of loneliness gripping his stomach as he attempted to breathe through the pain. And just this morning, he awoke to find himself sucking on his arm where the mosquito had stung him. Later in his morning meditation, dressed in black robes with an apron designating his complete devotion to Lucifer, he first felt too warm, then too cold, then sweaty as he tried to sit erect and quiet his mind.

These events made him surlier than ever. Han knew the beginning from the end of the telestial world. He had attained that level of consciousness. But he did not know how God worked nor did he know what specifically would become of him. But his most recent dreams offered some suggestion; scenes like Bosch's *Last Judgment* would wake him from a dead sleep. He would find himself naked, carried along on a pole like a pig prepared for roasting. In the blue sky far away, a beatific Jesus was surrounded by adoring beings. In between there were people being sawed in half, tortured with white-hot rods, and stretched backward on the crossbar of a cross left to die. There was no sound except a faint chorus in the background.

There were nights when he could not fall asleep at all, so petrified was he of these night visions.

The other dream that left him in a terrible mood in the morning was one where he was utterly alone on a small planet, except for a pursuer who had been commissioned to kill him. He would flee over flat land to mountains—and his faceless assassin would be right behind him. He would find a cave and huddle in the back, but he was not safe. He could hear the sound of heavy breathing coming from the front of the cave and the scraping of footsteps. The Chinese emperor would thrash around in his large, silk-sheeted bed until he awoke breathless, heart racing.

Chapter Thirteen

Do they (the Gentiles) remember the travails
and the labors, and the pains of the Jews,
and their diligence unto me, in bringing forth
salvation unto the Gentiles?

2 Nephi 29:4

The rail-thin, white-haired woman who stood, head bowed at the entrance to Zion, knew the questions she had to answer truthfully before being admitted. How easy it had been the first time—the daughter of an apostle—to breeze through, give lip service to the promises. Now each word of each question burned in her mind as Laurie listened and struggled to make sure she could answer the questions truthfully. They were not difficult—basically the Ten Commandments—actions any peace-loving person could agree to. *They didn't even ask if one believed in Christ,* she noted. *I could have brought along some of the people at the ashram.*

As she was escorted down the path to a waiting van for transport to Independence, Missouri, she did get a glimpse of her tall, rugged-looking oldest son talking to a couple of other guards. Her heart raced. *Should I call out to him? Does he still love me?* Before she could decide, she was being hurried down the small slope and placed in the center seat, the middle row, of a dusty Dodge van. *Bye, Neddy,* she silently called out as she strained to see him through the back window.

She felt sick most of the long ride from the plains of Colorado to the hills of eastern Missouri. Although she was provided with sandwiches and fruit for the two-day journey, her stomach could not handle the "ordinary" food. The food at the ashram was vegetarian and mostly consisted of rice and beans.

Laurie worried about how she looked—long, ocher-colored dress to her ankles, headband, sandals. She was afraid her parents would immediately think she was some kind of hippie and judge her harshly before she could talk to them. Obsessed with this scenario, she decided to create a scene as the group of eight (driver and seven passengers) began their approach to Topeka. She would force them to get her a new dress.

Laurie surreptitiously slipped the knife used to cut the oranges from its resting place between driver and front side passenger. With it she began to stab holes in her dress around her stomach area so that she began bleeding from these wounds. She had made six quick holes before being subdued by a Colorado rancher seated behind her. He first grabbed her shoulders, then her arm, squeezing it hard enough to force the knife from her hand. "Hey, what the…? Lady, are you crazy?" the gnarly, old man called out as he struggled with her.

The driver took a quick look back, then eased the van to the side of the abandoned road. As soon as it rolled to a stop, this young man from Toledo jumped out of the car, ran around the front and slid open the van door.

"Have you gone nuts?" he yelled at the white-faced Laurie. She said nothing, but slowly smeared the blood around her front of the dress.

"Look, Miss Whatever-Your-Name-Is, we're not going any farther until you tell me what you are doing?"

Laurie opened her mouth to tell the truth, then shut it. *Maybe I am crazy,* she thought. *Why don't I have them put me in a psychiatric hospital somewhere, then I'll be in a hospital gown when my parents come for me.*

But this was a primitive world that she found herself in. No mental hospitals had been established. People were just managing to get food and shelter together. Unless she was a real threat to others, there was nowhere to take her.

Because she did not respond, the rancher and the driver decided to tie her hands together for the rest of the relatively short ride into Independence.

"Where did you say you wanted to be dropped off?" the driver demanded. But Laurie decided silence was the best policy, so after securing her hands, the driver got back in the van and checked the list on the clipboard. "Freda Winthrop. Drop off at 365 Fir Street in downtown Independence."

She was mortified. Not only was she clothed in her ashram outfit, now it was covered with blood and punctured with holes. She had not given her real name for fear someone might know how she left— excommunicated and ordered out of Zion. *Maybe I'll have them leave me at Nate's instead.* She considered her options. The dark clouds that had accompanied her exit rolled back in. With set jaw, she schemed as the miles rolled on. Finally she spoke to the driver, "That's right. Fir Street."

The driver could not wait to dislodge her from her middle seat. He quickly untied her hands and nearly shoved her into the street. Staggering to right herself, Laurie quickly covered the front of her orange, blood-stained gown with her arms and headed across the tree-lined to her parents' house. There was no response to the light taps on their front door, so Laurie headed down the side driveway to the back door. The back door did not open to her repeated twisting of the knob. Back at the front door, she tried unsuccessfully to get it to open. Her parents were not at home; they were working at the temple.

"It's not like I can call a taxi in this town," she murmured. After giving up the idea of finding a phone to call Nate, she managed to shimmy in through a bedroom window. *Why they lock their doors in Zion is a mystery to me*, complained the definitely sullen returnee.

After finding a short-sleeved green dress of hers in a trunk in the basement, Laurie decided she would get the ball rolling and call her kids. It was just Laurie's luck that both Elder Whitmer and Nate had a telephone in each house, for telephones were still a rare commodity. But since both held important positions in the Church's structure, the two were accorded the necessary communication devices.

It was also a stroke of luck that all of Laurie's nine children were at home that afternoon. Neither Ned nor Cristina had returned to their welfare duties after yesterday's baptism. So, when the phone rang and it was Laurie on the other end of line, this rocked the Winder family to its core. Nate was not there; he was attending to some shipments of grain that were being readied for the massive population influx with the arrival of the ten tribes.

Cristina answered the phone. "Hello?"

"Who is this?"

"Ah, Cristina Winder. May I ask who's calling?"

"This is your mother, honey."

Cristina turned white and nearly dropped the phone. "Mom? Where are you?"

"At Grandpoppy's house."

"In Missouri?"

Laurie could hear several young voices calling out the background. "Is that Mom?" "I think she said, 'Mom'." Her heart raced. *Could they possibly love me still?* she wondered. Then she heard the phone being passed to another, and Ned came on the line.

"Mom, where are you?" he asked with a little suspicion in his voice.

"I'm here in Independence."

"How did you get here?"

"By van. From the border. How are you, son?"

"Fine. What border?"

"The Colorado one. How are you all?" she strained to keep it light. She felt like he was a cop who had pulled her over for a speeding ticket.

"We're fine. Want to talk to the others?" he asked, apparently satisfied with her answers.

The younger ones were shy. It seemed a very long time since they had talked to their mother. But Laurie did get to speak to each one and tell each one that she loved them. They agreed to have Nate call her when he returned home. As she hung up, she realized that none had asked to see her. *What have they been told?* she agonized as she waited in the empty house for her parents to return.

A radiant Peg and a flushed-face Ben sat on the third row of a fairly large meeting in the Tribe of Judah wing of the temple. They were being briefed at their first mission presidency meeting by Elders Dawahoya and Stewart. After the roll call at 7:30 A.M. (way too early for Ben's tastes) and the opening hymn, there was an invocation by Michael Levine. He was Presiding Bishop when Peg and Ben entered Zion. A Jew, he too had been called to a mission, in south-eastern

Canada. Then President Dawahoya, acting president of the twelve apostles, stood to address the assembled couples.

"Brothers and sisters, this is indeed an historic moment. How we had longed for this day when we could begin taking the gospel to our Jewish brethren and sisters. After this meeting, you will be released to go to a presentation on the Jewish religion, which, of course, you will need to understand to begin this journey. After that presentation, we will begin looking at scriptures and the approach you will be taking to reach out and teach these members of the tribe of Judah. But for right now, Elder Stewart and I have no agenda. We are going to be led by the Spirit. And we want to have time for your questions."

There was no immediate response from the audience, just a quiet murmur.

"Well, I see you are shy," Elder Dawahoya kidded. "We have four hours, so I'll fill in a bit until you find your tongues."

Ben had been an admirer of the Hopi apostle since he was called into the Council of the Twelve nearly twenty years earlier. The apostle looked like an Indian warrior with piercing brown eyes and a square jaw. Lines ran down the sides of his jaw, making him look more fierce than he actually was.

There was this teasing, funny way he had of making people laugh at what he said and at themselves which helped people get near to him. Ben was especially grateful for this personality trait during the time when he first was translating the Tibetan plates. He was such a nervous wreck, and it was Dawahoya that kidded him, called him nicknames, and generally defused the very tense situation.

Now, here Ben was, sitting twenty feet away from the head apostle, as a newly set-apart mission president—something Ben would never have even remotely imagined for most of his time as a member in the Church. He even thought his translating ability was a fluke—a product of the acid he took in his youth. But there was no mistaking this calling.

"We don't want to restrict your questions. We're in the temple, and we are free to discuss what you want."

After some preliminary questions from the audience, the Hopi apostle began to bear down on them. "You are a representative of the Church, called by prophecy and revelation, and the laying on of hands. You have been given the keys of the presidency of your mission. You men have been set apart in the highest quorum of the priesthood in the order of the son of God..."

The room began to fill with a peaceful lightness and a slight tingling. As the apostle went on, Peg began feeling light-headed. There was discussion of the logistics of reestablishing the missionary system, food and transportation problems presented by the new World Government's crackdown on buying and selling, and all the while she worried, *How will any of us survive for any length of time out there?*

Now Elder Stewart was speaking, "The blows that these people of Judah have taken have softened them as no other time in history—no, not even during the Holocaust. There will be more than a few who will be baptized and come to Zion. Once here, we can teach them further about the temple covenants and how similar they are to their earliest ceremonies. But you are to teach only faith, repentance, and baptism. The Book of Mormon will be an enormous assistance, particularly 1st and 2nd Nephi. We will be presenting you with lesson plans for using these scriptures, but brothers and sisters, you can do wonders if you will listen to me about one subject and one subject only—revelation."

When the Scottish apostle said "revelation" Peg saw out of the corner of her eye a man suddenly standing just at the corner of her peripheral vision. He was leaning against the wall, and she was sure he was not standing there a second before. But she was pulled into what Stewart was saying, "You have the right and responsibility to receive revelation for the members of your mission. When my wife and I prayed when we were called to head the mission in South Africa, we always included this prayer: 'Father, bless us that we may have the power of revelation, that the Lord will guide us and that we will be corrected when we have misunderstood.' I still pray that same prayer for my children and grandchildren."

Peg turned her head slightly to the right and saw that the man standing against the wall was Andrew. Her heart raced. She poked Ben and tried to get him to turn around, but he was immersed in one of the most important lessons he had ever heard.

"...you have to look at yourself as the leader of the mission and ask yourself, 'Can I accept correction?' Brethren, I speak mostly to you. You must find out if you can. The hallmark of a person placed in a leadership position in this church is their humility." The tall, elegant apostle was now leaning forward on the pulpit and pointing a finger. "You are of the Jewish tribe. You have had to fight with every breath and fiber of your being to survive as a people. And in the process, you collectively have become hardened. Even you in this congregation, even converts to the gospel."

A number of men stirred in their seats. Ben, sweating in his blue suit, pulled a handkerchief from his vest pocket and wiped his brow.

"If you are to be great servants of the Lord, you must feel the promptings of the Spirit. Do what you should do and don't do what you should not."

Elder Stewart looked up and smiled in the direction of the back of the room. Peg again poked Ben. "It's Andrew, honey. Look."

The couple, along with most of the members of the audience, turned and watched as the powerful brother of Peter approached the stand. The two apostles shook hands. Then Elder Stewart indicated he was yielding the podium to the courageous apostle who had deserted his fishing nets to follow the Savior.

Andrew stood for a long moment, looking out at the crowd. He had a slight smile on his face. "Once I saw President Hinckley address a crowd of newly called missionaries. He looked out at the crowd and said, 'You're not much, but you're all the Lord has. I feel that way today.'"

The crowd had a good laugh at that. Then Andrew opened the Bible and began to preach, first in English and then in Hebrew. Peg could imagine him standing in front of an open Torah with a prayer shawl on his shoulders. Instead he wore a simple white suit and tie.

"*Shema, Yisrael. Adonai elohenu, Adonai ehad*," and Ben could follow him. Just that one semester of Hebrew study and he understood. But then he looked at Peg, and she was bobbing her head as if she understood Andrew. So Ben glanced around the room, and the entire audience was enthralled, clearly understanding the Hebrew that was being spoken.

"This is the day that Isaiah has spoken of," the apostle intoned. "This is the day that Judah will be redeemed. The supper is well prepared." Then he began quoting the *Doctrine and Covenants* in Hebrew, "And also that a feast of fat things might be prepared for the poor...that the earth may know that the mouths of the prophets shall not fail...yea, a supper of the house of the Lord, well prepared, unto which all nations shall be invited..."

The effect on the men in the room who were Jews by birth, if not by religion at this point in their lives, was so profoundly moving, tears flowed freely over their Semitic faces. There was something so primitive, so right about being taught the Gospel in this language. They were filled and changed in the moment. All trace of Jewish self-contempt was washed away. And the outpouring of the Spirit produced an audience who needed no interpreter to understand each word spoken. The miracle was not lost on them; they understood what it was to be humbled in the presence of such power and authority.

"Don't be hesitant to make promises to your missionaries. You hold the keys and the authority, and you must not be hesitant. There is so little time left until our Lord returns, we must be bold in our leadership. Remind these young men of the war in heaven, that they were valiant warriors held back until this time. Remind them how they overcame Satan."

By now the members of the audience were ready to be lifted right out their seats.

"They will become discouraged. This is quite possibly the hardest mission call yet. Remind them of their patriarchal blessings. And tell them that this is the most important thing they can be doing for the whole world at this moment. That should relax them!" That brought laughter and a momentary release from the intensity of the message.

But that was not all. He went on, "Educate your missionaries about Perdition. Lucifer and Cain are both called that name. It means 'destruction.' Something you may not know is that Cain, when resurrected, will rule over Lucifer. The boys need to be made aware of the subtleties and snares that the embodied as well as disembodied spirits can use. And the Jewish teachings stress this, needless to say."

Peg looked to Ben, surprised to see him struggling with tears.

"Those who do have bodies have been saved to come to the earth at this time. They are not merely wicked, they are incorrigibly evil. They willfully and utterly pervert gospel principles. Your boys may run into one of these sons of perdition before the electronic 'veil' is dropped over all of North and South America. They may be clever and seductive. Remind the missionaries that these people 'will rise to the damnation of their own filthiness,' as Joseph Smith has taught. And to trust the Spirit to bear witness of their spiritual filthiness." Peg pulled her chair closer and slipped her arm under Ben's. *Thank heaven for priesthood protection*, she thought and shivered. *I've got to really warn the kids about such things.*

After the group had been divided into smaller groups for instruction on the Hebrew religion in its purity, each of the four groups were instructed by an apostle from the meridian of time: Andrew, Bartholomew, Thomas—and Ben and Peg's group by Paul.

Short, dark-haired with a large hooked, nose and piercing, nearly black eyes, the apostle held the room captive with his teachings for nearly two hours. It was very pleasing to him to become a rabbi again. And the students were among the most eager and well-educated of any he had taught.

"This is the difference between the oral Torah and the holy writ..." Paul was explaining in his high, nasal-sounding voice as Peg's mind wandered to the kids. *What are they learning?* she thought. *Are they learning from apostles, too?* "And, of course, one of the most important similarities that I know you are aware of has to do with the belief in the Messiah," Paul continued. Judaism says that God has not yet brought the Messiah or his age to the earth. Your job is to convince them otherwise."

Danny and Miriam, in her best navy blue dress with the sailor's collar, had been separated after the opening exercises. They met first in the chapel of the temple, and they then descended the stairs to rooms off to the side of the baptistry. Danny did not mind, but

Miriam felt out of place at first. She sat with a knot in her stomach as the other girls nearby talked to each other. She had just moved into the Young Women's organization as a twelve-year-old and felt like she did not belong.

The crowd quickly became quiet when two tall, well-built men, one of whom Miriam knew quite well, walked into the room from the baptistry side door. He smiled warmly at the twenty-two girls, ages twelve to seventeen who had gathered there. They were precious daughters of individuals called to go into the world to teach the gospel to the Jewish nation. They were to go to different parts of the United States, Canada, Europe, but not to Israel. Not yet.

Matthew and Timothy stood in front of them in white jumpsuits, hands folded in front of them. "Ladies, this is an honor and a privilege," Matthew began. "I am Elder Matthew who lived to minister with the Lord when He walked the earth. You have been called to fulfill an important mission for Him, and we have come from Him to share with you what He would have you know."

Timothy smiled in Miriam's direction and she relaxed. He took over the discussion. "While the boys are being taught about the various duties that they will be called on to perform as Aaronic Priesthood holders, I want to talk with you about your important role. Never in the history of the world have young women as spiritual and capable as you been called to participate in the gathering of the Lord's elect. Most of you are at least one quarter Jewish, something you should be proud of. I am half Jewish. My lineage goes back through Nephi to Lehi. My mother was a native of the area where we lived."

Miriam found her arm in the air. "Yes, Sister Taylor?" She looked around, expecting to see her stepmother. "No, you..." the apostle said and smiled.

"Oh, I was just wondering just where you were from."

"When I was in mortality, I lived in what today is called the Guatemala Highlands, in Central America."

"Wow. And is it true that you were at Bountiful when Jesus came after he was killed?"

"Yes."

And with those questions, a torrent of questions filled the room from eager young women who suddenly had teachers whose experiences, not just theories, were available. There were many questions about Book of Mormon times, what the Lord is like, would they be in danger when they went to the various locations, what their duties would be as daughters of a mission president. Two hours flew by.

"Well, my dear ones, I have to go to see to your parents," Timothy said, holding up a hand to indicate their time was up. "But I will see you again, I assure you. For, as Miriam Taylor knows, my assignment as well as Elder Matthew's is to help oversee the youth in this great missionary effort."

The girls all called out a thank you to them as they strode out the door. Then Miss Miriam found herself to be the center of attention, which she, ever the extrovert, of course, abhorred.

The young men were first treated to a history of the Jewish nation from the Old Testament to modern times. Two key individuals who played a part in the Aaronic Priesthood were their instructors: John the Baptist and Aaron himself. The group of seventeen could not contain their joy and amazement when the men introduced themselves. Their jaws dropped.

Aaron taught the boys the real stories about many of the Old Testament stories. "I want you to understand what your ancestors suffered so that you could have the knowledge you have of the gospel and its teachings. Without the preservation of the Old Testament writings, there would have been no prophecy and no longing for the Messiah from the beginning of the world." When John the Baptist stood to talk, the crowd came to understand very quickly why he attracted so many to him before the Lord began his ministry. He was so intense, charismatic and funny. Yes, funny. With an understanding of the adolescent male that made every story he told zing with excitement and passion.

"I want you to understand the Hebraic mind—a mind that looks for meaning in every major event in an individual's or society's life. Let me illustrate. There are seven major festivals that are celebrated each year in Jewish society. Each of those festivals has a theme. Let's take the bombing of New York on September 11, 2002. That was in the season Teshuvah. According to tradition, each day during the month of Elul (the beginning of the festival) a shofar is blown and Psalm 27 is read. It is a time of repentance. Yom Kippur is the most holy day."

The boys began shuffling a bit in their seats, so the cousin of the Lord asked what a shofar was.

"A curved horn," Danny answered with not much confidence.

"Exactly right. Where else do we see a horn or trumpet being blown?"

"I don't know. On the top of temples," Danny again offered timidly.

"What is your name, young man?" John asked.

"Daniel Taylor."

"Well, Daniel Taylor. You have a perceptive mind."

Danny blushed but was pleased.

"Daniel, do you know why Moroni is shown blowing the trumpet?"

"To call people to repentance, I guess."

"Exactly. And for all of you now, when did Moroni appear to the boy prophet?"

"Sometime in September 1829, I think," guessed the Levine boy sitting near Danny.

"It may please you to know that it was the very holy day of Yom Kippur that year when Moroni appeared, and to a Jewish audience, the significance would not be lost. In fact, it would move them. Now let's look at Psalm 27. Let's have each of you read a line."

"The Lord is my light and my salvation..." read a stub-nosed boy whose voice was just changing. Then around the room, each boy reading, looking for meaning in his life at this dangerous and exciting crossroad.

When it came to Danny, he softly read, "For in the time of trouble he shall hide me in his pavilion; in the secret of his tabernacle shall he hide me; he shall set me up upon a rock." And he formed the words, they became like a chant, a song that filled him with warm assurance.

"Awesome!" was the consensus.

"When the terrorists attacked the World Trade Center and the Pentagon," the Baptist continued, "people were in complete shock. In essence the American public had been in a state of slumber. These attacks were a 'wake up call' where many went to churches and synagogues to seek comfort from the God of Israel and to seek His face. So the blowing of the shofar accomplished its deed."

Another fourteen-year-old priest sitting near Danny asked, "And what about the 9/11. Wasn't that some sign? I mean, that's the number we used to use for emergency help."

"Yes, Jewish mystics noted that, and they also noted that the 27th Psalm was read in a prayer service in the National Cathedral. They would say that the God of Israel was trying to get a spiritual message to His people."

"Cool," uttered a few of the boys. John now had them eating out of his hand.

"And, as a good student of the Torah would do, we will continue to look for meaning, after the obvious is stated. You might not know, being as young as you are, that the national day of prayer was called by President Bush on a Friday. The entire United States was being called to be in Shabbat."

"In Shabbat?" a fascinated Danny blurted out.

"To observe the Sabbath, beginning on Friday night."

"And don't they have some kind of numbering system?" another boy asked excitedly.

"Yes, but that is the subject for another day. And there *will* be other days, I promise. We will continue to be your guides and come and go to assist you in your duties," Aaron said, trying to end the meeting.

"But can't you give an example?" several boys begged.

Aaron sighed and smiled. He remembered his own experiences with Moses, when he had to be pried from his brother's side, eating up the fascinating insights that Moses provided. "Okay, how many of you are old enough to remember the HAMAS—the radical arm of the Palestinian opposition to the state of Israel?"

Most hands shot up. "Let's look at Psalm 140." Boys rustled the pages of their precious scriptures. (Sometimes they were the only books that the boys managed to bring with them when they fled to Zion.) Aaron pointed to Danny, "Son, please read for us."

And the red-faced son of Ben, the translator, read, "O Lord, from the evil man; preserve me from the violent man; which imagine mischiefs in their heart; continually are they gathered together for war."

"Good. Thanks. Now the Hebrew word for 'violent' is the Strong's number 2555, and that is the Hebrew word HAMAS. Thus the 'violent man' and the 'evil man' are the radical Islamic terrorists. Now we really must stop, gentlemen. I'll explain about Strong's numbers in another session. You have been wonderful students, and I know you will be excellent assistants in baptizing and helping to bring many souls to the Lord."

Everyone left the room but Danny. He sat looking at his hands for a few moments until Miriam found him. Big tear drops fell into his palms. He repeated over and over, "It's true. My dad didn't make this up. It's true… It's true."

Chapter Fourteen

For they are the spirits of devils, working miracles,
which go forth unto the kings of the earth
and of the whole world, to gather them to
the battle of that great day of God Almighty.

Revelation 16:14

The Chinese/Russian yogic adept looked around the table at his home in Odessa at the ten men who had made up a deadly and ruthless shadow world government for many years. All wealthy beyond counting, they were completely devoted the Lu Han, whom they called the lord of 10,000 years. These members of the ultra-secret Order of the Dragon were they who in effect dealt the death blows to the United States as a world power. They had manipulated the Muslims to hate the Americans and gave them the money and means to bring the nation to her knees.

Although these devotees had followed their master to South America, they did not meet often as they were busy in different parts of the continent creating such a drug trafficking trade as was unparalleled in history. Now Han had all of them around *his* table and they were *his*. For dramatic effect, he turned on a large candelabra over the table even though the sun shone under the low laying cloud bank along the coast. He materialized a sumptuous spread for them, plus a gem of considerable weight at each place setting. These were gifts of thanksgiving which were to be used later in the evening at a special priesthood anointing.

"...but we may not really know. The only data we have to work with came from the fallout of an atomic bomb. It did not have all the biochemicals mixed in," said the Japanese member cautiously.

The emperor scowled at him with such fierceness that the man quickly changed his tune. "However it is my belief that we will have a healthy population base to work with once the effects of the disaster have dropped down to acceptable levels. And the cancer and birth defects should be negligible, now that the initial population has been eliminated."

Now Lu Han looked pleased.

"Those near the hypocenter at the time of the explosions were of course killed," explained the nervous devotee. "But strictly speaking, it has been difficult to tell whether death was due to the radiation or from injuries."

"What about birth defects?" asked the East Indian, a pasha with a palace rivaling the Taj Mahal.

"Exposure to radiation in *utero* increases the incidence of small head size and severe mental retardation, particularly among fetuses exposed during the period from eight to fifteen weeks after conception. Also studies involving body measurements show a slight weight and height reduction."

Lu Han stood up from the table and walked to the floor-to-ceiling window to look out at the seacoast.

"So, if I can summarize," he said with a great deal of irritation in his voice, "the first few months were the worst, correct? There already has been the vomiting, the diarrhea, the reduction in the number of blood cells, etc. Then cancer may become the next killer some time in the five-to-ten year range. Am I understanding you correctly?"

With that question, the black-rimmed glasses on the nose of the Japanese man slipped further down to its end. The emperor had asked in such an accusatory way that the quaking man expected to be beheaded. "Yes, sir," he said, pushing the glasses back up, his voice quivering. "Particularly leukemia. But I must add that there is also the possibility of temporary sterility, severe epilation, and a lens opacity."

"What?" Han turned and asked, clearly more irritated.

"Hair loss and a clouding of the lens of the eye, but that would only be for those who were near the epicenter of the blast."

"Enough!" Han waved his hand, and the man sat down and shrunk into the chair.

Han let out a heavy sigh and returned to the table. *I've escaped most everything except possibly the leukemia.* "Well, that is what we have to work with," he said in an upbeat voice. "I know you've heard me say that the way to world domination is to come in when people are frightened or have suffered and offer to be a savior to them."

The men along with Gornstein remained secluded at Han's stately dashau for nearly a week. What the "Snow Leopard" did not reveal was his knowledge of the oncoming comet which was likely to destroy a large number of the already weakened population. He estimated he had about a year's time to see that the populace was adhering to his BBB (666) policy before further disaster visited Earth's door.

But there were troubles with the implementation of the implants. Pockets of resistance among Christians and Jews immediately rose up. Although there were also international laws that allowed Han to imprison them as terrorists, local law enforcement authorities were few and far between. And the kind of sophisticated international intelligence network that had previously existed went down with the demise of the UWEN.

"Once the computerization is in place, we will be able to track any one on earth by satellite," boasted the elegant, white-haired Turkish man. "The specter that haunts the world..." He paused for effect, "...is the specter of migration. It's what the UWEN attempted to stop. In a world with multiple diasporas, people create multiple identities and loyalties. We must see that they have a singular loyalty to you, my lord."

Another Eurasian member with a long moustache spoke up, "You know the Christians call you the anti-Christ."

"Yes, I know because of their Bible's statement, which goes something like, 'No man may buy or sell, except that he has the mark or the name of the beast on him,'" Lu Han said with a broad smile on his face. "A delicious thought. The Christians in fear of me. Now if I could just get the Jews in line..."

"Labelling them enemies of the state won't hurt for starters," Gornstein said emphatically. The emperor looked hard at him for a moment. He was never completely certain that Gornstein, a Jew by birth, would not desert him. But he could never intuitively discern anything but an energetic disgust for the race. "Yes, Dmitri. But I have plans for them which I don't want to go into here."

The emperor in yellow silk robe and black silk pants paced to the far end of the room. "The question I have for you now is how to win their hearts. We can and will control them, but we must make them utterly worship me. I have decided to have a tattoo of the BBB design, symbol of the new economic order, placed on the back of my left hand so that I can show to the world that I am one with its all-embracing benefits."

The group showed their appreciation for his idea by raising their glasses in his direction. They then spent the rest of the afternoon discussing details of the implementation of the complete economic domination, the UFO idea, and how to take advantage of the fact that Han had already convinced nearly a third of world's population that he, in fact, was a god with his demonstrated miracles. They were not finished by dinnertime.

After another mouth-watering meal that Han materialized, he led them to a large room used as the library. He had placed ten chairs in a semicircle with two chairs in the front. As he opened the double doors, they were caught up with the scent of exotic incense. At least a hundred candles graced a long table at the far side of the room.

Excited to the point of being breathless, they moved quickly to fill up the chairs. The emperor and servant of Perdition walked to the front with the swishing sound of the black robes that he had put on. He, too, was excited. He had received permission from his unseen master to initiate these members of the Order of the Dragon into a higher priesthood order. Then he would not be alone at this level of power but could call on others' energies to carry out what was needed to rid the world of enemies of his master. He hoped that now that there would be ten, besides Gornstein and himself, they could generate enough energy to remove the electronic net over Zion and greedily pick off those who resisted his plan.

"Before I place my hands on your head and gift you with this power of the Dragon's priesthood, I promised you that I would tell you of my conversion."

He folded his arms so that they disappeared in the sleeves of his robe.

"This was after the miraculous healing of my throat after I had been attacked by a machete. That was in India. After that ordeal I returned to China, to the monastery where I was trained as a boy. One day, while in meditation, I was pondering on the lie that the fake, Jesus, told that he had bled from every pore of his body, which we all know would have killed him on the spot. Suddenly I began to feel my psychic heat rising. It was good that I was sitting in the yogic posture with the right leg crossed over left, because the heat swiftly moved up my spine and tore into the interior of my head with such force that had I not been sitting thus, I am sure I would have died on the spot from a brain aneurysm. But I was able to ground myself quickly and, with disciplined breath, began to push the energy back down."

The gathered group sat mesmerized by the descriptive details of the story. Han continued, "I began to chant: 'Ye objects of worship, the Duality and the Faith-Guarding Deities, and more especially ye Eight Orders of Spiritual Beings and Elementals...Come!'"

For dramatic effect, the emperor turned around and pinched out eight candles at each end of the table. Then he returned to the front of the room to face his enrapt followers. "Appearing before me, by miraculous power, first a skull-drum, a cloth of human hide, a human thigh bone, bells and finally vultures flocking around a dead female body. I cried out what does all this mean, O Master?"

"Then I beheld with my own eyes the form of Master Cain, who in his glorious spiritual frame called me by name and said, 'Son of the snow leopard, your sacrifice has been accepted of me and mine.' And then I 'felt' hands on my head and heard the words that I am going to repeat here for you now."

The men looked to each other, both excited and with some fear.

"You have nothing to fear," Han assured them. "You will be given more power than you can imagine. You will not be able to manifest yourself as I do, but you will able to read minds and know the future to a greater degree. All men's minds will be open, yours for the taking."

Then he gestured for Gornstein to sit in the chair. Then the first of the ten sat down before him. In the time it took to pronounce the words, the world was darkened by eleven power-hungry minions, now with even more power to do evil.

Laurie sat in the quiet house all afternoon surrounded by pictures of Jesus, Mormon scriptures and the knowledge that she had nothing and was absolutely nobody. About seven o'clock, she heard the crunch of tires in the driveway, two doors slam shut and the low voices of her parents as they walked up the flower-lined sidewalk to the door.

She had decided to just sit in the living room and call out softly to them as they came in the house, hoping that she would not cause one or the other to have a stroke or heart attack.

"I'm hungry. What about you, sweetie?" Elder Whitmer asked his wife as he held the door open for her.

"Absolutely. I'll..." was all the farther Dorothy Whitmer got out when her gaze fell on the sallow creature on the couch. "John," she called out in alarm and pointed.

Laurie could not utter a sound.

Her father rushed ahead of his wife, ready to expel the intruder. He was only a foot away from his only daughter when he finally recognized her. "Laurie?" he asked plaintively.

Her round, grey-haired mother reached his side and peered over to look more closely at the white-haired, emaciated figure.

A quiet "Hi" was all that Laurie could manage to get out of her dry mouth.

The two stepped back and stared. Several seconds went by before anyone spoke. It was Dorothy who broke the silence. "Honey, how did you get in?"

"The side bedroom screen. I don't know why you still lock your doors," Laurie said with a slight whine in her voice.

That immediately revived those defensive, hardened feelings her father had experienced when he was escorting her out of Zion. "You've caused a lot of grief, Laurie."

"I don't want to hear that from you, Dad. I know that. I can't tell you how much I know that."

He was surprised at the repentant tone in her voice.

"Well, I'm going to cook," Dorothy said spryly. "For three!"

The three ate without many words. "It's weird not to sit here and watch TV while we eat like we always used to do when I was a kid," Laurie ventured once.

John Whitmer was trying to get centered and take a spiritual measure of his daughter. *She got back in,* he reasoned. *Couldn't have done that without sincerely answering the questions.* But he could not squelch a bitter feeling that kept coming up in his throat. *All that pain those children have gone through—for some Chinese shaman!*

"Will you be staying the night?" Dorothy tried to keep the family on a low emotional keel.

"If it's okay with you. I don't have anywhere else to go." Oh, how those words burned.

"And the children?" Elder Whitmer asked. "Do they know?"

"Yes, I called them when I arrived."

"I see," was all he could say. Previously Laurie would have been all over her father for his "judgmental attitude," but she did not or could not rise to the occasion now.

"Well, let's get a good night's sleep, and then we'll take you over there tomorrow," Dorothy said as sweetly as she could under the circumstances.

After the three went to bed, Laurie could hear her parents arguing in urgent, low voices, but she could not hear what was said. All she knew was that there was no one who cared about her struggle to get back to Zion. She lay quietly in her former bedroom and said in monotone, "All I know is that I feel like a piece of garbage…no…a piece of ripped up cardboard."

After the group had retired for the night, the emperor retreated to his suite where he took a second shower for the day. Then he took a syringe and drew blood. He had secured a device for monitoring his red blood count. All the yogic high states of consciousness had not helped raise the rather anemic count. And that, plus the occasional return of the fever, frightened him and infuriated him. *I need to be immortal,* he silently raged. He was nearly fifty now and beginning to feel the mortal pangs of embodiment.

"Dimi, come in here," Han called out down the darkened hall.

After several minutes, a dishevelled and sleepy Gornstein came padding down the hall. "Yes, master. What do you desire?" he asked.

"I desire company. Sit with me."

Dmitri could not hide his surprise at this admission of need coming from the ever stoic emperor. He sat down on a large beige ottoman at Han's feet and held his breath. He did not know what would happen next. Han had been so erratic in the last month, sometimes intimately warm and others so violently out of control angry, he feared Han would strangle him without a thought. He waited.

"What do you know about the Chinese population control at the end of the last century?" the emperor asked his startled follower.

"I do not know much. It think the government tried to control the population by limiting families to one child."

"Partially correct. The policy was limited to rural areas. And the couple could have a second child if the first was a girl."

"Yes. I remember. But most of them let the female babies die."

"And now we have how many surplus males?"

"I don't know now that we have had this disaster. Maybe fifty million."

"And we have taken advantage of the surplus of males for our army?" Han continued without paying attention to his companion's answer.

"Yes. We used them in our colonization attempt of the U.S."

Han was quiet for a moment. "I know we've just spent the day talking about saving the world population for our own designs, but I must ask this one favor of you...I want a half million people killed...healthy people...who have not suffered from the fallout."

Dmitri almost let a thought come to mind questioning Lan's sanity, but he caught himself and waited.

"You do not know what I know. These are Europeans and Asians who are in the northeastern part of Mongolia right now. I want them slaughtered." Han looked away; the lines down the side of his mouth looked like a slashed goatee in the dim light of the bedroom. Gornstein shivered slightly. The room seemed to grow colder.

"We are days away from having the satellite system up. Shall we focus on that area?"

"We can't waste days. They may be out of my grasp. I want the poorest, most uneducated and unskilled of the army population assembled. We can afford to lose them. Besides, many are the result of incest, you know."

"Yes, there were men in my army division who were the product of a brother/sister union. Not enough females to go around," Gornstein replied.

"I'd like to rid the earth of their defective genes," Han stated matter of factly.

After further planning, the Russian left for his room. For the very first time, he felt like running for the back door of the villa, but he feared that he might be stabbed in the back before he could reach the end of the hall.

He felt Lu Han had become more cold-hearted and devoid of light than any man he had ever encountered. And Gornstein had been with the Muslim bands when they took over southern Europe, slaughtering indiscriminately. He was no stranger to fellow soldiers who could murder without a moment's conscience pang.

He made it to his bedroom and climbed back the bed. Before he fell asleep, he slipped his hand under the pillow to feel the cold of his favored pistol. Later that night, his eyes flew open and he instinctively reached for the gun when he found his bedding being slowly pulled back. The emperor slid in next to him in black silk pajamas and said in low voice, "You do not have to fear me, Dimi."

The white-haired patrician of the Whitmer clan, descendant of the family who were witnesses to the authenticity of the Book of Mormon, walked slowly down the driveway to the trash can. It was early morning before he was scheduled to work in the temple. The apostle carried the trash from last night's dinner. He was still stewing about what he was going to do with Laurie. *She's been excommunicated. Just this morning she admitted to giving a false name to enter Zion—one morning after her arrival!*

When he opened the lid to the trash barrel, a flash of something orange caught his eye. Putting down the bag he carried, he fished through the trash until his hand reached Laurie's blood-stained orange dress. She had placed it at the bottom and covered it with the rest of trash, but not well enough for her father's sharp eyes.

"What in the world?" he asked aloud as he pulled the garment out of the trash and held it up to the light. "Laurie?" he called out in his unhappy father's voice.

"Oh, oh," she responded as she heard his tone. She scrambled to her feet, from her yogic posture, and headed out the door. As she turned the corner, she could see the dark clouds around her father's face and, of course, the dress that she didn't want her parents to see. *I'll tell him I was stabbed and I barely escaped with my life*, she quickly thought. But then a sick pull on her stomach made her stop speaking, probably the first time since she was young girl that she let herself be stopped by her conscience, and she asked in an even voice, "Yes, Dad?"

"What is this?" He was angry.

"The dress I arrived in. I didn't want you and Mom to see me in it."

"These holes... Is this blood?"

"Yes."

"Yours?" His voice softened.

Now was her opportunity to get her father on her side. "Yes."

"What happened?" the apostle asked as he walked to her side. There was no going back. If Laurie wanted to remain in Zion, she had to start telling the truth. *He always knows when I'm lying*, she thought. *So, here goes nothing.* "I stabbed myself in the stomach because I was desperate to get the driver to stop. I wanted to get a new dress so you wouldn't have to see me in this outfit."

John Whitmer was so accustomed to his daughter's lies, he was completely taken aback not by the answer as much as by knowing that she had just spoken the truth.

Tears filled his eyes and he stretched out his arms to her. "Honey, don't you know that we love you no matter what you're wearing?"

Laurie did not answer. She entered his embrace and started sobbing uncontrollably. The left shoulder of her father's white shirt became soaked through to his garment. The two remained standing in the driveway in this embrace for a good five minutes—the orange dress at their feet. Finally Laurie said, "I don't know what I believe any more."

To which her good and long-suffering father responded, "That's all right, honey. We'll start at the beginning."

Chapter Fifteen

The visions and blessings of old are returning,
And angels are coming to visit the earth.

LDS Hymn #2

The 613 commandments or Mitzvahs, known as the Mitvot, were given collectively to the Jewish people to perform."

"By whom?" Ben's arm flew into the air before he realized that he was interrupting Timothy.

"Well, that's a bit long to explain. As I said, it's part of the Hasidic tradition. Because this group of Jews believes that the Mitzvahs correspond to spiritual energies, when a Jew is doing one of them, it is not only the physical meaning that matters; they believe it also has an effect on the cosmic vibration of the universe."

John the Baptist spoke up. "This is based on the mystical meaning of the Hebrew alphabet. There are three 'mother letters' which represent air, water and fire. It is out of these elements that God created the earth. The seven double letters represent days of the week..." While Peg could not continue straining to follow the discussion about the kabalistic system, Ben was so absorbed, he let the red pen he held in his hand drop to the floor. She leaned over and picked it up. *I'll get him to explain it later.* She rustled around in her seat, then stared out at the darkening afternoon. *We're leaving in three days and I still don't know how they expect us to survive out there, particularly those boys who will be out on the streets trying to preach the gospel.* They were already her boys that she was worrying about.

"Now, Hasidic Jews believe in reincarnation. They believe that a core group always come back as Jews and that it is a step backwards on the spiritual ladder to be born as a non-Jew." John was finishing.

Aaron smiled appreciatively in the Baptist's direction before continuing. He, too, was appreciative of the powerfully built cousin of Jesus and his way of both entertaining and explaining difficult concepts. "This group believes that the thing that travels from one incarnation to the next is a soul, but there are five different levels of a soul: 1) *nefresh*, the biological life force; 2) *ruach*, the emotional part or ego; 3) *neshamah*, the higher consciousness of the individual; 4) *chayah*, the collective unconscious, as in the psychotherapist Jung's system; and 5) *yechida*, the oneness with both creation and God. They do not believe the first two levels survive death."

"But like Latter-day Saints, they believe that an earth life is a precious opportunity for spiritual growth," Timothy added.

Peg found herself staring at the three clean-shaven men in ordinary white suits and ties seated in chairs in front of the room. Somehow they were supposed to have long white beards to their chests and have fire issue out of their foreheads. But they were as ordinary as stake presidents, only they were translated or resurrected. And that meant they shone. Oh, how she longed to be translated, then going to L.A. would not mean worrying about hand cream and how to keep Miriam and Danny from marauding gangs.

The presidency of the mission to Judah finished their final lecture on the various branches of Judaism, and it was time to go to the meeting room next door to be joined by their families and a final talk by President Ueda.

"Rest assured, dear people, we will come to you from time to time. You will not be without seen and unseen guidance in this most important matter," Aaron assured them. "And one day in the near future we will meet back here with those good and faithful members of the tribe of Judah who have longed for this day all of their lives."

The last topic of his talk surprised both Ben and Peg. After the prophet announced that the temple in Jerusalem was still standing in spite of all the opposition from the Arabs, he then revealed that part of their mission was try to convince Evangelicals in the U.S. and Canadian cities that were not shielded by Zion's electronic net that they should join the Church. Most had not left their homes, believing that the Rapture would take them up into heaven. There was no reason to flee anywhere, they believed. In the process, they had suffered terribly.

"We have been given a mandate from the Lord that we do everything in our power to get them on the busses that regularly leave from major East Coast and West Coast locations. Even if they choose not to join the Church, we can more adequately care for them in our organized centers throughout the middle of America." *And we will be out there trying to get them to come to Zion and die in the process.* Peg began to feel shaky, like she was going to throw up.

"And many Evangelicals believe that the Rapture has already occurred, that they have been left behind to work out their salvation as best they can. This is a terrible waste," President Ueda said emphatically.

A few last words, then the prophet asked, "So are there any questions?" Most in the room chuckled, knowing that there were a million questions running through their minds.

"Yes, sir," Peg blurted out. "I have one. Just how are we going to survive, sir?" She was half out of her seat. Ben, embarrassed, pulled her down.

"Sister Taylor, we will discuss that privately in a few moments. Would that be all right?"

Peg felt like a fifth-grade girl who stupidly had offered to go to the board to do an arithmetic problem and found she did not know the answer. She leaned down and put her hands to her burning cheeks. Ben was not of any help. Embarrassed, he sat straight up, not touching her as another ten minutes passed of questions and answers.

"Now, if you will be so kind as to wait here, we will call you by family," Elder Dawahoya then said and smiled in Peg's direction. She moaned under her breath.

The group left the room in alphabetical order. "Taylor" was the third from last. Danny and Miriam began picking at each other's hair. Ben admonished them sharply under his breath, "Stop that! Show some respect here, for heaven's sake."

"Sorry, Dad," they said quietly in singsong voices.

Peg picked at her fingernails. Finally Elder Stewart put his head into the room and called out, "The Taylor family?"

The four quickly stood up. Ben smiled back at the two other families still waiting, now nearly an hour. As they walked down the hall behind the tall, white-haired Stewart, Ben got butterflies in his stomach.

What happened next satisfied every one of Peg's fears. Individually, each member of the Taylor family sat down on a chair surrounded by Presidents Ueda, Dawahoya and Stewart. The men laid their hands on each head and pronounced a blessing. All different—each appropriate for the individual—but in the end the blessing was the same: "In the name of our Lord, Jesus

Christ...I confer upon you a special blessing that your body be changed, so that no disease can enter it, nor darts from the Evil One can penetrate your mind. No harm of any kind will come to you until you return safely to Zion."

Peg was embarrassed when, after she had been blessed, the prophet squeezed her shoulder with fatherly affection.

During Ben's blessing, he first felt the weight of the six hands on his head, but as they began to pronounce the special blessing, it was as if the three had lifted their hands off and another set of hands had been placed on his head in their stead. A burning sensation, which was both hot and pleasant, shot down from his head, down his spine, and out his legs. It was just that simple, but Ben felt sure those hands were the Lord's somehow. And he believed.

The four Taylors sat back down in their chairs and the president said, "You won't feel much different, but I assure you there has been a change in your biochemical makeup that will make you impervious to the environment you find yourself in. A gift from the Lord."

"Is this like the miracles He did in the Bible?" Miriam wanted to know.

"Exactly," the spritely president replied, a twinkle in his eye. "Isn't it great?"

"Does this mean that we are translated?" Danny asked excitedly.

"No, son, those changes will occur at the Lord's coming. But this is definitely a step up," Elder Dawahoya kidded him.

"I'll say," Ben said, standing to shake each man's hand.

"Although you will soon be under the blanket of Zion, it may be many months before that occurs and we want you to be able to carry out your duties," President Ueda said.

Out in the car, Peg wanted to confess to her doubts. "I felt like such a doubting Thomas," she moaned.

Danny reached over the seat and patted her shoulder, "Mom, don't beat up on yourself. You are always looking out for everybody. How could you know that this would happen to us?"

"I should have," she said, inconsolable.

Ben changed the subject. "You guys want to go with us out to the Dubiks?"

"Yes!" they both said.

"Okay, let's get something to eat at home and head out there. You know we can't be at their temple wedding, so we're going to take them some gifts."

Out on the broad plain in the Chukotka Peninsula, it was getting hot as the day wore on. The sun rose that day at 2:45 A.M. and by 11:00 the travellers were shedding layers of clothes to keep cool except for the translated ones—John the Beloved, who walked along with Sangay and two of the translated heads of the ten tribes. They walked in the front of the 100-mile-long phalanx of people streaming toward the Bering Strait in hopes of reaching Zion.

Seen by air the area they were walking in resembled an elongated triangle pointed to the east, toward Alaska. Curiously, the region is located in both the eastern and western hemispheres, on both sides of the Arctic Circle and is the northernmost point of the Pacific Ocean. A symbolic point, to be sure, for one of the very last major battles in the war between Lu Han's forces and the Saints.

"How far back are the stragglers?" John asked Sangay.

"They are still coming down the river."

"Well, we will all be out on the tundra by tomorrow evening, I estimate. That will make it easier."

"How do you think they are holding up, Brother Sangay?"

"Some are very weary...losing hope, I think."

The four men looked to each other sadly, and then out onto the gentle mountain range and the fog bank that indicated they were near the sea. They could hear the barking and bleating of seals and walrus along the shoreline. Another twenty minutes and they were there among a myriad of birds, puffins, sukelts and kittiwakes, all taking to the sky in surprised and angry protest.

"This feels good," the head of the tribe of Dan exclaimed. "Cooling off."

"I didn't think I would be so sensitive to warmth and cold, now that I have this translated body. It's not that I'm afraid I'll catch cold..." said the head of the tribe of Reuben. "It's just I...I don't know. It's just interesting, that's all."

"A lot of this land is gone." John changed the subject. "We had early warnings from both the Arctic and the Antarctic at the end of the last century. Scientists were able to build computer models about unstable sea ice, permafrost, and so on."

"But they never released them to the general public, did they?" Elder Dyachenko asked.

"No. In those days there were satellite images of, say, the St. Lawrence Island showing polynya breaks or openings in the sea ice that predicted the rising sea levels. What they did not tell us was that the island would most likely disappear early in this century."

The four had reached the destination that they had seen in a shared vision: a bay, a large patch of tundra with a million small flowers, and sloping mountains in the background. "What do you think?" John asked. "This is it?"

The three agreed.

"And if man with all his ecological destruction can reduce the polar regions to mush, then the Lord can surely raise the land wherever He pleases."

The three men agreed with him, thrilled that the long-awaited prophecy that predicted a land mass would rise out of the sea as an escape route for the ten tribes was nearly upon them.

They walked around the area for a few minutes, then John said, "Okay, brethren, place your standards on that small rise so that when the tribes come in that is what they will see."

The four men walked a short distance, dug out the tundra and placed each of their tribes' standards. They were modeled on ones used originally by the ten tribes in their journey to Israel. Large antler horns, a kite-like structure, a wolf head...each symbolic of the tribe's contribution to the twelve tribes.

"The others couldn't leave their positions right now. They are having difficulty keeping up the spirits of their travellers," Sangay said sadly.

"Is that cranberry?" Elder Grudzinski asked, pointing to small, dark red objects on a low-lying plant.

"I believe so. I know I saw Labrador tea as well."

"This whole area used to be used by the Chukchi for reindeer herding. Half a million domesticated reindeer. There are still a handful of herders, but with the rise of the sea, whole sections of the peninsula have been lost and with that, reindeer populations have dwindled."

"Is that the man we're waiting for?" Elder Hovanec asked, pointing to a figure emerging from the fog.

"Yes," John answered. "Him and his small party."

The men squinted to see a party of twelve men dressed in traditional garb. In front a man dressed in a reindeer skin coat, decorated with tassels and embroidered designs. White spots ran down the front of his outfit from neck to knee-length skirt. His leggings and boots were decorated with Venetian trade beads used only for very special occasions.

The groups waved to each other. The translated beings held their ground and let the group approach.

"This the Koryak shaman. He speaks both Chukchi, which is a Paleo-siberian language, as well as Russian. The party consists of his helpers who have come to speak with us about *Quikil*, or Big Raven."

John greeted them in Chukchi. The others joined in, using their gift of languages to immediately speak and understand an unfamiliar language.

The parties sat down on the tundra. The shaman's men set down their spears and retreated to the background.

"I am called Quikinnaqu. But that is only my ceremonial title. The real Quikinnaqu or Big-Raven is the Father and Protector of our tribe."

"We call him Jesus Christ," John explained. "He is a supernatural being who is the Great Transformer of the world."

The shaman turned back to his men and grunted in surprise. He turned and said, "You white men know of the Big Raven?"

"Yes, we do. And we have come from him to bring you a message that you have been waiting for."

Once again, the shaman turned around sharply. "How is it that you know of such things?"

"Because the Big Raven has watched over the Koryak for many thousands of years. He watched as you went across the ocean in your kayaks and travelled to the Big Country to the east. We call that land America."

"America," the group said in unison and nodded.

"Yes, and he watched as the Koryak returned to this land and he protected your journeying. Then he told you many things about the land of America and said that one day you would be called to go back there."

The shaman lunged forward. "No white man knows these things. You are an evil trickster." In a flash he had pulled out a knife and thrown it at Sangay. Sangay deliberately let it hit him. No blood oozed from the opening in his arm.

The Koryak scrambled to their feet and began to flee. John called out to them. "Wait! Look!" He snapped his fingers and a snarling wolf appeared on the permafrost.

That stopped the shaman in his tracks. He returned slowly, eying both the wolf and the beloved apostle who had nothing but love and sincerity in his face.

"You have come for us?"

"I have. We will be joined by many, many people. When the time comes, the sea will open up and land will appear. Just as in your prophecies." John snapped his fingers and the wolf disappeared. This brought surprised cries from the shaman's party.

"Now I know you are a true messenger from the Big Raven. We will go to prepare our people." And in what seemed like a moment, they had disappeared back into the fog bank.

"Right!" John said with satisfaction. "That was the last group. I'm pleased. They, along with the Chukchi, have been true to their tribal myths. I believe we will bring their people with us. In the records of Ephraim and Manasseh, there is a story very similar to this."

"Oh, yes. I've read it," Sangay said. "It's about a missionary named Ammon and a king who believes in the Great Spirit. Do you remember that, Rudolf?"

"Of course. I read the Book of Mormon from cover to cover in one sitting. I can't wait to place our records in their hands. We have similar spiritually uplifting stories, to be sure," exulted the head of the tribe of Dan.

Turning to Sangay John said, "Thank you for your courage with these people. I know you are still unaccustomed to being in a translated state. It took a very disciplined man to stand and allow himself to be hit with a deadly weapon."

Sangay demurred. "I prefer to think of it as slow reflexes." That brought a collective laugh. Then, at a signal, they said their goodbyes, and instantly there was nothing but four colorful standards waving in the coastal breeze.

Chapter Sixteen

I'm really a very good man,
but I'm a very bad Wizard.

The Wizard of Oz

General Gornstein looked out the window at the scene below as his transport plane began swooping down on Proventiya, the southernmost coastal town on the Chukya Peninsula. From here he could not see the purported half million people out on the tundra. But they had been spotted by satellite the very first day it was up and running. In fact, the first pass over the area showed a massive dust storm and the second a clearing and the mass of emigrants on a southeast trajectory toward the Bering Sea. The Russian had not doubted his master, Lu Han, but it did help that the masses were spotted. He did not have to look like a fool, ordering a massive call-up of the Chinese army just on what had appeared as a whim.

Near him on the plane were his chief of staff, Lt. General Dankevich; Vice Admiral Abashvili, head of naval affairs; General Davidkov, head of air defense; and General Garbuz, head of intelligence. All Russians. He didn't trust the Chinese officers; for such a venture, he returned to his old comrades with whom he had fought in their successful bid to overthrow the UWEN.

The plane was loaded with a total of 200 men ready to set up a command post at Proventiya, which had been a Soviet administrative and military center during WWII. Abandoned in recent years, partly because of the rising sea level and partly because of its isolation, it was only accessible by air and water. But it was a perfect place to begin the extermination of this large mass of refugees.

The plane set down on a old runway that was now just tundra. After a bumpy landing, it turned around and deposited the men at the entrance to an empty city, with whole apartment blocks still intact. These would serve as barracks. More than 50,000 infantrymen and border guards had been housed there during the Cold War.

While the tired travellers worked their way to the sea, the Chinese army was on the march. At the rate the army of 250,000 men was moving, they would intercept the refugees within a few days.

"I know we've got weaklings and idiots in this army," Gornstein nearly shouted at their first debriefing. "The men in the cities were killed off or are so sick that they are useless. We had to call up these village idiots. But at least we have the numbers. And they are expendable."

The Russian veteran of thirty-seven years of war looked over the reports from the field. His chief of staff reported, "The 211th Submarine Brigade will be in place by day after tomorrow. That's seven submarines, sir."

"And launchers?"

"Six is all that we could pull together, sir."

"Aircraft. Thirty-second Fighter Aviation Regiment. How many MIGs?"

"Forty, sir."

And so it went. A massive call-up of manpower with limited war-making material. Assuming that there would be armed resistance from the refugees, both the 43rd and 181st Missile Regiment had been reactivated. Gornstein was frustrated by the lack of materials, but he had been successful in the battles in Turkey and Iran with a limited amount of guns and ammunition, so he knew it could be done.

"When can we begin the flybys?" he asked impatiently.

"We are working on clearing a runway in Uelen. Three days at the least."

"Where is an aircraft carrier when you need one?" Gornstein asked sardonically. The assembled men chuckled.

"Of course, when they reach the land bridge, we can pick off those who've managed to elude us. But let's see what damage we can do to the majority so it doesn't come down to man-to-man combat." Gornstein was absolutely in his element with his Russian mates, speaking the mother tongue. These men he understood completely.

Peg's feelings of humiliation and embarrassment filled the car on the way to the Dubiks'. The kids tried to joke around; Ben ignored her, but she just couldn't shake the fact that she had made a fool of herself in front of *that* assembled group of people. A feeling like a white-hot knot seared her just below her breastbone. So, when the family arrived at the Dubik house with its springs and artistic-looking outbuildings, Ben and the kids quickly spilled out the car and disappeared. They were escorted around the property by Alex with Adam in tow. Moira met Peg at the entryway and gave her a hug. "Come in. You look like you could use a friend."

Peg gave her a dozen jars of strawberry jam as a wedding gift, then said, "I've been doing so well, until today..." Peg began to explain what had happened at the temple as they walked down the stone walkway to the large family room. By the time they reached the family room Moira decided to offer Peg one last therapy session using a newly constructed area in her study.

"Look. I've just finished putting together a sand tray area. Why don't you come and see what I'm up to?" Moira sounded quite like her deceased mother, Grace, at that moment. This was particularly soothing for Peg who had relied on the Maori grandmother.

"You sound just like Grace," Peg said.

"People have been telling me that lately."

"Do you sometimes try to count the days until you can see her again?"

"Truth? Yes, I do. I figure another three and a half years, give or take. That's..."

"One thousand one hundred sixty-eight days," Peg interrupted. The two laughed lightly, then grew sober.

Peg continued, "I can't wait to see Rachel. That seems like a lifetime."

"I know. Sometimes I wonder if I'll make it through. People are dying here in Zion, you know."

"But just from old age, right?"

"No, not necessarily. We don't have communicable diseases, but if people brought weak hearts or a predisposition to have a stroke— they are dying."

"Isn't that an irony? Get all the way here, and then die," Peg said glumly. Then her eye fell on the hundreds of small miniatures displayed on shelves around the back of the room and she exclaimed, "Wow! What fun!"

"I wish there were more," Moira moaned. "But this is the best I can do under the circumstances. I've begged and borrowed them and Alex has constructed quite a few. I'm feeling like I have enough to at least start."

"How does it work? What goes on?" Peg asked as she began to stop and look at each shelf.

"Well, it was used mostly for children in the twentieth century—children who couldn't express how they felt made pictures with the miniatures. A follower of Carl Jung, Dora Kalff, started it in the 1930s, I think. Then toward the end of the century, people began using it with adults who were physically ill. It was an adjunct, for example, to conventional cancer treatment."

"And what did it do?" asked Peg incredulously.

"Well, there is a psychological component to physical illness. And this enabled people to express the unconscious factors that might have been contributing to their sickness."

Peg had stopped at a figurine that particularly caught her attention. It was a copper-colored pumpkin that was drawn by two horses.

"Like it?"

"I want to take it home." Peg laughed.

"Then that is your first piece. Take it and put it on the table. The criterion for choosing an object is whether it 'calls' to you or not."

"Okay. This could be fun," Peg said as she moved to the next shelf and picked out three shells and placed them on the long table. When she had put fourteen objects down, she paused, surveying each of the shelves a second time. After a bit, she said, "I think I'm done."

"Good. Now you have a choice between a wet tray and a dry one."

Peg picked one in which the sand had been wet so that it could be molded into mounds quite easily. Moira pointed out that there was a blue bottom to the large rectangular plastic tray if Peg wanted to make lakes or rivers. Then the therapist sat back and watched as Peg began to move the sand around.

She pushed and she mounded, first in this corner, then in the other. She took two of her fingers and began making a large sideways 'S.' Wider and deeper she went, lost in the construction of a road that wound from the upper left-hand corner around to the lower right-hand one. She began to hum to herself, forgetting that Moira was sitting there. The refrain of a song by Sting came to her: "I did not love you." This she sang or hummed repeatedly as she placed objects along the path in the tray that she had made. They were mostly shells and rocks. A timepiece, Darth Vader and Dorothy from the *Wizard of Oz* were clustered in the lower left. And in the lower right a cameo and black crane.

This took about fifteen minutes to complete and when Peg had finished, the knot in her stomach was gone and her pupils were dilated with pleasure. "There, I think that's it."

The two sat for a few moments, then Moira asked, "Anything else on the shelf? Anything you want to do?"

Peg looked over the collection, got up and pulled out the Wizard of Oz. "I think I need to replace him with Darth Vader."

"Okay." The two sat again in silence. "Now? Done?"

"I'm not sure."

"Well, what shall we call this creation?"

"Ah…I guess, 'My Journey.'"

"And that's got to be on your mind—you leaving in a couple of days and all."

"I guess so, but what does this mean? What am I saying?"

"Like the dreams we've worked with, it's first up to you to say, and then I'll throw in my two cents' when you are done."

"Well, I think this is my life's journey," Peg said, picking up the carriage and moving it slowly through the sand. She followed it around the S-curve and to the end with the cameo and the crane. "There isn't much here after I get past Dorothy and the Wizard. It feels like I have to hurry past them."

"You've put a timepiece there."

"Yes." Peg thought for a moment. "Well, if this is like dreamwork I'll say that Dorothy reminds me of me right now. My goodness, if I'm not living in Oz, I don't know who is. I mean, with translated beings giving lectures on ancient Judaism and ancient apostles teaching our mission lessons."

The two laughed. Peg continued, "Dorothy was brave, enlisted helpers, and...managed to get back home. Wow! Well, that certainly describes what I'm worried about."

"And the Wizard?"

"Well, he was a fake. He pretended to be someone he wasn't." Peg began to tear. "Just like my father. And I believed him!"

"You were just a girl."

"I know what I'm saying. I'm saying that it's time I stopped believing my father."

"And what would he have you believe?"

"That nothing works out. That something is always going to trip you up. People will always disappoint you because they are human. Whooeee!" Peg nearly shouted as she threw her arms in the air. "Yes! That's it." She jumped up and grabbed some miniature fencing from the shelf. She bent it into a triangle so that the trio were fenced off from the rest of the figures. "Okay, that feels great. Keep them out."

As she moved the carriage around and down toward the bottom right corner, she seemed to hesitate. "I don't want to finish this."

"Why?"

"Because I think I understand what's there at the end. My mother loves cameos. I think the crane is a messenger of death. I think I'm saying to myself that my mother may die when I'm gone and I'm going to have to meet her at my journey's end." She fell quiet. "You know how that Sting song ends?"

"No."

"'I must have loved you,'" she sang softly. "Wow. That is powerful. So my guilt today wasn't so much about being embarrassed as much as it has to do with shutting out my father's voice and doing something about my mother before I leave?"

"What do you think?"

"Yeah. That feels right."

Moira squeezed Peg's arm who said, "I'm going to set up a sand tray room in the mission home. Then we can all really know what's going on."

Moira smiled. "I'd like to add one more observation."

"Yes?"

"You see the configuration of the road?" Moira draw her fingers along the path. "It looks like a uterus. Sometimes sand tray has been used to help with an early diagnosis of an illness or pinpoint a part of our body that holds blocked emotions just as dreams do. Perhaps you are mourning the loss of your child-bearing years or you may be going into early menopause. Why not check out your estrogen and progesterone levels before you go?"

"You know, I think the first interpretation is very telling. But as far as I know, physically all systems are go. We had a blessing just a couple of hours ago that said our bodies would be healthy."

"What a comfort, Peg!"

"It was. I don't feel any different right now, but I have faith that when it's important, we'll know it."

"I envy you this adventure."

"And I envy you your plantation."

"I guess the Lord decides we need to go against our natural inclinations in order to grow," Moira said. "If it were up to me, I'd be on a bus to the east or west coast in a flash, but I've got to learn to be domestic."

"Well, I'm really going to have to look at the journey beyond having children. That's so helpful."

The two looked at each other lovingly.

"Don't you let that Wizard convince you otherwise, you hear?" Moira said in her mother's voice.

"I won't. Promise."

The Taylor family returned reluctantly to the car and waved goodbye to the Dubiks as long as they could. Ben drove the car down the main highway, stopped, looked both ways, then abruptly turned the car to the right, away from the way to their house.

"Hey, Dad!" the two kids yelled in unison. "You lost your mind?"

"No. I want to make one more stop on our way home."

"Where, honey?" Peg wanted to know. "It's getting late."

"Won't take more than twenty minutes," Ben said refusing to reveal where he was headed.

They drove along in silence for a short time; then Peg said, "I'm really sad we can't go to their wedding."

"Me, too," Ben added. "Who's officiating?"

"President Ueda. And there's talk that Sangay and Pema may make an appearance," she replied wistfully.

"Yeah, and Adam said he was getting sealed," Danny said leaning forward from the back seat.

"He thinks that that means he's going to get stuck to his parents," Miriam laughed.

"And where did he get that idea?" Peg asked in the slightest accusatory tone.

"Not from us," the pair replied.

"Yeah, sure. Come on, 'fess up. I know you guys. You like to tease little kids," Ben joined in.

"Well," Danny said, then started laughing.

"I knew it," Peg kidded him. "Honey, I hope you corrected the impression."

"I did."

Silence. Then Miriam broached a touchy subject. "Are we ever going to get sealed to you guys?"

But Ben jumped right in. "You guys have to be twenty-one and temple worthy. Then you can choose what you want to do, remember?"

"Yeah," her voice flattened. "But what if you die? Am I still your kid?"

"Absolutely, positively, marvelously, fantastically forever."

Miriam let out a sigh and fell back against the back seat; she stared out the window at the passing scenery.

About eighteen miles down the road to their destination, their car began to climb hills—hills that had been created by the great quake. Although not as high as the ones they could see in the distance, these unexpected hills still jutted up five hundred feet. When they reached the top of the rise, they all cried out in joy. Here before them lay a beautiful valley, surrounded by high mountains to the north and hills on all three of the other sides. The valley appeared to be about eighteen miles wide and about twenty miles long. It was completely empty.

"This is Adam-ondi-Ahman. I wanted you to see it before we went, because there is going to be an astonishing event in this valley very soon. Guys, get out your scriptures. Let's get out and sit down over there," he said, pointing to a large rock formation.

Peg pulled out an orange sleeping bag, unzipped it, and laid it out for them to sit on. They stared at a rounded hill jutting up from the valley floor—a knoll with one tree overlooking a great open space. Ben indicated that that was Spring Hill, the place where Adam built an altar and prayed to the Lord when leaving the Garden—and where Joseph's party found rocks piled on one another in the 1840s. Although the geography was different than when the prophet looked out over the landscape, the sacredness of the spot had not changed.

"I heard that there used to be a big sign off the major freeway that said, "Adam-ondi-Ahman. Turn right here," Peg said.

"Weird," Danny said. "I wonder what people thought. They weren't Mormons, not around here."

"I don't know. Let's make this Family Home Evening time," Peg said folding her arms. The family prayed and asked for safety to Los Angeles; they asked for the softening of the hearts of the Jewish people that they were going to approach; and most of all they prayed that they might be worthy to see the face of the Savior at the time of his coming.

"Okay, let's look at scriptures," Ben said enthusiastically. Opening his red travelling quad to the index, he looked through references for Israel, Ten Lost Tribes. "Danny, you read Doctrine and Covenants 133:26 through 34."

The family looked out at the long, empty valley as Danny read, through the part about the ice flowing down at their presence and a highway being cast up from the deep. When he read "and the boundaries of the everlasting hills shall tremble at their presence. And there shall they fall down and be crowned with glory, even in

Zion, by the hands of the servants of the Lord," it seemed like his voice echoed out and back at them. It was as if they could imagine the valley being filled with crowds of people in colorful garb, carrying banners, crying out, "Hosanna, Hosanna, Hosanna unto the most high God."

Peg filled them in on what she and Ben currently knew about the ten tribes' movements and how they would probably arrive in Zion before the fall.

"Something else we won't get to see," Miriam said grumpily.

"Oh, we'll get to see the ten tribes. They aren't going anywhere."

"But there is one thing we won't see happen here," Ben said.

"What's that?" Miriam asked.

"The council at Adam-ondi-Ahman," Danny replied. "It's only for translated, resurrected or people in the spirit world. No humans invited."

"Why is that?" she asked.

"Because there is going to be a most amazing ceremony that is so sacred, only those kind of evolved souls can attend."

Miriam folded her arms and hurrumphed. Ben put his arm around her and pulled her to him. "One day very soon, we'll get to see more amazing things than you can even imagine, sugar."

"Try me," she said, trying to stay sullen. The four laughed heartily, and this time the sounds they made did echo out in the valley and return to them.

"That might be the first family laugh in this valley. Think about that," Ben said.

Peg, ever the teacher, wanted to go with the lesson. "Okay, what about this council? What do you guys know?"

"I know that in the Doctrine and Covenants it says that Adam will return here. That he first gathered all of his descendants to this valley and blessed them, and now he's coming back again," Danny said.

"Good. That's section 116. What else?"

"Well, this was the Garden of Eden," Miriam said. "Wow, that's freaky."

"No, that's south of here in Jackson County. When Adam and Even had to leave the Garden, they went north and settled here."

"And it's in Daniel that we learn what's going to happen here," Peg added.

"Hey, couldn't it be happening right now and we don't know it?" Miriam asked.

"Could be, silly." Ben tussled her hair and tickled her a bit.

"Let's look at Daniel 7." Peg took the scriptures and handed them to Danny. "Aaronic Priesthood holder, you read."

When they were done, Ben took the scriptures and opened randomly. "I like to do this sometimes, just to see if there is anything relevant to my life right now. Let's see what I've opened to." He squinted a bit to read the small script. "Isaiah 43. Ah, let's see. Verse one: 'Oh, Israel (Oh, Ben and Peg and Danny and Miriam)," Ben added. "'Fear not: for I have redeemed thee, I have called thee by thy name; thou art mine.'"

No one said anything. Peg teared up and took Danny's hand, who uncharacteristically let her hold it. Then a bird, perhaps a falcon, swooped down the valley from right to left, taking several long moments to complete its arc. "That's a sign," Peg said quietly. "I think we are acceptable to the Lord."

"I think we are," Ben said, reaching out to touch her shoulder.

Chapter Seventeen

And it shall come to pass that the Jews shall have
the words of the Nephites, and the Nephites
shall have the words of the Jews; and the Nephites
and the Jews shall have the words of the lost tribes...

2 Nephi 19:13

The emperor sat very still and probed Gornstein's thoughts across the globe. He was pleased with what he experienced. His Russian general was doing just what he expected he would. "Good. That will do nicely," Han said aloud. "The television programming will report that defectors in Northern China were trying to escape without submitting to the economic system and put up armed resistance. Of course the army had no other choice but to *slaughter* them." He chuckled.

He walked out onto the balcony and looked up into the night sky. *No comet yet.* "I've decided to take the extraterrestrial route," he said to no one visible. "I'm going to say that they, the superior beings, have appointed me as their earthly representative because of my superior spiritual nature. I hope that pleases you, Master."

He waited to see if he perceived a reply from Lucifer, the master of the unembodied. "I will tell them that they must watch the television at certain times each day. I will appear daily to give them the extraterrestrials' instructions. There will be severe penalties for non-compliance: the World Government will use our new satellite system to see that the set is turned on."

The tall, lithe martial arts expert walked to the end of the balcony and returned. "Then I will drop the proverbial bomb: if the people do not comply with all of their demands, the beings have threatened to send a comet to destroy the earth." He laughed as he searched his pockets for a match. "And, of course, when it hits, I can say that there were pockets of resistance—the Jews, the Christians. And, if everyone does not comply, the next comet will destroy all life."

The end of the cigarette briefly caught fire as he lighted it and took a long drag. He did not smoke in front of anyone, lest he appear to be addicted to any substance. But in private, he found comfort in the smoke, the inhalation, the slight burning sensation in his throat. More importantly he waited for the nicotine peace that descended on him and helped him grow numb. A particular blend of Turkish tobacco, sprinkled with a little hashish, suited him perfectly.

After a few long inhalations in which he held his breath before blowing the soothing smoke out, he slid open the glass door, stepped back into the living room, then made his way to a back room which he kept locked. The smell of heavy incense wafted from the room as soon as he opened the door. An ornate altar filled one wall. He moved to a corner closet, pulled out a black martial arts jacket along with a black sash and apron. In these he planned to do his daily ablutions to the dark god of the underworld who guided and sustained him.

He poured goat blood into a goblet from a plastic pitcher that had been stored in the small refrigerator he kept in this forbidden room. He lifted the golden container toward the altar and swore, "May this be the moment when the world is yours, Master."

As members of each of the tribes reached the grassy peninsula's edge and placed their banners on the rolling hilltops, the colorful icons could be plainly seen by the rest of the tribe trekking up the river valley and out onto the broad plain whose soil resembled a gigantic assembled picture puzzle because of the permafrost.

The tens of thousands walked slowly along over the sparse grass and scattered dwarf vegetation, like cotton grass, dwarf birch and willow. Some were singing simple uplifting songs. Others trudged, heads bowed, in a rhythmic, almost hypnotized state. Every so often they would look up to survey the horizon. As the forward group smelled the sea air before they caught sight of the fog along the coast, they spied the icons and cried out. They were suddenly filled with renewed energy to reach the water's edge.

Near the banner hill the ten translated men huddled together. "This is the part I dread," one said.

"We cannot do anything to protect these wonderful people by miraculous means until they journey across the land bridge," another reminded them.

"We can *pray*, however, that the elements may cooperate with us," Sangay said. "That is not supernatural. All apostles have that ability in their telestial form," He reached out his hands to them. "The Savior has indicated this is the test that every one of our people must pass through. And, if they die, they will not be long in the spirit world before they will have a triumphant return along with other Christian martyrs."

215

"It's still hard, knowing what's going to happen," Elder Hovanec said. The rest agreed.

Without a sound or warning, John the apostle stood outside their circle. They quickly created a place in the circle, comforted by his presence. "Shall we pray, brethren?" he asked.

It seemed to Sangay that the very atoms of the air danced in response to John's heartfelt plea. Soon after, the vast plain began to be filled with masses of people in colorful garb, lowing livestock, and children—all of them hot and dragging their feet. They began to erect tents and work together to create a temporary camp site. These were just the front runners of those who looked like an army of ants marching up from the river valley.

Not more than a half hour after John's prayer, a piece of the Arctic Circle ice cap the size of Delaware broke away from the main ice sheet and plunged into the Arctic Ocean above the Chukchi Sea, an area of about 200,000 square miles. The tsunami wave generated by the impact into the ocean began travelling at a rate of about twenty-five miles per hour down the Bering Strait until it hit the Bering land bridge connecting Russia with Alaska. The land bridge acted like the end of some titanic bathtub whose water was being swished back and forth by a thousand-foot-tall toddler. The water crashed up against the land with a deafening roar and powerful trembler, then returned in a great wave which swept over the city of Uelen, covering it with ten feet of water and wiping out both the air landing strip and the hundreds of Gornstein's forces who were working on its construction.

When word reached Gornstein, he was furious and frustrated. Timing here was everything. If he could not stop them, he assumed the emigrants would pass over the Bering Bridge and into rugged Alaskan terrain. His army would have much greater difficulty exterminating them there than they would on this broad, open plain. Satellite photos rolled in on the fax machine in his office, indicating that the bulk of emigrants were now out on the Chukchi Peninsula and could be surrounded and slaughtered. His orders to his land troop commanders, now only two days out, were that they must press on with greater speed (with severe threats if the operation was not carried out to his liking).

As the giant iceberg, as tall as a skyscraper, brilliantly white, floated farther and farther south, it moved into the Bering Strait where it began to act like a solid wall pushing water in front of it. Flooding became the norm along with coastlines and particularly on the Bering Bridge. The division of the World Government's troops which had been situated on the land bridge soon found that they could not find any higher ground to which they could retreat. They radioed for help and were transported out of the area by ship and submarine. After the evacuation, Gornstein ordered the sub commanders to maneuver into position along the bridge, for he expected a mass exodus of the ten tribes at any time.

John the Beloved called for a council of the ethnic peoples who had declared their intention to travel with the ten tribes. Within the hour, heads of the Chukchi, Koryak and Yupik, who were Siberian Eskimos, responded. John explained the gravity of the situation regarding any stragglers who would soon fall into the Chinese army's grasp. "Could you possibly help?" he asked gravely. "I know what I'm asking of you. I know you are the only ones who know the lay of the land and have weapons, albeit primitive ones. I know it won't stop the enemy altogether. But, if you were to make a stand against them, it may delay them long enough for the rest to join us."

These noble warriors did not hesitate. This was the Big Raven's desire. A small army of 700 natives slipped quickly through the assembled crowds, headed toward the full oncoming thrust of the Chinese divisions.

John watched, tears forming in his eyes. "God be with you," he said under his breath. Then with a sigh, he turned and walked to the coast. Followed by his ten translated leaders, he stopped and stared out at the empty ocean, crashing up against the bluffs. In one powerful motion he raised his arm and commanded in a loud voice, "In the holy name of Jesus the Christ, let there be land where there is sea. May the ice flow down before us."

At that moment the gigantic iceberg broke in pieces as if smashed by an unseen hammer. As it flowed over and submerged the Bering land bridge, it also knocked the submarines against the coast, rendering them useless. Further down the coast where the small group of translated men stood, they watched as St. Lawrence Island, which had long been submerged, began rising up, slowly and steadily, along with land forty miles wide. It formed a brand new land bridge spanning the ocean as far as the eye could see. All the way, in fact, to Sheldon Point on the Alaskan coast. A thunderous cry filled the earth from both man and animals, birds and angels who stood as witnesses to the miracle.

All these massive earth and sea changes created a wall of ocean water twelve feet high that swept through Proventiya, taking everything and everybody with it. Gornstein and two of his closest attachés had been warned by Han in a dream to leave, so they were in the cargo plane high over the Siberian landscape headed back to Constantinople. They missed the miraculous reconfiguration.

By the time the small army of warriors of the Chukchi Autonomous Area reached the tired and discouraged travellers, the Chinese army was upon them. Horrified, the villagers could only watch as the soldiers picked off members of the ten tribes like lions do when they race across a plain and pull down a sick, straggling antelope.

The small native army ran charging down the hills into the middle of the surprised and better-armed Chinese. Some of the Chinese soldiers fell. However, for the most part, they easily mowed down men armed with rocks, spears and homemade hatchets. This encounter with these brave martyrs, however, did slow the Chinese sufficiently to allow the rest of members of the tribes to reach the camps. (They were to talk about this valiant sacrifice all the rest of the journey to Zion. It quickly became known as the "Chukchi Massacre.")

Even before word had arrived at the coast that the slaughter had occurred, the ten translated men walked out on the newly formed, still wet land and signalled for their people to follow. Although a bit panicky, they obeyed. John led the way.

At the point where the International Date Line artificially separates one day from the next, John the Beloved created a permanent separation. In another sweep of his arm, he called on the Father in Heaven to bring Zion's "electronic net" this far north. In an instant, this was accomplished, so that once the travellers made it through the portal of the shield with its slight, high vibratory hum, no harm could come to them.

An unusually dense fog formed from the ocean's edge inland into the river valley. That impeded the Chinese army even more. By the time they reached the coastline, they could only see the backs of the final entrants into Zion. Although they moved quickly across the new land barrier, they could not penetrate the net. All they got for their troubles was an electric shock when they tried to push past the invisible but potent border of Zion.

When the first group of the ten tribes arrived in Alaska, at Shelton Point on the south fork of the Yukon River, they were met by a flotilla of boats sent by the prophet to bring nursing mothers, young children, the elderly and ill to Zion. The rest would continue walking their way to the center stake in Missouri. Busses were dispatched from all around Zion to head north and join up with them.

Triumphant members of the tribes picked up the pace, anxious to see the prophet's face, give him their records, and do the temple work that would seal them together and finish all the ordinances necessary for them to be able to rise in the morning of the first Resurrection along with Ephraim and Judah.

Never had the world seen such a large miracle where 476,093 people, who should never had been able to move more than twenty-five miles from home, escaped from the Anti-Christ's grasp and travelled 8,000 miles to set up new homes in the Lord's kingdom. Their songs of thanksgiving *did* shake Zion's hills as they neared Adam-ondi-Ahman. "How gracious is our Lord God! How he remembers his people."

Peg looked around the living room of their house. She remembered the first time she laid eyes on it. It was in shambles due to the series of earthquakes that preceded the establishment of Zion. They had really had their way with the 100-year-old farmhouse at 398 North Orchard Road. White stucco with dark green trim, it was still standing, technically. The whole south side was fully exposed. The walls lay in a heap on the ground; interior stairs dangled precariously from the second floor. The kitchen was covered with debris from the collapse of the ceiling. How quickly the building crew had put it back together, and how much Peg loved to have a house that she could paint and decorate the way she wanted. She had never owned a house before. She had promised the kids they would never leave; they would always live next door to the Winders.

"Suck it up, sweetie," she said to herself in a voice that her father had used with her when she acted "like a girl." "Okay, Dad. Just this once," she said aloud to the empty room. "But I'm telling you there is going to come a time when I have a real house, one that no one can knock down or take away from me."

She tightened her jaw, pulled back her shoulders and walked to the back door. Out in the back yard, Ben and the kids were piling the last of their belongings into a new shed built for their move. The house would be used by a yet-unknown family from one of the ten tribes. Knowing that part was satisfying for Peg.

"Okay, the bus will be here in about five minutes," she called out. "Let's have a family prayer."

Standing on the porch, bags at their feet, they clung together in a tight circle as they prayed. It was not long after that they could see the dust kicked up by the bus as it turned down the lane and headed for their house. "By the way, I want to say again what a wonderfully generous thing that was to give Mom the car," Peg said. "I know how important it was to you."

Ben blushed slightly. He put his arm around her shoulder and said, "She certainly needs it more than we do now."

Peg turned her head and kissed his hand. Then they were walking down the steps and boarding the bus already filled with twenty-five of the forty young missionaries they were taking with them. The family took the front seats. The boys called out, "Hi, President Taylor, Sister Taylor!" It gave the two a rush to hear themselves spoken to in such deferential tones. The missionaries also greeted Danny and Miriam, who responded in quiet embarrassment.

As the bus passed by the Winder house, they were brought to tears—the whole family (minus Laurie, of course)—nine children and Nate came out on the porch holding a long, handmade banner which read, "Bon voyage, Taylors. We love you."

Miriam stuck her head out of the window and waved vigorously to his close friend, Missy, who jumped up and down and waved until the bus was out of sight.

The Taylors were delighted to find that their driver was none other than Jed Rivers, longtime friend from California. After the rest of the boys had been picked up, the bus headed out across the plains. "How long does this take?" Ben wanted to know.

"Two days if all goes well. We have a motel in Durango, Colorado, that we usually use. They do a good job there," Jed replied.

Ben settled back into the seat and looked out the window. On one hand it was comforting to know that Jed had driven this route many times, as part of a shuttle service from West Coast cities into Zion. On the other hand, it was a bit disconcerting to think that he *himself* was the authority in charge.

Peg wanted to talk. "Can I catch you up on the latest?"

"Okay, honey, five minutes, then I've got to zone out. I've been dealing with people all day."

"Good. I'll talk fast." She knew that she had to say what she wanted to and then leave him alone for awhile. He was such an introvert, he needed hours a day to be alone. "Well, first the O'Boyle girls did get baptized last night. Nate did it. People said the room was filled with spiritual presences."

"Great," Ben tried to sound pleased, but he was tired and emotionally raw. "And second?"

"Second, Laurie came to the house to see the kids. Nate deliberately wasn't there. I heard that it went pretty well, considering. But she is so frail that she's staying at her parents' for now."

"That's good." Ben's voice was now fading. "Is there a third?"

"Yes, just one more item. Mary Margaret has been called to head a program for single moms and their kids. Kinda like a nunnery, but with kids. They are taking over apartments and building simple housing. She couldn't be more pleased."

The response was a slight snore. Ben had gone into overload and blessed sleep. He had not had much the night before.

"Mom?" Miriam asked, tapping Peg on the back. "I want to know. Will the O'Boyles have to move?"

Peg turned around and smiled at her stepdaughter. "I didn't get that impression. You really like Sarah, don't you?"

"Yes. I'll miss her. Can we write letters?"

"You betcha. You know, you are growing into such a beautiful young woman."

Miriam blushed, but she took the compliment. Just to keep talking to Peg helped her with the knot in her stomach. She was homesick already.

Danny, shy at first, got pulled into a scriptural argument that was happening in the seat behind him. Elder Berry and Elder Green had taken sides about when the Holy Spirit would get his body. Danny could not keep from offering his opinion that it would not be until the end of the Millennium. He sounded like he had given it some consideration.

"Hey, Danny, you could go on splits with us. Want to?" Elder Berry offered. Danny started to demur, but more of the missionaries jumped in and soon Danny was included in this new family configuration with a total of forty new older brothers. Then the boys started in on Miriam, kidding her about the stuffed bear she insisted on carrying. And she shot back insults about their haircuts.

Peg smiled and put her head against the back seat. *I can see how this might be really good for these kids*, she said to herself. She let her mind drift to a time in the near future when she would be able to homeschool both of them. She could see them having great discussions about history, politics, their creative writing. She reached down into her large black bag with the embroidered kittens on the sides and pulled out a worn and beloved copy of *The Poems of Dylan Thomas*. She thumbed through the pages until her eye fell on #17, "Since, on a Quiet Night."

She began to whisper as she read the lines, "Since, on a quiet night, I heard them talk/Who have no voices but the winds'/Of all the mystery there is in life/And all the mastery there is in death…" She let the book drop into her lap, snuggled up next to Ben, and let herself be lulled to sleep by the swaying of the bus as it travelled southwest to the proverbial land of oranges and starlets.

The stay in Durango was uneventful and a welcome relief. The boys ran and played rock soccer for a couple of hours to get some of the kinks out. Then the bus headed down to the Four Corners area, out across Navajo country and onto into the desert that separates Arizona and California. All this territory had been under the Zion "umbrella" for some time now. The forest lands that had been so badly burned in years past were showing green growth. The occupants of bus #221 were both excited and nervous, knowing that they would be leaving the protection of Zion after they crossed the Mojave Desert, whose extreme temperatures had been moderated under the climactic benefits of the shield.

The kids and missionaries were in the back of the bus singing "Michael, Row Your Boat Ashore." That gave Peg and Ben a few moments to have a quiet, serious discussion.

"About the rebuilding of the L.A. temple, why do it?" Peg wanted to know. "Why not have people come to one of the temples in Arizona? There can't be that many Latter-day Saints left in Southern California."

Ben leaned toward her and lowered his voice. "Because very soon the whole of the Western Hemisphere will be under Zion's net. And because as many people as possible need to have their calling and election made sure. That seems to be necessary in order to meet the Lord at his coming."

"Oh." Peg wanted to ask if they would be worthy to have that crowning ordinance, but she did not think Ben had the answer, although it was strange to see how he was subtly changing now that he had been set apart. It was like a real mantle of authority had dropped on his shoulders.

Ben asked, "Remember when we had the rededication of the Nauvoo Temple?"

"Who could forget. It was so emotional. Especially when President Hinckley said he might never return to Nauvoo," Peg said as she sat up straight and turned toward him.

"I thought it was amazingly synchronistic when Elder Oaks was talking about the last days and the reception was interrupted."

"Yeah, what did the message read on the screen?"

"Something like, 'Reception not authorized,'" Ben recounted.

"I remember shivering. I thought, 'Boy, if *that's* not a sign!' Soon we won't be able to use our satellite system, and then that's exactly what happened."

The two looked out at the flat desert landscape. "I'm really curious about L.A. I hope I'll be able to go back to Lakewood," said Ben.

"You remember how we talked and talked about the dedicatory prayer which spoke of the Father's presence in the temple—about what it meant?" Peg asked.

"I think it's pretty clear that it was momentous in the history of the world; it was one of only a few times when the Father made an appearance."

"Things really sped up after that, didn't they?"

Ben slipped his hand under her arm. "They still are, baby."

The scene on the Los Angeles freeways was like something out of a bad science fiction movie. Old cars rusting out on the sides of the road, dead palm trees looking like forty-foot-tall straw broom sticks, foliage overgrowing the median and spilling out onto the road, potholes and very few cars. Busses were used as the major means of transportation when people travelled from one part of town to another, which was infrequent.

Miriam came up to her parents' seat and squeezed in between them. "I'm scared."

"Hey, you don't have to be," Jed interjected. "This isn't a bad place. It's just a sad one."

"I came here to go to Disneyland one time," Miriam said sadly. "It definitely *did not* look like this." Everyone chuckled.

"No, I'm sure it didn't," Jed replied as he exited off the freeway onto Santa Monica Boulevard where the temple stood.

There was a palpable excitement when the bus wound its way up the driveway and onto the grounds on which workers were applying plaster and stonework to the sides of the temple. Others were working on the Visitors Center. The activity helped release the knot in Ben's stomach. Here was real proof that there was to be a mission and a temple. *Up to this moment, all that has happened could have been a dream*, he thought.

Several of the missionaries were let out at that stop; then the rest boarded the bus for the Rancho LaBrea area where most of the missionaries would have their apartments and the Taylors their mission headquarters.

"Ho, I remember this place," Ben said excitedly. "Hey, kids, this is where the LaBrea Tar Pits are located." He pointed out the window as the two moved to the right side of the bus.

"These were prehistoric tar pits in which dinosaurs got trapped, and sabre-tooth tigers and a dire wolf, if I recall. There was a museum that had displays. We'll have to go sometime and see what's still there," he said, sounding like the young boy he had been the first time he was taken there by his mother.

Jed pulled the bus up to a large complex of apartments that had been called Park LaBrea Apartments, built during World War II for military personnel, but then used for the general populace until the last few years. Twenty had been cleaned out, disinfected, furnished and readied for the missionaries.

The Taylor family, feeling somewhat forlorn in the empty bus, watched as the rambunctious elders bounded across the parking lot and disappeared in the building. Jed got back in and pulled the door closed. "Next stop, Pan Pacific Park and new home of Mission President Benjamin Z. Taylor and his lovely family."

"It isn't Z, dude," Ben said, leaning over and tapping Jed on the arm affectionately. "It's X. That's X for X-ray vision, X-ray Man."

The two laughed. "That's the park over there, Pan Pacific. Used to have a beautiful walkway all around it. Still has soccer and baseball fields (dead grass, of course) and I think there's a few basketball standards around." Danny perked up. Jed continued, "And think, you and the missionaries will have healthy bodies to be able to play out there. That will bring crowds, believe you me. They are still so sick, they can't run back and forth one time across the court."

He eased the bus onto Poinsettia Street. It was Saturday and they were surprised to see so many people walking down the sidewalks.

"This is the orthodox neighborhood I was briefed about," Ben said. "This is Shabbat. We stick out like a sore thumb."

Danny and Miriam each looked out of one side of the bus. Families were walking together, somberly and obviously headed for a significant destination from the look on their faces. Fathers wore dark suits and hats; mothers were in long-sleeved blouses and long skirts; boys dressed in suits with yalmakas on their heads; and girls dressed similarly to their mothers.

"They are wearing wigs!" Miriam nearly shouted and pointed at a mother and daughter.

"There's a guy my age with sideburn curls. There's another," Danny joined in.

Peg broke in with her teacher's voice. "Just as we were told they would be. Don't point. It's rude."

The kids pulled back from the windows and Peg continued, "Remember, they don't carry things on the Sabbath; they don't use electricity or cook. They take the Old Testament really seriously."

The bus was now slowing down at a large Spanish-style house that had been built in the 1920s. "Here we are," Jed volunteered. "Your new home for the next three and a half years."

"That long?" Miriam asked in alarm.

Ben put his hand on her arm. "Jed is a kidder, honey. We don't know how long the Lord has in mind."

As they stepped down off the bus, a family walked by. Peg decided she would try out her newfound knowledge and called out, "Good *Shabbas*."

The family looked a little startled, but called out, "Good *Shabbas* to you."

Peg was pleased with her performance; Ben and the kids were embarrassed. They hurried up the walk. Ben turned the key in the lock and opened the large wooden door for the family. Then he went back to help Jed with the bags.

"You take care," Jed said. "You're a better man that I am. I would not be dropped down in this town for love nor money."

"Nonsense. Why, you and Jody would go anywhere if the Lord asked you. Look at you. You drive a mean bus, brother."

The two laughed. Jed asked, "You remember when you baptized me?"

"Can't ever forget that. That was my first baptism, and I'd only been in the Church a few months."

"Well, you told me then that I would end up doing great things for the Lord."

"I did?"

"Yes, and I have. I'm a glorified bus driver. Glory be."

The two guffawed, shook hands and patted each other on the back.

"When's your next run?"

"Depends. I'm going back to Independence for maintenance. Then headed north to pick up some of the ten tribes, I think."

"Well, I'll miss you, dude," Ben said, walking backward up the sidewalk to his house.

Jed climbed back into the empty bus. Before shutting the door, he called out, "God bless, President Taylor," and saluted him.

Tears sprung to Ben's eyes as he returned the salute. He watched until the bus rumbled out of sight. His eye fell on an Orthodox family walking rapidly down the street. He sighed as he turned to open the door to his new home. "They don't even use electricity, Lord. How am I going to get them to come into the twenty-first century Church?"

The Spirit welled up in him, and he distinctly heard, "That is not your care, my son, but Mine. You have only to invite Judah to the wedding feast."

Afterword

And his princes shall be afraid of the ensign,

saith the Lord, whose fire is in Zion.

Isaiah 31:6

hat followed was such a rush of cataclysmic events that it seemed as if each new morning brought with it some shocking, unimaginable headline. Indeed, the saying started to circulate across the United States that "every day is 9/11 now." In brief, the following events occurred before Zion's net was finally dropped over all of the Western Hemisphere.

As prophesied by Joseph Smith, Boston, Albany and New York City along with Boston were devastated by natural disasters. Another disaster with more positive results was an infestation of various sorts of bugs and insects throughout the world, ridding it of that cancer that had afflicted it for generations—namely, illicit drugs; for the poppy, coca and marijuana crops were entirely wiped out. Other plagues, some old and some new (such as the grotesque hybrids of the AIDS virus with other viral strains), added to the populace's misery.

When the massive migration of the ten tribes reached the southern borders of Canada and the translated leaders felt they could safely leave them for a brief period of time, the ten men went to the great gathering in the valley of Adam-ondi-Ahman. Not only did all of the prophets of Israel fill the valley, but also certain spiritual adepts from all cultures and all times who had accepted the Restored Gospel on the other side of the veil.

These sages and holy men and women from both indigenous cultures as well as from the world's great major religions shouted praises in that sacred valley to the Lord Jesus Christ as the Supreme Master of the Universe. It was as if the very force of those hymns of praise rent the veil that separates the earth from the spirit world on this solemn occasion, thereby allowing individuals from the spirit world to appear along with translated and resurrected beings at this momentous meeting.

As prophesied, Adam did return the keys of the earthly kingdom to the Lord, having received them from the heads of each dispensation. Joseph Smith, honored by all those assembled as the greatest revelator of all times, was the last to hand over his keys to Adam.

In a gruesome parallel to the splendor that was quietly emanating from the valley of Adam-ondi-Ahman, Lu Han's comet smashed into the Indian Ocean off the coast of Madagascar. This event consolidated his hold on those frightened, gullible, and godless masses who lived outside the protected zone of Zion.

And thus began the final redemption of the earth, this tiny planet—which, although it is just one of an infinity of planets, is so specially favored by its Messiah that he was born (and died) here. First, however, had to come the preaching of the gospel to every soul. To this end President Ueda would soon ordain 144,000 high priests. They along with many other Latter-day Saints, including Ben and Peg Taylor, would be called to play a pivotal part in the concluding telestial drama before the coming of the Millennium.